She was getting to close to the truth, or at least someone thought she was...

The rain had started in earnest as Tonya reached the dark back parking lot. The smell of rotting garbage emanated from the battered green dumpster, and a mangy orange cat peered at her from underneath it. Lightning flashed and illuminated the eerie scene, followed by a clap of thunder that made Tonya jump.

Fumbling with the key in the lock of the driver's door, she was suddenly jerked backward by something around her neck. She staggered back, her hands instinctively going to her throat. Then she had the sensation of someone behind her holding her close. She felt hot breath on her neck as a raspy voice whispered viciously in her ear. "Stop asking questions. And stop playing detective. Or you and that nice little farm of yours will go up in smoke."

Then she was pushed violently against the door, her head banging hard against the metal. Lights danced before her eyes, and she had the sensation of falling. She slid to the ground face first, gravel grinding into her mouth as blood poured from her nose. Her last sensation was of something sharp striking her across the neck.

With their winnings from the local racetrack last season, jockey Tonya Callahan; her trainer father, Royce; and his new bride, Lexi, buy a farm where they plan to breed racehorses. But their peaceful life is shattered when a strange man shows up at their home, claiming to be Lexi's husband. When the man is murdered, all the evidence points to Royce, and newly promoted police lieutenant, Adam Abarca, hauls him off to jail, leaving Tonya no choice but to conduct her own investigation. Again. As she follows a trail of betrayal, cruelty, and deceit in her quest for the truth, she discovers that someone who has committed murder once won't hesitate to kill again, and her odds of surviving this new investigation are slim to none.

KUDOS for *Three to One Odds*

In *Three to One Odds* by D. M. O'Byrne, Tonya Callahan is spending the winter away from the racetrack on the new farm that her father, Royce, and stepmother, Lexi, bought and where they plan to raise horses. Into this idyllic scene on Christmas day comes a ghost from Lexi's past—a man claiming to be her husband. When he gets himself killed, Lexi can't help but be relieved, until Royce is arrested for his murder. The cops think they have their man they don't seem to care whether or not he is innocent, so Tonya decides to investigate on her own to clear her father's name. But this time she has few suspects and almost no clues, although someone thinks she does, and they don't like it. With superb character development, a solid plot, fast-paced action, and a number of surprises, this one will keep you on your toes all the way through. A really great read. ~ *Taylor Jones, The Review Team of Taylor Jones & Regan Murphy*

Three to One Odds is the story of Tonya Callahan, apprentice jockey and daughter of a racehorse trainer. Tonya now has a new stepmother, Lexi Parr, another trainer, and together the three of them purchase a horse farm on the outskirts of town. With the local track closed for the season, Tonya helps her father and Lexi on the farm, along with Mike Torres, a jockey friend to is staying with them while studying to, hopefully, become a vet. Their life is peaceful, and Tonya is happy, eager for the new foals to start arriving, but on Christmas, a man named Luca Caine shows up at the farm claiming to be Lexi's husband and saying he will not leave town without her. As if that isn't bad enough, a short time later, Caine is murdered, and Royce, Tonya's father, is the prime suspect. When he is arrested, Tonya decides to investigate on her own and prove his innocence—a decision that may well get her killed. O'Byrne does an excellent job of weaving the multiple subplots together. Combining mystery, suspense, and action with charming characters and a solid, well-thought-out plot, *Three to One Odds* is one you won't want to put down. *~ Regan Murphy, The Review Team of Taylor Jones & Regan Murphy*

THREE
TO ONE
ODDS

D. M. O'BYRNE

A Black Opal Books Publication

GENRE: MYSTERY-DETECTIVE/WOMEN SLEUTHS/SUSPENSE

THREE TO ONE ODDS
Copyright © 2018 by D. M. O'Byrne
Cover Design by Jackson Cover Designs
All cover art copyright © 2018
All Rights Reserved
Print ISBN: 978-1-626949-09-6

First Publication: MAY 2018

Published by Black Opal Books **http://www.blackopalbooks.com**

THREE
TO ONE
ODDS

CHAPTER 1

A thin layer of frost, glittering in the morning sun, covered the lawn in front of the old farm house, the driveway, and the pastures. The colored lights framing the porch and doorway reflected red and green on the icy drive.

Hibernia, the farm that was Tonya Callahan's new home, although old and weather-worn, seemed like a palace compared to the single-wide mobile that she and her father had lived in for as long as she could remember. Now they were settled in the farmhouse that had once belonged to the Warrens, the old couple who had sold the farm to them.

As she headed for the barn that Christmas morning, the frost on the driveway crunched under her boots, and she zipped up her jacket against the chill.

Sliding open the double barn door, she was greeted with whinnies and the impatient stamping of hooves. Her eyes scanned the length of the shed row where twelve heads craned out of their stalls, their ears pricked up and all staring intently at her. *I'm never as popular as I am in the morning*, she thought.

Tonya inhaled the warm, sweet smell of hay, horses,

and leather that reminded her how lucky she was. She was a licensed apprentice jockey, she had a new stepmother, and her father was positively glowing with happiness. Then there was Mike Torres, the former jockey who now lived in their old trailer, that had been moved from the track to the farm, as he studied to fulfill his lifelong dream—veterinary medicine. All was right with the world.

Mike was right behind her as she started for the feed room. *"Buenos dias,"* he called to her.

"Morning, Mike. Merry Christmas. Or should I say *Feliz Navidad?"*

"Very good. Your accent is getting better."

A loud whinny and the banging of a feed bucket against the wall signaled that JK's Imperial Count, Hibernia's resident breeding stallion, was in his usual demanding mood.

"Okay, Jake, keep your coat on," Tonya called as she wheeled the hay-laden wheel barrow down the shed row to the last stall. Tossing the hay bundle over the stall door, she said, "Here you are, your majesty." Jake tore into the bundle then looked up, wisps of hay hanging from his mouth as he chewed it. Tonya smiled at his comical appearance, his long ears, and thin face reminding her of a skinny mule. But he was hardly a mule. He was a champion racehorse and the owner of the record for a mile and a quarter at the local track. On him rode all the hopes and dreams of the Callahan family.

"What time is dinner?" Mike called to Tonya from a stall he was cleaning.

"About noon. But come at any time. We're going to open our presents first." Tonya couldn't wait to see Mike's expression when he opened the gift she had for him. Pleasing Mike was important to her, but she was still somewhat confused about her feelings toward him. Were they romantic feelings? Close friendship? Or just the affectionate longing of an only child for the sibling she never had? Whatever it was, she looked forward all day to their study sessions in the evenings.

"Anything I can bring?"

"Nope. We've got it covered. See you in a while," she said as she finished up her chores.

She hurried to the house, wrapping her scarf more tightly around her neck. The West Texas sunlight was trying to penetrate the cloud cover, making the morning seem chilly and raw. In the house, her father, Royce, was building a fire in the brick fireplace. The scent of evergreen from the Christmas tree mixed with the smells of apple cider, pumpkin pie, and cinnamon coming from the kitchen.

Tonya joined her new stepmother, Lexi, in the kitchen to help prepare Christmas dinner. Lexi wore a bright red apron over her jeans and sweater, her long dark hair tied back with a blue ribbon that matched her eyes. Although there were fourteen years between their ages, they had become close friends in the past months. "This turkey ought to be more than enough for the five of us," Lexi said as she brushed the bird with butter.

"Five?"

"Doc Frey is joining us. Didn't I tell you?"

"Oh, that's right. I forgot. It'll be good to see him again."

"We'll be seeing him a lot in the spring once the foaling starts."

Doc Frey was the kindly, gray-eyed veterinarian from the racetrack who had offered to fund Mike's education through college and vet school, seeing in him an extraordinary talent for the work. Mike and Tonya studied together every night, Mike racing through his GED courses while Tonya desperately tried to master Spanish. Her high school French classes had proven to be worthless at the Southwest racetracks where her father trained Thoroughbreds.

Tonya's two cats, Clive and Henry, prowled the kitchen sniffing the delicious and unfamiliar smells. "And there will be plenty left over for you two as well," Lexi said. She reached down to scratch the little blue-gray patches between the ears of the identical white cats. They both closed their eyes and purred at her touch.

Once the turkey was in the oven and the other dishes started, they returned to the living room to find Royce asleep in his chair, his legs stretched out toward the fire. He and Mike had been up until two a.m. with a colicky mare. Lexi looked at him affectionately. Then she jumped into his lap, kissing him and messing his hair, shouting, "Merry Christmas!"

Royce woke with a start, grabbed Lexi, and began tickling her while she shrieked. Tonya smiled at their antics. Never did she think her father would find love again after his first wife had died when Tonya was little. But here they were like two teenagers with their first crush. Tonya was happy for him, even if she was still a little jealous at having to share his love with another woman.

Mike tapped on the door and came in, carrying several brightly-wrapped boxes. He put them under the tree and sat on the sofa with a shy smile. "*Feliz Navidad,* everyone." He had replaced his barn clothes with a soft gray shirt and his best jeans. His thick dark hair was neatly combed.

Tonya plopped down on the floor next to the tree. "Let's get to those presents! Here's one with your name on it, Dad," she said, tossing a box to her father. Lexi slid off his lap as he began tearing into the wrapping.

Tonya played Santa, distributing gifts to each person

until they insisted she open her own. Everyone got something useful, and there were "Ooo's" and "Thanks" enough to go around. Tonya had struggled with what to get for Mike and finally settled on a brass name plate for his future office engraved, "Miguel Torres, DVM."

He tried to hide his emotions as he caressed the beautiful plate. The joy on his face was unmistakable as he looked up at Tonya and said, "Someday."

Doc Frey arrived with a bouquet of flowers for Lexi's table, a bottle of wine, and a gift box. He sat on the couch next to Mike and handed him the box. "Just a little something to help you on your way." Mike tore through the wrappings to find a leather-bound copy of *Merck's Manual*, the Bible of veterinary medicine.

"Wow! Thanks a lot." Mike thumbed through the 3000-page volume with awe. Doc Frey put an arm around his shoulders.

Lexi went back to the kitchen and came in with cups of steaming apple cider which she passed around.

Tonya's heart was full of the joy of Christmas. She stole glances at Mike's eyes, always expressive but today more than ever, as they reflected his gratitude for his new life among people who loved and accepted him.

He had become an integral part of the life of the Callahan family and a valuable asset to the training/breeding operation.

The morning flew by. Doc and Mike were deep in a discussion of the causes of colic in pregnant mares while Tonya played with the cats, tossing bows and balls of wrapping paper for them to chase. Royce snoozed by the fire until Lexi came in carrying the turkey on a huge platter. "Dinner's ready, so let's sit down," she announced.

Tonya went to the kitchen, and the two women carried in the rest of the side dishes.

As they pulled out their chairs at the table, Mike said with a grin, "What? No tamales?"

Royce stood and began to carve the turkey. "Sorry, *amigo*. Not today. Maybe for the New Year's dinner."

Clive and Henry prowled around the chairs, hoping for a few tidbits. Tonya felt Henry rubbing on her legs and lifted him into her lap. He curled up, watching her adoringly as she ate. Clive hopped up on a nearby shelf where he sat purring with his tail curled around his front legs and his eyes half closed.

Late that afternoon, they were all settled in the living room enjoying the fire, full of turkey, wine, and good cheer, when there was a sharp rap at the front door.

Royce got up to answer it. "Now who could this be?" He opened the door to reveal a stranger standing in the doorway.

Lexi gasped, and her face turned white. Her knees buckled, and she slid to the floor, landing in a heap next to Royce's chair. Doc Frey kneeled down next to her, taking her pulse. Tonya stared at her in shock then at Royce who stood open-mouthed at the door.

The stranger finally spoke. "Sorry to break in on you like this. I wasn't sure it was the right house. My name is Lucas Caine." He offered Royce his hand, and Royce shook it then hurried to Lexi's side.

Caine was slim and nearly six feet tall with thinning blond hair, a mottled complexion, and watery blue eyes. He smiled readily. *Almost too readily*, Tonya thought. Not really knowing why, she took an intense dislike to him. He lingered by the door, surveying the scene, and Tonya thought he looked somewhat smug as he watched Lexi struggle to her feet, helped into the chair by Royce and Doc.

"What is it, honey?" Royce asked with concern. Lexi just shook her head and stared at the floor.

"Maybe I can explain," Caine offered, closing the door behind him. "Diana is surprised to see me here." He looked at Lexi. "Aren't you, Dee?"

Royce stared at the stranger in confusion. "There must be some mistake. My wife's name is Lexi. Lexi Parr Callahan."

"No," Caine said with a smirk. "Her name is Diana Wilkins Caine. And she's my wife, not yours."

Tonya and Royce exchanged bewildered glances. Doc cleared his throat, "Mike, why don't we go out and check on that mare again?"

Mike got up quickly and followed him to the door. "We'll be in the barn if you need us, Royce," he said, glancing at Caine.

Royce nodded dumbly, turning back to Lexi who still sat staring at the floor in silence as though trying to make herself invisible.

Not bothering to wait for an invitation, Caine sat on the couch, stretching his legs in front of him and looking around. "Nice place you got here, Callahan." He gave Tonya an appreciative glance, looking her up and down in a way that made her skin crawl. "This your daughter?"

Tonya moved closer to her father who ignored the question. "Look, Mr...Caine, is it? I don't know who you are or what you want, but you've made a mistake."

The man pulled some papers out of his jacket pocket and laid them on the coffee table. "I thought you might say that. Here is our marriage license and our wedding picture."

Royce stared dumbfounded at the items. "But what—where—"

Caine seemed maddeningly nonchalant. "I've been looking for my wife for several years. Just happened to see this in a racing magazine." He handed Royce the

winner's circle picture from the Traveler Stakes, the race
Jake had won in record time. Tonya, the winning jockey,
sat proudly on his back while Lexi held his bridle, and
Royce hoisted the trophy. What a glorious day that had
been. Never could Tonya have dreamed when the photog-
rapher snapped the picture that one day it would lead to
this nightmare.

Royce gave back the picture, his eyes smoldering. "I
don't know what your game is, Caine, but I think you
should leave."

Caine glared at him for a moment then shrugged his
shoulders and stood up. "Okay. But I'm not leaving town
without my wife. I'm staying at the Wagon Wheel, Dee,
when you're ready to talk. I get off work at Jenkins's feed
store at five."

He strolled arrogantly toward the door. "Merry
Christmas, all," he said with a smirk. "I doubt it will be a
happy new year." They heard him whistling as he closed
the door.

The silence in the room was palpable. No one
moved. After a moment, Tonya murmured, "I'll go see to
those dishes." As much as she wanted an explanation for
what had just happened, she knew this was a time for
Royce and Lexi to be alone.

As she puttered about in the kitchen, she heard Lexi
say, "I need to lie down." She and Royce went to their
bedroom just off the living room. After a few minutes,
Tonya could no longer restrain herself. She tiptoed to
their door, listening intently. Lexi was sobbing as though
her heart would break.

"Why didn't you tell me?" Royce was saying. "I
knew you'd been in an abusive relationship with someone. But married? How could you marry me when you
were married to him? And is Diana Wilkins your real
name?" He sounded both bewildered and hurt.

"Oh, Royce," Lexi sobbed. "I'm so sorry. I guess I just convinced myself that Diana no longer existed. I was someone else. My old life was dead. I never dreamed I would meet someone...that I would want to marry again. I never thought he would find me this time."

"This time? You mean this has happened before?"

Lexi blew her nose. "Oh, yeah."

Tonya stood riveted by the door, hoping that whatever story came out would not jeopardize their idyllic life. But she sensed that things would never be the same again.

"About ten years ago I got an assistant trainer job at a small track near Cleveland. Lucas was a trainer there. Oh, he was so charming. I fell in love with him, at least the man I thought he was, and married him. I left my job to work with him. Almost immediately, things went bad. We were always at odds over the horses and how he treated them. I tried to do the best for the horses, but he usually overruled me. He would do anything to win, legal or not. We fought constantly. Worst of all, he began to be abusive, more and more possessive and controlling. He really started to scare me, so I decided to leave him. I packed up and headed back to my parents' farm, but he followed me. At first, he tried sweet-talking me into returning with him, then he threatened to kill me if I didn't. I stayed there and refused to see him again, but he caught me on my own one night and broke my jaw. That was when I realized I would have to disappear forever."

"My God. I had no idea."

"I left again and moved to Colorado where I got a job on a ranch. Within weeks, he found me again. I don't know how. I knew that wherever I went, I'd never get away from him, that somehow he would always trace me. That last time, in Colorado, he put me in the hospital. But he was in jail temporarily for assault, so once I got out of the hospital, I left town again."

She stopped talking for a moment. Tonya could only guess at the look on Royce's face. But he was silent.

"That's when I decided to change my name. I went to the local cemetery and found the grave of someone who was born the same year as me. I applied for her birth certificate then a driver's license in her name—Alexis Parr. I headed for Texas and got a job at the track here. I moved around to the tracks on the circuit. I kept a low profile and hoped he wouldn't be able to trace me. I got a couple of horses to train and began to think of myself as Alexis. Diana was just someone I knew in a former life."

Lexi sighed. "Then I met you. I was so happy. It never dawned on me that in marrying you, I was doing anything wrong. Or illegal. I guess I just put it out of my mind." She hesitated, and Tonya heard her sigh again. "I'm so sorry, Royce. I love you so much. But I've hurt you and brought you into my mess. Can you ever forgive me?"

Royce was silent for a moment, and, when he finally spoke, his voice cracked with emotion. "Honey, there's nothing to forgive. I'm just thankful that you ended up here. You are my wife, no matter what that man says. We'll get through this together. You'll file for divorce, then we'll marry again, this time legally. Nothing will ever keep us apart."

"Lucas will never agree to a divorce. You heard him. And he won't leave town without me."

"You leave Caine to me. Now lie down and get some rest. I'll help Tonya and Mike feed the horses. Then we'll talk some more. And don't worry about anything. It will be fine. Trust me."

Tonya scurried away from the door and back to the dishes. Royce came into the kitchen, his face etched in sorrow and anger. She decided not to press him. When he wanted to tell her, he would. He stood at the sink, gazing out the window at the purple and pink streaks the setting sun painted in the sky.

"Let's go feed the horses," he muttered through a clenched jaw. "It's getting late."

Tonya had seen her father angry before. She understood the Irish temper she had inherited from him. But his expression tonight reflected more than temper. There was a steely resolve in his eyes.

"Is everything okay, Dad?"

"No, but it will be." He put his arm around her shoulders. "Don't worry about anything, kiddo. We'll get through this." He left the kitchen and headed for the front door. She followed him, pulling on her jacket.

Once outside, Tonya noticed that Doc Frey's truck was gone. The lights were on in the main barn, and Mike was already starting to fill the feed buckets with molasses sweet feed. Tonya loaded several bales of hay into the wheelbarrow and started down the shed row. Royce went to the stall of the colicky mare to check on her.

Mike caught up with Tonya and asked quietly, "What was that all about?"

"Long story," she replied, tossing hay over the half door to one of the mares.

"Is that man really Lexi's husband?"

"It seems so."

Mike whistled low. "What's going to happen now?"

"I don't know. It depends on what the guy does, I guess."

"I don't trust him. He's a bad *hombre*."

Tonya marveled at his insight. Not only did he have a special feel for animals in distress, he seemed to have a sixth sense for people as well, especially their character.

"You may be right," she said. "I don't trust him either."

"Maybe we should take a break from studying to-night. After all, it is Christmas."

Tonya glanced at her father who was cleaning stalls. "I don't know. Maybe they do need to be alone tonight."

Mike looked a little disappointed. "Or we could study in the trailer."

"But the computer is in the house. No, let's try to act as normal as possible. We can have some turkey sand-wiches and get to work on the algebra."

Mike seemed eager to agree. "Okay. See you in a few minutes."

After all the horses were fed, Tonya walked back toward the house, her boots sliding a little in the muddy yard. Just like the frost, it seemed that their Christmas joy had evaporated in the harsh winter sun.

CHAPTER 2

The next morning, Tonya, Royce, and Lexi sat at the table eating breakfast. Tonya looked out the window at the weak sun struggling to break through the clouds. It would warm up by mid-morning, but now the kitchen was chilly, and the atmosphere felt oppressively bleak.

Lexi's eyes were swollen and red, and Royce looked older, his face more lined than Tonya had ever seen it. Her heart ached for them. Only married two months, and they were already sharing sorrow. Were they even married?

Royce set down his coffee cup. "I need to go into town and get something to take care of those rats in the hay barn. They're building tunnels everywhere. I swear the whole dirt floor is going to collapse one day."

Tonya was glad to have something to talk about to break the tension. "Yeah, I saw three of them together the other day. I suspect they're plotting a takeover." She smiled and glanced at Lexi, who seemed not to hear Tonya's little joke.

Royce cleared his throat. "I'm sure Jenkins has some kind of rat poison."

"Maybe I'll go with you," Tonya said. "I love wandering around the tack section. Jenkins has a good selection."

Lexi just kept staring at her plate, looking pale and strained, saying nothing.

"I have an idea. Lexi, why don't we go to that new salon and have our hair done? We could go while Dad is at the feed store."

Lexi sighed. "I don't know. I'm not much in the mood."

Royce encouraged Tonya with a slight nod of his head.

"Oh, come on," she said. "It will be fun. And it'll take our minds off—"

Lexi looked up at them. Sadness filled her normally bright eyes. "Off the mess I've made of our lives?"

"I'm sure Tonya didn't mean that. She just wants to look nice for Mike," Royce teased. "Or maybe she's planning to see Sergeant Abarca again soon. But I hear Adam's a lieutenant now. I guess helping you solve those murders at the track last summer gave his career a boost."

"I'm not trying to look nice for either one. I would just like to feel like a girl for a change. I mean, jeans and boots and a ponytail are okay for the farm, but a change would be nice. What do you say, Lex? Please?"

Royce caressed his wife's arm. "Do it, honey. You'll enjoy it."

Lexi looked at the two of them, and a faint tremulous smile played on her lips. "I guess I'm outnumbered."

"That's my girl." Royce sat back and winked at Tonya. "I'll tell Mike we'll be gone for a while." He left the table and headed for the barn.

They heard the front door close, and Lexi's eyes widened. "Wait a minute. Didn't Lucas say he works at Jenkins's feed store? What if Royce runs into him?"

"What if he does? He's probably seen him there before now. Dad just never knew he was."

"Yes, but now that they know each other—"

"Don't worry about Dad. He's pretty level-headed." Tonya got up from the table and put the breakfast dishes in the sink, trying to push thoughts of Royce's Irish temper to the back of her mind. "Let me just feed the cats, and we'll get ready, okay?"

"Okay." Lexi left the table and went to her bedroom.

Clive and Henry came into the kitchen, yawning and stretching. They meowed and rubbed on Tonya's legs as she poured their food into the bowls. She bent down to stroke their silky fur as they ate. "You guys don't know how good you have it. Just eat, sleep, and be loved."

She sighed. Six months ago, all she had wanted out of life was to ride Thoroughbreds in races. Even the three murders at the track and the attempt on her life by Alton Jeffers hadn't shaken her world as badly as the past twenty-four hours.

She gave the cats a final pat and went up the stairs to change.

cₒℓ

The ride into town was a quiet one. Tonya gazed out the window of Royce's old pickup at the white painted fences and the rolling pastures, brown now in the winter sun. Lexi sat between them, appearing small and vulnerable.

It seemed like years since the day Tonya first met Lexi at the track. She had approached her in hopes of riding one of her two horses in races. She found Lexi to be a smart, no-nonsense trainer who lived hand-to-mouth, struggling to make ends meet. Lexi had made tea for

them in one of the stalls where she lived to save money.
She told Tonya that day that racing is a man's game and
that women would always be trying to break into it. That
was before Jake came into their lives, giving them the
success they had never dared hope for.

Royce drove down the main street of the little town
of Centerville and pulled up in front of the hair salon.
"Take your time, girls. Come over to the feed store when
you're done. I'll shoot the breeze with Jenkins for a
while."

"Okay, Dad. See you later."

Tonya and Lexi got out of the pickup and stood on
the sidewalk gazing at the storefront. The sign announc-
ing *Michelle's Boutique* seemed a hopeful attempt at an
impression the rundown little store really didn't warrant.
The new owner had tried her best to spruce up its appearance, repainting the wooden siding and cleaning the old
windows until they gleamed. But like the rest of the small
Texas town that baked in the brutal sun most of the year,
its age was hard to hide.

As they entered the store, Tonya saw two young
women sitting in side-by-side swivel chairs. They both
bounced up and hurried toward the door, their heels click-
ing on the tile and resounding through the empty room.
The older one was a chunky, well-groomed woman in her
mid-thirties with a sunny smile and warm manner. "Good
morning! Welcome! I'm Michelle. This is Tissy." She
gestured to the other girl, a delicate waif-like creature
who was probably in her twenties but looked younger.
She was wearing a blue smock. "What can we do for
you?"

"Hi," Tonya said. "I'd like to have my hair trimmed
and styled. What about you, Lexi?"

"Oh, I don't know. Maybe just a wash and style?"

"Great!" Michelle beamed. She pointed Tonya to one

of the chairs. "Sit right here. Tissy will take care of your trim." She led Lexi to the sinks along the back wall. "And let's get you shampooed over here."

Tonya sat down, and Tissy buttoned the drape around her neck. She undid the tie on Tonya's ponytail and ran her hands through Tonya's long auburn hair. "How much did you want me to take off?"

"I'm not sure. Someone told me it would look good in a bob, but I don't know."

"Well, I'll take off a couple of inches, and then we can see."

Tonya watched Tissy in the mirror as she worked, her brow furrowed in concentration. Her light brown hair was short on the right side and long on the left. Her ears and lips were studded with cheap piercings. When she bent over slightly, her hair moved away from her face to reveal a six-inch scar running from her left eyebrow almost to her chin. The scar was so red and brutal-looking that Tonya gasped slightly.

Tissy looked quickly up at her in the mirror. "Am I hurting you?"

"No. No, not at all."

Tissy self-consciously pulled her hair over the scar. She seemed nervous and insecure, her eyes full of pain and mistrust. Tonya wondered about her background and how she got that scar.

Michelle bustled over with Lexi, whose wet hair was in a towel, and sat her down in the adjoining chair. They chatted about the style Lexi wanted, and Lexi seemed to be relaxing, perhaps temporarily forgetting the misery of the previous evening.

"So. Are you girls from around here?" Michelle asked.

"We bought the old Warren farm just outside of

town. We've been there about two months now," Lexi
said.

"Oh, I know that place. An old couple owned it,
right? Joy and oh, what's his name?"

"Clyde," Tonya answered, smiling at the memory of
the lovely old couple who had lived there for forty years.

"That's right. Clyde. Such nice old folks. Joy came
in here one day with her two granddaughters just before
she and Clyde moved away. They were the cutest little
things. Acting so grown up. They had their hair done.
Grandma's treat. Moved to Florida, right?"

"Yes."

"Just a sweet old couple. They raised racehorses,
didn't they?"

"Yes. That's what we'll be doing."

Michelle looked skeptical. "Just the two of you?"

"No, my Dad, Royce, is a trainer. So is Lexi, his
wife," she said, nodding at Lexi. "And I'm an apprentice
jockey. We're going to breed Thoroughbreds and train
and race some of our own and some for other owners. At
least that's the plan."

Tissy's face clouded. Tissy looked out the window
onto the street and declared suddenly, "I have to get
something. Be right back." She tried to toss the scissors
onto the shelf, but she misjudged the distance. They fell
to the floor with a metallic clatter that made them all
jump. An awkward silence filled the room. She hurried
toward the back room, apparently eager to end the conversation.

"See if you can find that gallon bottle of alcohol
while you're back there," Michelle called after her. She
shook her head. "Damned if I know where that thing
went to. Just bought it last week, too." She glanced toward the back of the store, watching Tissy's rapidly re-
treating figure. "You'll have to excuse Tissy," she whis-

pered. "She's a little jumpy. She had a bad experience of some kind before she came here."

"Is that where she got that scar?" Tonya asked. "It looks pretty nasty."

"I don't know. She never told me. She's only been here since November. She's a very private person. Hasn't made many friends. Keeps to herself. I don't like to pry."

"Oh, my God," Lexi broke in, turning pale. "Look." She pointed out the window. Lucas Caine was standing across the street staring at the salon. His hands were in his pockets, and a cigarette dangled from his lips.

"Who's that?" Michelle asked.

"Someone we don't want to see," Tonya explained.

"He's stalking me!" Lexi whispered, starting to panic. She looked around frantically as though searching for some place to hide.

"Take it easy, Lex. I'll call Dad when we're done and have him come over to pick us up. Caine won't do anything in here. If he does, we'll just call the cops."

"Hey, I don't want any trouble with the cops," Michelle objected, peering uneasily out the window. But Caine had moved on, strolling nonchalantly in the direction of the feed store.

Lexi breathed deeply. "He must be on his way to work."

Tissy came warily out of the back room and resumed working on Tonya's haircut.

"Did you see that alcohol back there?" Michelle asked.

"What? No, no. I didn't see it." Tissy's face seemed to have grown paler, making the scar stand out even more.

The two stylists worked for a while longer, the conversation having turned to the weather and other innocuous topics. Tissy styled Tonya's hair in a long bob, curled under at the nape of her neck.

"That looks great," Lexi admitted.

"Thanks." Tonya admired the new style in the mirror. "I like it. And it's still long enough to put in a ponytail."

When they were finished, Lexi and Tonya paid and thanked them.

"Sure enough!" Michelle exclaimed. "Please come back. We're open every day except Sunday. We do nails, too."

"We will," Tonya said. "Thanks again."

Out on the sidewalk, Tonya looked up and down the street. "Well, that went well," she smirked. "Really took our minds off Caine, huh?"

Lexi laughed, and the tension was broken. She linked her arm through Tonya's. "Oh, to hell with him. Let's go meet your father."

Jenkins Feed and Tack was only a few blocks away along the main street. They strolled down the sidewalk, stopping to look at the Christmas sales and decorations in the windows. They passed the tiny police station on one corner, and Tonya noticed Adam's cruiser parked near the front door. Memories of their one date last summer came flooding back to her, making her wonder whether they would ever have another one. He hadn't called or visited since they moved to the farm. *Maybe making lieutenant has gone to his head,* she thought.

Royce's pickup was the only vehicle in the parking lot in front of the feed store. Tonya opened the door and held it for Lexi. The old building had wooden floors and smelled of leather, horse feed, and animals. Free-standing metal shelves were crowded into the small store, creating tight aisles. The shelves were crammed with bags of cat and dog food, birdseed, and vitamin supplements for all kinds of animals, as well as small tools. Sacks of molasses sweet feed and alfalfa cubes were piled next to one wall. A small adjoining room held the tack and grooming supplies.

A large green parrot called out from a cage near the counter where Royce was standing talking to Leo Jenkins, a stocky middle-aged man with a receding hairline and a huge stomach that hung below his belt. "Watch your step, buster!" the parrot exclaimed repeatedly.

"Pipe down, ya silly bird," Leo said, "or I'll feed you to Diesel." An overweight black cat sat quietly beneath the cage, staring up at the parrot with intense yellow eyes, the tip of his tail twitching slowly back and forth.

"Watch your step, buster!" the bird shrieked again.

Jenkins finally muttered, "Cover him up, will ya, Alec? He's giving me a headache."

"Sure thing, Mr. J." Alec—a large, heavy-set woman with wild black hair and small dark eyes set close together—came from behind the counter. She appeared to be in her early fifties. Her face bore scars of a long-ago battle with acne. She pulled a canvas cover over the cage then returned to the counter and stared at Tonya and Lexi with a blank, noncommittal expression.

The parrot lapsed into silence, and the disgruntled cat stalked away.

"Here's my girls now," Royce said smiling. "Don't you both look pretty?"

"Thanks, Dad. We had a nice time. Hello, Leo."

Jenkins nodded. "Hey, Tonya. I've got some new tack you might be interested in. A couple of blankets, an exercise saddle, blinkers, and a few new whips. Although one of them seems to have gone missing. A good one, too. Forty bucks. Who would steal a whip?" He shook his head. "I don't know about people these days. Anyway, feel free to browse around in there."

"Thanks. Maybe another time. We should be getting back soon."

Lexi was looking around nervously as though she was afraid Lucas Caine might jump out at her any moment. But he was nowhere to be seen.

The old manual cash register dinged as Jenkins opened the drawer. "Okay, Royce. That'll be twenty-nine, ninety-five for the arsenic trioxide. Just mix it with sugar or sweet feed and spread it around the barn. The rats will love it. In no time, you'll be up to your butt in dead rats. But be sure no other animals get into it." He put the tin into a paper bag and handed it to Royce.

"Thanks. Ready to go, girls?"

They piled into the pickup, pulled out of the lot, and turned onto Main Street. Tonya looked out her window just in time to see a large white van with heavily tinted windows pull out from behind the store and turn onto the same street. Then she saw Lucas Caine watching the van. He crushed out a cigarette under his boot and spat on the ground. Tonya was grateful that Lexi hadn't noticed him.

CHAPTER 3

That afternoon, Tonya admired her new hairstyle in the mirror of her bedroom on the second floor of the farmhouse. The room was small, but compared to the one in the trailer, it seemed enormous. Her single bed and tiny dresser were dwarfed by the space. Tonya often thought about adding some more furniture one day. The walls were papered in a flowered pattern that reminded her of Joy Warren. Maybe this was Joy's daughter's room at one time. It had a girliness about it that was somewhat foreign to Tonya. Growing up on the racetrack with her father, Tonya had been a tomboy, committed only to the horses and to her dream of becoming a jockey.

Taped to the mirror over the dresser were the winners' circle pictures from Gus's win in the Futurity and Jake's smashing victory in the Traveler Stakes. In Jake's picture, his tongue was hanging out of his mouth as though he was making a statement to all those who had doubted him.

Henry and Clive were curled up on her bed, barely opening their eyes at her voice. "What do you think, boys? It's called a bob." As she uttered the word "bob," her mind went back to the night her best friend, Alana, had styled her hair with the tortoise shell comb she had given Tonya for her twenty-first birthday. Alana had said that Tonya's hair would look nice in a bob.

Tonya sat on the bed, and a wave of raw grief washed over her recalling the loss of her friend a few months before. Alana's body was found in the parking lot at the track, the third victim of Alton Jeffers, the maniac with a murderous hatred of Hispanics and female jockeys. Even the memory of successfully identifying him as the killer from a series of clues would never soften the pain of losing her best friend.

She sighed and changed into jeans, boots and a light jacket. She was grateful to have plenty to do on the farm to keep her mind from dwelling on the sadness of the previous summer.

Coming down the stairs, she noticed Royce and Lexi sitting on the living room couch. Royce's arm was around Lexi, her head resting on his shoulder. Her sadness seemed to fill the room. Tonya didn't want to disturb them, so she slipped quietly out the front door and crossed the yard to the main barn.

Mike was nowhere around. *Probably studying*, she thought. Mike was so intent on taking his GED test and applying for college and then veterinary school that all his spare time was devoted to his books.

Tonya stopped at Gus's stall to give him a pat on the nose. The little chestnut colt, who Royce liked to refer to as "the shrimp," had won the Sprint Futurity by a nose on the last day of the summer meet. His winnings, plus those from Jake's race, had made it possible for them to buy the farm. But Gus had suffered a bowed tendon that day and had been recuperating ever since.

She opened the door of his stall and leaned down to examine his left foreleg. The leg was healing, but it would take another couple of months before he was ready to begin training again. He had grown a little, but he would always be small compared to other colts his age. She straightened up and stoked his sleek neck. Gus nosed her jacket pockets hoping for the carrot she usually remembered to bring him. His huge fawn-like brown eyes regarded her hopefully.

"Sorry, not today." With a final pat on his neck, Tonya left the stall and went to the tack room, where she pulled down Jake's exercise tack and her helmet. Jake had been in the barn all of Christmas day and needed some work. Although he would not be racing again, as a breeding stallion, he needed to be in peak condition.

She walked down the shed row, admiring each of the six mares and four weanlings in their stalls. These were the horses that had come to the Callahans as part of the sale of the farm. The mares would all be bred to Jake in the spring, and the weanlings, who would be yearlings on January first, would be sold at auction.

Jake was waiting impatiently in the end stall for Tonya. He pawed the stall door, tossing his head up and down, eager to get out of his confinement. Tonya ran a quick brush over his glossy brown coat then saddled him and led him into the aisle to the mounting block. Climbing onto the block, she slid onto Jake's back, marveling once again at the view from atop a seventeen-hand Thoroughbred.

She headed him out of the barn, past the hay barn and foaling sheds toward the half-mile training track at the rear of the property. Jake walked eagerly along the path to the track. Galloping around the track wasn't terribly exciting to him as there was no competition, but he always seemed happy to get out of his stall or paddock. Tonya thought how much fun it would be to ride through the area's fields and woods, but Jake was just too valuable to take on a trail ride.

Tonya jogged him onto the dirt track and let him decide on his own pace. Soon he broke into a rolling gallop, eating up the ground with his long legs. Tonya allowed him to make four circuits around the half-mile oval then walked him another half mile to cool him down.

She wondered if Jake missed the thrill of competition as much as she did. Her mind wandered back to the last day of the race meet last summer, the day he won the Traveler Stakes by twenty lengths and set a new track record for the mile and a quarter. That was the most exciting moment of her life, especially considering she had almost lost her life just a half hour earlier to Alton Jeffers. She shuddered at the memory of the man's hands closing around her throat until Lexi bashed his head in with a heavy mirror from the locker room wall. After Jeffers was taken away by the police, Tonya staggered out of the locker room to ride Jake to his smashing victory, only to pose for the winners' circle picture that would change their lives forever.

Tonya rode Jake back toward the barn, passing Royce who was just entering the hay barn with what looked like the tin of rat poison and a bag of sugar. She waved at him, and he waved back.

After their ride, Tonya unsaddled Jake and brushed him. Then she led him to his outside paddock and turned him loose. At once he lowered himself to the ground and rolled over several times, scratching his itchy back.

She was just hanging up her saddle when Mike entered the tack room. *"Buenos dias,"* she said to him.

"Dias is really for morning. *Buenos tardes* is better."

"Oh, that's right. I'll get it one of these days. *Buenos tardes, Miguel."*

"Muy bueno." He tilted his head and looked at her. "You cut your hair. It looks great."

"Thanks," she said self-consciously, her hand going to the back of her hair. She cleared her throat. "How's the history homework? Is it making sense?"

"Sure, but I'd rather be reading about the causes of laminitis in horses," he admitted with a grin.

"Patience. One day you'll be in vet school, and that's all you'll be thinking about."

Mike sighed. "Yeah. One day."

Tonya looked at him sideways. "You're not getting discouraged, are you?"

"No, not exactly. It just seems so far away."

"You'll get there," Tonya said. "At least you know what you want," she added.

"Don't you? I mean, I thought being a jockey was all you ever wanted."

"It was. I mean, it is." She smoothed the saddle cloths hanging on the racks, the bright red RC sewn onto each one. "I don't know. Things are kinda weird right now. I'd hate to see my dad get hurt. Like you said, Lucas Caine is a bad *hombre*. What if he makes trouble for us? What will happen?"

Mike came closer to her and spoke quietly. "Tonya, we can only do what we can do. Let Lexi and your dad figure it out. You'll make yourself *loco* trying to fix everyone's problems."

Tonya felt comfort in Mike's nearness. The depths in his eyes always calmed and disconcerted her at the same time. She felt her face grow warm and her heart beat just a little faster.

Suddenly he turned away. "I'm going to take Gus out for a walk. He'll be happy to get out of his stall. One of these days, we'll be able to ride him around the property. Then maybe he can start galloping again."

"Okay. See you tonight."

Tonya left the barn and returned to the house just in time to see Royce's pickup pulling out of the driveway.

She took off her boots and left them by the door. Then she padded into the kitchen where Lexi stood staring out the window, her eyes vague and unfocused. "What's up?" Tonya asked.

"Nothing much. Just trying to figure out what to have for dinner."

"Don't make a fuss. There's enough leftovers from Christmas dinner to last us a week. We can just make sandwiches or something." Lexi seemed to not hear her. "Why don't you make us a cup of tea? Just like the first time we met. Remember our little tea party in the stall?"

Lexi turned from the window and reached for the tea kettle. "Seems so long ago."

Tonya took down the cups from the cabinet. "Where did Dad go?"

"Back into town. He forgot something."

"What'd he forget?"

"He didn't say."

Lexi looked so depressed and listless that Tonya's heart went out to her. Desperate to take Lexi's mind off Caine, she chatted about Jake's workout. Lexi seemed to perk up as Tonya reminded her of Jake's previous antics on the racetrack and his aversion to rough handling from men. The two women had succeeded with the stubborn horse where his former trainers and jockeys had failed.

"So how's Dad doing with Jake's breeding schedule?" Tonya said finally.

"He's lined up quite a few mares, I think. After that track record race, the owners are calling from all over. It should be a busy spring for us. I just wish…"

Tonya patted Lexi's arm. "It'll be fine. Don't worry. Caine can't force you to do anything, no matter what he says. He can't drag you back to Ohio by the hair now, can he?"

"He would if he could." Lexi took a deep breath and began talking about Caine. Tonya listened while she poured her heart out, describing the man's evil temper and need to control. "He never loved me. He only wanted to dominate me. After I left, I have no doubt he found other women to abuse and bully. It's what he does. I heard a rumor that he once beat a girl so brutally that he put her in a coma. I don't know if that's true, but I wouldn't put it past him. He's a sicko."

"Did you ask him about it? The rumor?"

"No. I was afraid to. But after he turned abusive with me, I began to realize it was probably true. I didn't hang around long enough to find out. All I knew is that I didn't want to be next."

Tonya gazed into her teacup, wondering what attracted women to that kind of man. She thought about the two men she was attracted to. Mike once had a reputation for being ruthless jockey, intent on winning at any cost. But once she got to know him, she realized he wasn't ruthless at all. He was scared. She had begun to understand his need to win, doing whatever was necessary to be able to support his mother and sisters in Mexico. Since he had been able to pursue his real passion, veterinary work, he had become a completely different person.

Then there was Adam Abarca, the young, sad-eyed police lieutenant who had hinted about marriage the last time they were together. She hadn't seen him since they moved to the farm in early November. Was there some kind of hidden need to control in either of these men? Did all men have the potential to be abusers?

It was after seven when they heard Royce's pickup in the driveway. He came into the house, tossed his jacket on the couch, and dropped heavily into his chair by the fireplace. Lexi and Tonya came in from the kitchen.

"We thought maybe you ran away from home," Lexi teased. "We were about to eat without you."

Royce was silent, staring into the empty fireplace. Lexi exchanged glances with Tonya.

Tonya placed the plate of sandwiches on the dining room table. "Come have a turkey sandwich, Dad. There's plenty of pie left, too."

Still, Royce didn't move. Lexi went to him and kneeled on the floor in front of his chair. "What is it, Royce? Tell me."

He looked at her with a pained expression. Then he took her hands in his. "I went to see Caine," he confessed.

"No. Why?"

"To try to talk some sense into him. Or reason with him. Or something. But it was useless. The man is beyond reasoning with. I've never met anyone like him."

"What happened?" Lexi asked.

Royce leaned back in his chair and massaged his temples. "I went to Jenkins's and found him in the back of the store. He was just getting off work. He actually seemed pleased to see me, if you can imagine. He suggested we go to his motel room to talk it out, 'man to man,' he said.

"So I gave him a ride over to the Wagon Wheel. You know the place, a real dive. Anyway, we went into his room and started to talk. He seemed rational, even understanding at first. He even made coffee for us. Then he said something like he knows how much you mean to me and how this must be hard for me. I was thinking 'maybe he's not so bad.' Then he seemed to switch personalities. He claimed that you were his wife legally and always would be. I told him I would never let him take you away, no matter what the legal situation is. And that I wasn't going to let him abuse you anymore. That's when he got really belligerent. He didn't get violent or anything. Just nasty."

"That's Lucas all over," Lexi sighed.

"Well, I tried to control my temper and told him he really had no choice but to agree to a divorce. Even if he didn't, you would sue him in court. I told him there were medical records back in Ohio that would prove abuse so that any judge would grant a divorce."

"What did he say to that?"

Royce's eyes flashed. "He laughed at me. The little creep. He said you are his wife and he isn't leaving here without you. 'One way or the other,' he said. He seemed so sure of himself. Then he said he had a date and told me to get out. That's when I lost it."

"What do you mean?"

Royce rubbed the back of his bruised right hand that was starting to swell up. "I wiped the smile off his face."

Lexi gasped. "Oh Royce, you didn't."

Royce looked just a bit sheepish. "I'm afraid so."

There's that Irish temper, Tonya thought. "What happened then, Dad?"

"Nothing. I left him sprawled out on his bed rubbing his jaw. Then I just drove home."

Lexi's face was pale and her eyes wide. "He'll never give up. I'll never be rid of him. Oh, God," she groaned, hiding her face in her hands.

Royce pulled her hands away from her face. "Now listen to me. No one is going to separate us. No one."

Her voice became frantic. "You don't know him, Royce. He gets what he wants because he won't give up. He'll figure a way to get me back. Even though he really doesn't want me. He just doesn't want anyone else to have me."

"I don't care what he wants. Whatever he's trying to do, he'll never succeed. Never. Do you hear me?"

Lexi nodded bleakly, her eyes full of tears. "Yes. I hear you."

He stroked her dark hair. "Good. Now give me one of those sandwiches. I'm starving."

ℰↄℰↄ

Late the next day, Tonya came down the stairs for dinner, followed by the cats sniffing the air filled with the smells wafting in from the kitchen. She heard the doorbell ring. "I'll get it," she called. She opened the door to find Adam Abarca on the porch, his six-foot-three frame filling the doorway. He wore a dark suit and tie, his lieutenant's badge prominently displayed on his belt. His curly brown hair and blue eyes were every bit as handsome as Tonya remembered. She was shocked to see him after two months of silence, but she wasn't about to let him know she was disappointed about not hearing from him.

"Adam. How nice to see you. Please come in."

"Thank you," he responded, somewhat formally. "It's nice to see you, too."

Royce and Lexi came in from the kitchen. Royce seemed genuinely pleased. "Well, Sergeant Abarca. Oh, I guess it's Lieutenant now, isn't it? It's about time you came to see us." He gestured toward the sofa. "Please. Sit down."

Adam moved to the sofa. "I'm afraid this isn't a social call, Mr. Callahan. Although I should have dropped by before this." He glanced at Tonya as he sat down, and she thought his basset-hound eyes seemed even sadder than she remembered.

He pulled several pieces of paper from his pocket. "Do you folks know a Lucas Caine?" Without waiting for an answer, Adam spread the papers on the coffee table. It was the winners' circle picture from the racing magazine, a sticky note with the Callahans' address, and a map of the area with the location of the farm circled.

"Yes, we know him," Royce admitted slowly.

"We found these papers in his motel room. That's how we connected him to you. What is your relationship to him?"

Royce and Lexi exchanged glances. Lexi's eyes pleaded with Royce.

"Just an acquaintance. Someone Lexi knew years ago."

Adam narrowed his eyes. "Are you sure about that?" He looked from Royce to Lexi. Then he turned to Tonya and raised an eyebrow at her.

Tonya looked down at her hands and remained silent.

Adam took out another piece of paper. "We found this, too." He handed Lexi and Caine's wedding picture to Royce. Lexi sank into Royce's chair and sat quietly staring at the floor.

Royce stood with his feet spread apart. "Okay, so what? This is a family affair. We'll work it out."

"Not anymore. Lucas Caine was found dead in his motel room this morning. He was murdered."

There was stunned silence. Tonya looked at Adam in disbelief. Lexi stared wide-eyed at Royce who rubbed his hands through his graying red hair.

Adam continued. "I'm afraid I'm going to have to

ask you all to come to the station tomorrow. If you don't mind."

Tonya stared at him in disbelief. "You don't think that—"

Adam looked at her. "I don't think anything. It's just routine to question everyone who knew him. Or who had any contact with him in the past few days. That would include you three."

"We'll be there," Royce said, squaring his shoulders. "Will ten o'clock be early enough for you?"

Adam stood. "That will be fine. Thank you." He gathered up the papers and started toward the door. "See you in the morning." He nodded to Tonya and left, closing the door quietly behind him.

CHAPTER 4

They had talked well into the night about Caine, his past with Lexi, and who might have had a reason to kill him. Tonya had gone to bed exhausted, wishing she had never heard the name Lucas Caine. She could hardly believe that just forty-eight hours earlier, she was experiencing the best Christmas ever, passing out presents, and enjoying a turkey dinner with her friends and family. Now she was on her way to the police station to be questioned about a murder.

Lexi and Royce sat close together in the pickup, her arm linked through his. Royce had been trying all morning to keep their spirits up, whistling in the kitchen while he made coffee and offering to make breakfast for everyone.

"You didn't eat much this morning, honey," he said, stroking Lexi's arm.

"I'm kind of nauseous. I don't think I could have choked it down."

Tonya noticed that she looked pale and wondered if it was just the stress of the past few days. But what if it wasn't? What if she was really sick? Lexi had always seemed so strong, so capable, a petite dynamo of a woman who could handle fractious Thoroughbreds easily and confidently. Now she seemed sickly and vulnerable.

"What do you think he's going to ask us, Dad?" Tonya asked.

"I think he just wants the whole story of how we know him. We'll just tell him the truth and let him figure out what happened. Knowing Caine, there must be all kinds of people with reasons to do him in."

They pulled up in front of the small police station on the main street. As they got out of the truck, a stray dog eyed them suspiciously before slinking around the corner of the building. The normally sleepy Southwestern town had suddenly taken on a sinister air.

A chubby-faced, young uniformed officer sat behind a tall counter tapping on a computer keyboard. He asked their names and said that Lieutenant Abarca was waiting for them. He stood up and ushered them into Adam's office. Tonya noticed that Adam was in the larger office that used to belong to Lieutenant Kubisky, the now-retired cop who led the investigation into the murders at the track the previous summer.

Adam stood up when they came to the door, looking tall and imposing. "Good morning. Thanks for coming. Please sit down."

There were three chairs in readiness for them facing his desk. Once they were seated, Adam opened a folder on the desk and cleared his throat. "Now, let's start with you, Mrs...er...Callahan. Suppose you tell me how you became acquainted with Lucas Caine. From the beginning."

Lexi took a deep breath and related the same story she told Royce in their room Christmas night. Adam made notes as she talked, interrupting only occasionally to ask a question. She admitted marrying him, changing her identity to escape from his abuse, and eventually coming to Texas where she met and married Royce.

Adam gazed at her intently. "I have to tell you, Mrs. Callahan, bigamy is against the law. But since there was no intent to defraud anyone, and your husband is dead, there would be no point in pursuing it."

Lexi looked down at her hands. "Thank you," she whispered.

"Now, Mr. Callahan, what happened after Caine left your place Christmas night?"

Royce wet his lips. "Nothing happened. At least not that night. I mean, I did see him the next day."

Adam made a note. "That would be the day before yesterday. What time?"

"About five. I went to the feed store where he works—worked. We talked in the back for a while, then he suggested we go to his room."

"What did you talk about?"

"What do you think?" Royce asked, sounding peeved. When Adam gazed up at him patiently, Royce admitted, "I tried to get him to agree to a divorce and leave town quietly."

"What did he say?"

"He laughed and said that would never happen, that Lexi, or Diana as he called her, was his wife, and he wasn't leaving here without her. Then he said he had a date and told me to get out."

"A date? With whom?"

"I have no idea. A date. That's all he said."

"Then what happened?"

Royce hesitated and rubbed his right hand. "I punched him."

Adam narrowed his eyes at Royce. "You lost your temper."

"Maybe. For a second. I had to shut his smart mouth."

"Well, it's shut now, isn't it?"

Royce leaned forward. "Now look, he was alive when I left him. I might have bruised his jaw, but that's all. As God is my witness."

Adam made a note then turned to Lexi. "Was Christmas day the last time you saw him, Mrs. Callahan?"

Lexi nodded, but Tonya said, "Well, we did see him the day after Christmas. Remember, Lex? Outside the salon?"

"Oh, yeah. We were at Michelle's Salon having our hair done. We saw Lucas on the sidewalk outside. He was looking at the salon. I thought he was stalking us."

"But I'm sure he wasn't," Tonya added quickly. "When we came out, he was gone." Adam made notes as she talked. Tonya said, "Adam, how do you know he was murdered? I mean, how did he die?"

Adam looked up at her, his eyes revealing his distress with the whole business. "We're still waiting for the autopsy results for a definite answer to that, but we do know whoever killed him set fire to the room with some kind of accelerant. He was found still in his bed."

Royce narrowed his eyes. "You mean he just laid there and let someone burn him to death? That doesn't make sense."

"Like I said, we'll know more when the autopsy is finished. In the meantime, I'd like to take each of your fingerprints."

Royce bristled. "Why Tonya? She has nothing to do with this."

"It's okay, Dad. I don't mind."

Adam stood up. "Just routine, Mr. Callahan. If nothing else, it will help eliminate the innocent."

He led them into a small, drab room where a technician applied ink to each of their fingers and pressed them onto a card. Adam oversaw the process then ushered them to the front door. "Thanks for coming. I'll be in touch."

He gave Tonya a slight *I'm sorry about this* smile, but she was in no mood for pleasantries. She felt dirty, and not just from the ink stain on her fingers. She was sure Adam suspected her father of killing Caine, and it infuriated her that anyone could think such a thing. *Maybe his promotion has gone to his head*, she thought. *Maybe becoming a lieutenant automatically turns you into a jerk, like his former boss.* She shot him a withering look as she left.

The drive back to the farm was even quieter than the ride into town. They all seemed to be lost in their own thoughts. When they reached the farm, Tonya changed her clothes and headed to the barn, eager to get away and lose herself in the horses. She went to visit Gus, but found his stall empty, so she left the barn to walk around the property.

The late December afternoon was pleasant and mild. Puffy clouds drifted lazily from West to East across the vast blue sky, and a slight breeze was blowing off the hills. The grass in the pastures was a dull winter brown but held the promise of the lushness of spring to come.

Tonya started down the dirt road past the hay barn, the foaling sheds, and the other outbuildings. The calico barn cat that the Warrens had left with them followed her, trotting along beside her as though the cat sensed she needed some company. Tonya bent down to scratch behind her ears while the cat head-butted her hand and purred. After a few minutes, the calico shot off into the weeds after a rabbit. Tonya watched her go. *I'll have to give that cat a name one of these days*, she thought. The Warrens had always referred to her as just "the barn cat."

Turning to the right, she followed the dirt path to the half-mile training track. She found herself drawn to the three-stall starting gate parked at the head of the short chute. She climbed up onto the bars and sat there gazing down the wide strip of dirt. Since they had come to the farm, she hadn't worked any of the horses from that gate. Gus was still recuperating, Jake's racing days were over, and there were as yet no horses there to train. She felt a sudden wave of nostalgia for the racetrack and the thrill of competition. More than anything, she was nostalgic for the comfort and security of her previous life. Living on the track's backstretch in her father's single-wide mobile home, she would rise early, exercise the horses for her father and other trainers then watch the afternoon races, or—on a really good day—ride in one herself. It had been a long, hard summer of trying to convince trainers to give her a chance to ride their horses in races.

She squelched the memory of the fall in one race that had shaken her confidence badly, preferring instead to relive the thrilling victories on the last day of the meet. Then there was that awful day when Alana's body was found. That memory, too, was pushed to the back of her mind.

As she sat on the gate, she saw Mike lead Gus around the track's far turn and come toward her. Suddenly, she was overwhelmed with a feeling of relief. She hopped down from the gate and started toward them. Mike waved, and Gus's ears pricked up when he saw her.

"How's he doing?" she asked when they met.

Mike was wearing a snug T-shirt that showed off his well-toned upper body. "Good. Not limping at all. It's been what…almost four months now?"

"Yeah," Tonya said, running her hand down the back of Gus's left foreleg.

"Maybe we can ride him one of these days. He should be able to bear some weight now. But we'll have to wait and see what Doc says the next time he's here. What happened in town today? Royce said this morning you would be talking to the police. Did Lexi's ex really get killed?"

"Yeah, he did. The interview went okay." There was so much she wanted to say to Mike, so much she wanted to confide to him, but it was almost as though speaking the words would make her worst fears come true. She was afraid her father's happiness was crumbling, angry at Adam for suspecting him, and grieved that Lexi was in such pain. She looked at Mike and saw the questions and concern in his eyes. "I don't want to talk about it. Let's jog Gus a little and see how he goes."

They both started jogging down the track, with Gus trotting between them. The colt began trotting faster and faster, pulling Mike along by the lead rope. Soon they were both running to keep up with him, laughing and shouting "Whoa!"

Gus bucked and pulled harder on the rope, clearly enjoying this vacation from his stall. Once they finally got him stopped, they stood there panting and giggling like children.

Tonya held her side. "I guess he's on the mend," she gasped.

Mike laughed and patted him on the neck. "*A ciencia cierta.*"

"Does that mean 'certainly'?"

"Very good. Yes, he'll certainly be back on the track in no time."

"I wonder where I'll be in no time," she said, almost to herself.

This little jaunt had been a welcome refuge from the fears and grief of the past few days, but their pressures still weighed heavily on her.

Mike took her shoulders and turned her toward him. "Tonya, listen to me. You'll get through this. So will Lexi. And your father. You are strong people, you work hard, you do things the right way. Soon this will be over, and we can all get back to doing what we love. You'll be riding races again. I'll be on my way to college and vet school. Royce and Lexi will be running the farm, training and breeding horses. And they will be successful. This is just a temporary setback."

The intensity in his eyes and his nearness took Tonya's breath away, and she felt she would believe anything he said. He was so close that she was sure he would kiss her. But he patted her shoulder and looked away. "Let's get Gus back. I've got stalls to clean."

They walked back to the barn in silence. Mike turned Gus out into his paddock where he rolled and then settled down to searching for some edible grass along the fence. Then Mike picked up a pitchfork and headed for one of the stalls.

Tonya saddled Jake for his daily exercise. Jake was much calmer than he had been on the racetrack, but she could tell he was getting bored. He enjoyed his time in his paddock where he could roll in the dirt and race around along the fences, but Jake was the kind of horse who relished competition. Lexi had expressed some doubt about whether he would settle down to life on the farm. Would he miss racing, along with the crowds that cheered and followed him? "Don't be surprised if he gets a little cranky on the farm," Lexi had warned at the time. "After all, he's only just turning five years old."

After two miles at a slow gallop on the track, they rode past the rise under the elm tree where the Warrens' stallion, Major Domo, was buried. The day she and Royce had first come to the farm for the tour from old Clyde Warren came to mind. She had suffered a bad fall in a race the day before and was dealing with fears of being injured or killed if she raced again. The farm seemed so idyllic and safe that day. But that was months before Lucas Caine showed up. She wondered if she would ever have those feelings there again.

ଓଉଓ

That evening, Mike joined them for dinner. A fire crackled in the fireplace, warming the normally chilly room.

The four of them sat at the dining room table, polishing off the rest of the Christmas dinner leftovers.

Royce looked over at Lexi, his voice and eyes full of concern. "You hardly touched your dinner, Lex."

Lexi sighed, sitting back in her chair. "I know, I know. I'm just not hungry." Dark circles rimmed her normally bright eyes, and her face had a greenish tint. Tonya had never seen her look so sick.

"Mike and I took Gus for a walk around the track today," Tonya said.

Mike laughed. "More like he took us for a walk—or a run. He dragged us around pretty good. He should be ready to ride soon."

Royce watched Mike digging into a second helping of mashed potatoes and stuffing. "If you don't watch those calories, you won't be the one riding him." They all laughed, and even Lexi's eyes sparkled a bit.

"Well, I love not having to make the weights every

day. Worst part of a jockey's life. This is great, Lexi. Thanks for inviting me."

"You know you're welcome to come over for dinner any time, Mike. Don't wait to be asked."

"What are you two studying tonight?" Royce asked.

"Biology," Tonya said, smiling at Mike as he reached for another dinner roll. "I hated it when I did my GED. But Mike is plowing through it so fast I can hardly keep up."

"Biology's fascinating. I can't hope to be a vet someday without it."

Tonya got up and started clearing the table. "You sit, Lexi. I'll load the dishwasher."

Mike got up from the table, took some books from his backpack, and sat down at the computer in the living room. Tonya joined him but couldn't help overhearing the conversation at the table.

Royce was rubbing Lexi's neck, "Sorry you have to go through this, honey. At least now Caine is out of our life for good. Hey, why don't we go into town and apply for a marriage license?"

Lexi gave him a wan smile. "Again?"

"This time in your real name. Um, do you want us to start calling you Diana now?"

"No. Diana is long gone. I'm Lexi Callahan now. License or no license."

"What about your family? Do they know where you are and what's happened?"

"My dad passed away a couple of years ago. My mom lives with her brother, my uncle Jack, and his wife. Jack is a psychologist. I called them regularly but never dared take the chance of going back there. I was afraid Lucas would find out."

"Well, once we're married, we can go visit them. Would you like that?"

She smiled at him gratefully. "Yes, Royce. I really would." She sighed, staring out the window. "I can't help wondering what happened to those other women whose lives he ruined. How can a man do that? It's unbelievable."

Royce's eyes flashed. "Whoever killed him did the world a favor."

CHAPTER 5

Tonya was just leaving the barn after the morning feeding the next day when she heard a car's wheels crunching on the gravel driveway. She recognized Adam's car and wondered what news he might be bringing. As she met him at the porch, she wished he didn't always see her in jeans and boots, smelling like horses. There was that sage green dress still hanging in her closet that had certainly made an impression on Adam the night they had dinner at the country club. Would there ever be another occasion to wear it?

"You're up early," she said as she scraped the mud off her boots. "Had your breakfast?"

"Yes, thanks. Is your father around?" His basset-hound eyes had a serious look about them.

"Yeah, he's here. Come on in."

He held the door open for her, and, as she moved past him, she enjoyed the familiar smell of the brand of aftershave he always wore.

"Dad," she called toward the kitchen. "Adam's here."

Royce came out of the kitchen, drying his hands on a dish towel. "Morning, Adam. I was just making some tea

for Lexi. She's a little under the weather. Want some? Or
can I get you some coffee?"

"No, thank you, Mr. Callahan," Adam replied stiffly.
"I'm sorry to tell you this, but I'm here to place you under arrest." He moved toward Royce, pulling a pair of
handcuffs from his pocket. "Turn around, please."

Tonya grabbed at Adam's arm. "Adam! Are you insane?! What are you doing?"

He gazed down at her sadly. "Please don't interfere,
Tonya. I'm only doing my job."

Royce stared at the young policeman incredulously.
"You're joking, right?"

"No, sir. It's no joke. You're under arrest for the
murder of Lucas Caine. You have the right to remain silent. Anything you say can and will be used against you
in a court of law. You have the right to an attorney."

As Adam continued reciting the Miranda rights,
Tonya and Royce stared at each other in horror. Lexi
emerged from their bedroom wearing a flowered
bathrobe, shock and fear on her face. She tried to go to
Royce's side, but Adam held her at arm's length.

"Please, Mrs. Callahan. Don't make this any harder
than it is. Your husband is my prisoner now. After he's
arraigned, you'll be able to see him. He'll be in a cell at
the station until the grand jury meets."

Tonya glared furiously at Adam. "You can't serious-
ly believe my father had anything to do with this."

"He had motive. He had opportunity. His fingerprints
were found in the dead man's room."

"But I told you what happened there," Royce protested. "I wasn't trying to hide anything."

"You were heard arguing with him behind the feed
store that day."

"We weren't arguing. Who told you that?"

Adam ignored the question. "The preliminary autopsy revealed he had ingested arsenic, and you purchased arsenic the same day. That was verified by Leo Jenkins."

"Yes, I bought it. It was for the rats!"

Tonya fumed at Adam. "You bastard. How dare you? I thought you were our friend!"

"I'm sorry," Adam said, sounding weary. "I'm only doing my job." He took Royce's arm and ushered him toward the door. Turning back to the two women, he advised, "Get an attorney. He's going to need one."

Adam opened the door and held it for Royce, who looked back at the two women, his face etched with sorrow. "Don't worry. This is all a mistake."

Tonya stood in shock, staring at the closing door in disbelief. The room seemed unusually cold. Lexi suddenly turned and dashed toward her bedroom. In seconds, Tonya heard her vomiting in the bathroom.

Sinking down on the sofa, Tonya watched Adam help her father into the back of his cruiser, his hands cuffed behind his back. Tonya's breath came fast, her heart racing. She couldn't process what had just happened. *Her father.* Arrested for murder. What kind of nightmare was this? She suddenly burst into tears of frustration, pounding her fists on her knees.

The cats, previously lurking on the stairs, slunk into the living room, looking around warily. Henry jumped up onto the couch and began rubbing his head gently on Tonya's arm, as though trying to comfort her. Clive followed his brother but stood up with his paws on the back of the couch, watching Adam's cruiser roll out of the drive. Tonya grabbed Henry and held him close, her tears wetting his white fur.

After a while, Lexi staggered out of her room. She dropped wearily into Royce's chair and stared at the cold, empty fireplace. She wrapped both arms around her stomach, groaning slightly.

Tonya watched her with concern. Lexi was tougher than this. Tonya wondered again if this might be a serious illness.

"Uh, Lex. Are you okay? I heard you throwing up in there. Dad said you weren't feeling well."

Lexi directed her gaze at Tonya, the dark circles under her eyes even more pronounced.

"I'm pregnant."

Tonya didn't know whether to laugh or cry. What would ordinarily be wonderful news now seemed ironic. The father of her coming child had just been arrested.

"Pregnant? So that's why you've been sick. Does Dad know?"

"I've been saving it for a surprise. I was going to tell him New Year's Eve. I can't tell him now."

"But you have to. You can't hide it for long anyway."

"He's got enough to worry him. I don't want to add to it." She leaned back in the chair and turned her face toward the fireplace. "Oh, God," she moaned. "This is all my fault. What am I going to do?"

Tonya was suddenly gripped with fury. She stood up quickly, pushing Henry away. "I'll tell you what you're going to do. You're going to see a doctor and get something for the morning sickness. Then we're going to call around for the best lawyer we can find." She was pacing the room, becoming increasingly angry and resolved. "Then we're going to find out who killed Caine."

Lexi looked up at her. "How are we going to do that?"

"I don't know yet. But we did it once. We can do it again," she said, referring to their investigation the past summer that led to the arrest of Alton Jeffers.

Lexi looked skeptical but seemed a little less bewildered. She sat up in the chair. "But you had Adam's help last time. He's not likely to help again." Suddenly she started giggling. "Not after you called him a bastard."

Tonya burst out laughing. It was all so absurd. She went to Lexi's chair, and the two embraced, laughing and crying at the same time. After a few minutes, Tonya stood up and wiped her eyes. Then she realized Mike had slipped in quietly. He stood by the door, his eyes wide.

"Uh...what's up? Have I missed something?"

Tonya's eyes met his. "Sit down, Mike," she said wearily. "We have a lot to tell you."

❧❦❧

Late that afternoon, Tonya sat in the waiting room of the only obstetrician in their small town. The walls of the room were painted a light green with posters containing pictures of happy babies and their mothers. Two other women were in the waiting room, both heavily pregnant. One thumbed listlessly through a magazine while the other stared at her cell phone. Her eyes came up to meet Tonya's, and she smiled.

"When are you due?" the woman asked.

"Oh, I'm not pregnant," Tonya replied. "I'm just waiting for someone."

The events of the morning were racing through Tonya's mind, but even now they were beginning to sort themselves out in a logical pattern. Lucas Caine was a wretched man, the kind of person who made enemies everywhere he went. He was known to be a crooked trainer who used illegal methods. No doubt that involved drugs of some kind. That usually meant drug dealers and others involved in the seedier side of racing.

He also had a history of womanizing. Surely there were fathers, brothers, and husbands of his victims somewhere. Was he involved with some woman here who might have a reason to kill him? He did tell Royce he had a date the night before his body was found. Who could that have been with? Maybe it was a married woman. The jealous husband theory was certainly a possibility.

Her thoughts were interrupted by Lexi coming out into the waiting room. She looked a little less haggard than when she went in. She stopped at the desk and paid her bill. Then she took Tonya's arm, and they left the building together.

As they climbed into the pickup, Lexi said, "You know something? I don't think I've eaten a thing today. Why don't we stop at the diner and grab a bite?"

Tonya was encouraged. "Sure. What did the doc say?"

"I'm about nine weeks pregnant. The baby should be here in late July." She looked out the window. "Funny. That's the first time I've said the word *baby*." She sighed. "I wish Royce was here."

"He'll be home soon, and he'll be thrilled. Don't worry. What about the nausea?"

Lexi held up a small bag. "He gave me these and a prescription for when these run out. I took one in the office. I feel better already."

Tonya drove toward Hank's diner, wondering what it would be like to have a little brother or sister.

"He also said to take prenatal vitamins, get plenty of rest, and avoid stress." She rolled her eyes. "I wonder if having your husband arrested qualifies as stress."

Tonya pulled into the parking lot in front of Hank's Diner and shut off the engine. She gazed through the window at the booth in the corner where she had eaten hamburgers with a track worker named Billy O'Casey just a few months ago. Tonya had suspected him of the murders on the track, and she was trying to size him up as a suspect. Then Adam had walked in, causing her to cringe at his seeing her with Billy.

Hank's was a 1950s Retro place, complete with an old-fashioned jukebox with coin operated vintage boxes in each booth and along the counter. The floor was patterned in large black and white square tiles. The booths had fake red leather seats and Formica tabletops. Strains of Elvis Presley crooning "Are You Lonesome Tonight?" were coming from the jukebox.

They slid onto two stools at one end of the counter and picked up the menus. "Geez, I'm famished," Lexi said. "I could eat a rhino."

The waitress stood in front of them, wiping the counter with a cloth. She was about forty years old with tired eyes and dirty-blonde hair pulled back in a bun. Only her mouth smiled as she offered an obligatory welcome. "Hi there. Welcome to Hank's. Can I get you something to get you started? Coke? Seven-Up?"

Tonya noticed the name badge on her pink uniform. "Meggie."

"Just water for me, thanks," Tonya said.

"I'll have herbal tea if you have it," Lexi added as she perused the menu.

"Sure thing," Meggie said. "We've got meat loaf on special tonight. I hear it's pretty good. I'll get your drinks."

She walked away, and Tonya wondered what it would be like to be a waitress, stuck inside all day long trying to satisfy people's different tastes and personalities. *I'll never complain about cleaning stalls again*, she thought, shaking her head.

Meggie came back with the drinks and set them on the counter. "Do you need more time?"

"Wanna try the meat loaf, Lex?"

"Might as well."

"Two meat loaf platters," Meggie said, writing it on her pad. "It comes with mashed potatoes and mixed vegetables. Is that okay?"

"Sure," said Tonya.

Meggie turned to the kitchen window behind the counter and put the ticket on the metal wheel. A gruff-looking cook in a dirty apron over his dingy T-shirt squinted at it and mumbled something.

Meggie turned away from the window with a disgusted expression. "Crabby old geezer," she muttered under her breath. She began putting place settings in front of the two women.

"I don't think I've seen you here before," Tonya said. "Have you been working here long?"

"No. I just moved to this burg about a month ago. I got this job a couple of weeks ago."

"Where are you from?"

"Back East," she responded with a wary expression.

Tonya decided she didn't want to pry, so she turned to Lexi. "We're going to have to take over the stable operation now that Dad is...away for a while. The mares will be foaling starting in late March, and we'll have to get the yearlings ready for the spring auction."

Lexi sipped her hot tea. "Don't forget we have to get Jake's stud book filled. I know Royce was talking to a bunch of owners about bringing their mares to him. He must have set up a schedule somewhere."

"We'll have to get Mike on that. From jockey to stallion manager to veterinarian."

Meggie perked up and seemed suddenly interested in

their conversation. "Oh, do you gals have something to do with horse racing?"

Tonya filled her in on their past on the track and their future hopes for the farm. "Are you interested in Thoroughbred racing?"

Meggie's face clouded a bit. "My younger sister worked at a track near Cincinnati once. She was a hot walker. Isn't that what you call it?"

Lexi nodded. "Does she still do that?"

Meggie sighed. "No. She passed away."

Tonya's heart went out to her. "Oh, was it an accident on the track? Working with horses can be dangerous."

"No. It wasn't the horses. She had some bad experiences and turned to drugs. She died of an overdose." She turned away, suddenly seeming embarrassed at having shared so much with total strangers. "I'll see to your dinners."

"That's tough," Lexi murmured under her breath.

Meggie came back with two plates and set them down in front of them.

"Thanks," Tonya said. "This looks great." She looked up at Meggie who was still standing in front of them. "Say, do you happen to know a man named Lucas Caine?"

The stocky waitress seemed startled, and a wary look shrouded her face. "Why do you ask?"

"Well, this is the only diner in town, and everyone comes in here eventually. I just wondered."

"Sure. I know Caine," she admitted casually, appearing to relax a bit. "He comes in here a lot. What do you want him for?"

"I'd like to know who killed him."

Meggie's tongue flicked out and wet her lips. "Caine's dead?"

"Yep. When was the last time he was in here? Do you know?"

The waitress looked out the window for a moment. "He was in here last week. The day after Christmas it was. I remember 'cause old grumpy in there came in with a hangover." She nodded over her shoulder toward the window to the kitchen. "Caine was playing some loud music on the jukebox, and he told me to turn it down."

Now we're getting somewhere, Tonya thought. "He told someone he had a date that night. Did you see him with anyone? Did he meet someone here?"

Meggie shook her head. "No. He ate dinner and left by himself. That's the last I seen of him." She turned abruptly and walked away. She busied herself on another part of the counter but continued to steal glances at Tonya and Lexi.

"She's hiding something," Tonya said quietly. "Don't you think?"

Lexi gazed at the waitress thoughtfully. "She knows more than she's saying. That's for sure."

CHAPTER 6

About a week later, Tonya met Mike in the barn
early one morning and noticed he seemed quiet.
She knew that with Royce in jail and Lexi still
feeling weak, Mike was doing most of the work. Tonya
felt badly for neglecting him and was determined to make
it up to him. "Hi," she said, feigning a cheerfulness she
didn't really feel.

"Hi." Mike's gorgeous almond eyes were as mysterious as ever, tinged today with a little sadness. "Tonya,
we need to talk."

"Uh-oh. That's never a good opening." Before he
could speak, she continued. "Look, Mike, I know you've
been working hard, and I know I haven't been much help
in your studying lately, but—"

He touched her elbow. "That's not it. Come here. I
want to show you something." He led her to the door of
the feed room at the end of the shed row. Opening the
door, he said, "See that?"

"What?"

"See those four bales of hay? That's all we have."

"But what about what's in the hay barn?"

Mike shook his head. "There's nothing in the hay

barn. We used it all. Not only that," he added, gesturing to the corner, "but these are the last two sacks of sweet feed. We're running low on the bedding shavings too."

"How can that be? I know Dad orders these regularly. How can we have used them up already?"

"We've got six horses and four yearlings to feed and twelve stalls to bed. The supplies don't last long that way. I called Jenkins yesterday to order more, but he said he couldn't sell us anything unless we pay cash. He won't extend any more credit until our bill is paid."

Tonya sat on a bale of hay and chewed her lip. "He knows Dad is in jail. He must be worried that if Dad doesn't get out soon, the farm will go under."

Mike sat down next to her. "I have a suggestion."

Tonya looked up expectantly. "I hope it's a good one."

"Well, it will help. Let's turn the horses out and leave them in the pastures. There's not enough grass to sustain pregnant mares and yearlings, so we'll have to keep feeding them out there, but it will save on bedding at least. There's no reason to keep them inside in this weather."

Tonya thought about the acres of pastures sitting empty over the winter. "I don't know, Mike. Six mares in foal outside all the time. How will we keep any eye on them? Suppose one of them foals early?"

"So? Horses have foaled outside for centuries."

"Yeah, but so much of our income depends on a crop of live, healthy foals. It makes me nervous."

"Okay, we can turn them out until March. That's the earliest any of the mares will foal according to Mr. Warren's calendar. And we can turn the yearlings out too. It will be good for them."

"What about Jake and Gus? We can't leave them out overnight. They're too valuable."

"No, but they can spend most of the day outside. That will help some."

Tonya stood up and squared her shoulders. "I'm going into town to get Lexi's prescription filled. I'll talk to Jenkins. Maybe we can work something out."

e↷↻

After dropping Lexi off at the police station to visit Royce, Tonya drove to the feed store. The green parrot's cage had been moved closer to the door, and, as Tonya walked in, he shrieked, "Watch your step, buster!" Diesel, the fat black cat, was at his usual post just beneath the parrot's cage, his yellow eyes fixed on the bird, the tip of his tail flicking back and forth. Tonya bent down to pet him then headed to the counter where Leo Jenkins was going through some paperwork. He looked up just a bit warily when he saw her.

"Morning, Tonya."

"Hi, Leo. Can I talk to you?" She explained how much hay, grain, and bedding she needed and waited anxiously for his response.

Jenkins said as he leaned toward her, his stomach hanging over the counter. "Sorry, Tonya. I feel for you, but I have a business to run. I'm sorry your father is in this mess, but I can't extend any more credit until I know whether he will be able to run the farm. I mean, you and your stepmother don't have much help out there. You're not racing anymore, and from what I hear, you don't have much coming in."

Typical small town, Tonya thought. *Everyone knows everyone else's business.* "That's only temporary. Dad has lined up a bunch of mares to breed to Jake. They'll start arriving in April, and then we'll have plenty of money. We just need to get through the next couple of months."

"Jake, huh?" he said, his eyes suddenly wistful. "I saw that last race of his, you know. Won by something like fifteen lengths, didn't he?"

"Twenty. And he broke the track record, too."

"Man, that was really something. I won't see anything like that again in my lifetime."

Tonya was hopeful. "Just think how many mares will be lining up to be bred to him. In a couple of months, we'll be on our feet again. So what do you say, Leo?"

Jenkins straightened up, his eyes suddenly flashing. "You don't know what it's like trying to make a living in a place like this. There's a million ways to lose money. Someone's been stealing from me. I'm missing a halter, a forty-dollar whip, some of that rat poison I sold your father, some other stuff, too." He shook his head. "I'm barely surviving here. And with your father in jail, who knows when he'll get out or even—" He gave her an embarrassed look. "I mean—"

Tonya rolled her eyes. *Is money all that matters to some people?* "He'll be out soon. I'm sure of it. They can't keep an innocent man locked up forever. Don't worry. You're going to get paid. We'll be selling four yearlings at the auction in March. Just a couple more months, and we'll be able to pay the bill. Just help us out until then. That's all we ask. Please."

Jenkins rubbed his stubbly chin. Then he sighed. "I suppose you want it delivered, too."

Tonya turned her most winning smile on him. "Thanks, Leo. You won't regret it. Oh, can I get a couple of bales of alfalfa to take with me now?"

"Oh, why not? Pull your truck around back. I'll have Alec meet you."

"Thanks a lot, Leo. Really." She started for the door before he could change his mind.

"Watch your step, buster!" the parrot shrieked as she closed the door.

Parking the pickup behind the store, Tonya remembered that this was where her father had met Caine the night he died. But Royce had claimed their conversation was cordial. Where did Adam get the idea they had argued?

Alec, the store clerk, was standing at the back door, a scowl on her pock-marked face.

"Need some help?" Tonya asked as she pulled down the pickup's tail gate.

"I can manage," Alec declared curtly and easily swung a hundred pound bale of hay into the bed of the truck. The burly woman's arms were taut and muscular, and Tonya almost expected to see an anchor tattooed on one of them.

"Nice looking alfalfa," Tonya said, trying to make conversation.

"It's okay. Nothing like what we had in the Midwest, though."

"Oh, where did you come from?"

"Southern Ohio. Nice farms there." Alec stared at Tonya for a moment. "You're the jockey, aren't you?"

"Tonya Callahan," she said, extending her hand toward Alec, whose iron grip was a bit painful. Pulling her hand gently from Alec's, she continued, "I'm still an apprentice right now. I hope to get my license in the next year or two."

The woman shook her head. "Dangerous work."

"Sometimes. Are you interested in racing?"

"I used to be. My daughter worked at a track back home."

"Really? What did she do?"

"She was a workout girl. Exercise rider. She loved to ride. Even talked about getting her jockey's license one day. Not that it did her much good." She shrugged her shoulders and turned to get another bale of hay.

"Is she still trying to make it as a jockey?"

Alec's expression turned angry and sullen. "No. Now she's just trying to learn how to feed herself."

"What?"

"She's in a convalescent home. Brain damage."

"Geez, I'm sorry. A riding accident?" Tonya was suddenly overwhelmed with gratitude that her one accident had resulted in nothing more than a bruised shoulder.

Alec stared at Tonya for a moment, her lip curling in an angry sneer. "No. Not a riding accident." She tossed another bale into the truck as though it weighed nothing.

Tonya felt terribly sorry for this poor woman. In spite of her size and strength, she was just another damaged human being dealing with sorrow and loss. "That's too bad."

"Yeah, too bad," Alec said sarcastically. "Anything else that needs loading in your truck?"

"No, just the hay. Thanks." Tonya cleared her throat. "Uh, Alec, you knew Lucas Caine, didn't you? The guy who worked here and got killed?"

Alec looked suspiciously at Tonya. "What about him?"

"Remember my dad who bought the rat poison that day? He's been arrested for killing Caine. But he's innocent. Someone told the police they saw him arguing with Caine behind the store. Was that you?"

Alec glared at her. "I mind my own business. If I was you, I wouldn't go snooping around where you shouldn't."

"This *is* my business," Tonya countered, trying to control her temper. "It's my father who's in jail. Now, what did you mean by snooping around where I shouldn't?"

Alec hesitated for a moment, looking around warily. "Only that there's more business going on here than just selling hay, and Caine was up to his eyeballs in it." Alec slammed the tailgate of the pickup and stalked toward the back door of the store. In the doorway, she turned briefly to glower at Tonya then closed the door behind her.

Tonya climbed into the cab of the pickup and sat there staring at the store's back door. Whatever happened to Caine, she was sure there was a link to the feed store somehow. Just then the same white van she had seen before pulled up and parked near the door. A dark-haired man in laborer's clothes got out and stood near the van for a moment, staring at her. Then he went in the back door.

She started the engine and noticed the gas gauge read Empty. "Damn," she muttered. She searched through her wallet and found only a twenty-dollar bill. She sighed and turned the truck toward the drug store, hoping that Lexi's prescription wouldn't be too expensive and that she would have a few dollars left to put fuel in the truck.

಄಄಄

Centerville's only druggist, Orville MacNeil, a mousy little middle-aged man with thick glasses and thinning hair, squinted at the prescription and frowned. Peering down at Tonya from his pharmacy window, he said, "Do you have insurance?"

"Uh, no."

"Well, before I fill this, you should know it will be over three hundred dollars."

Tonya swallowed and felt her jaw tighten. *What next?*

The druggist continued. "Even if I give you only half what the doctor prescribed it will still be about one hundred seventy dollars."

"Oh. I had no idea. It's for my stepmother. We just can't afford that."

MacNeil eyed her as he handed the prescription back to her. "Tell you what." He reached for a brochure from the rack on the counter. "There's some suggestions in here that might help her morning sickness. Supplements mostly." He handed the brochure through the window. "Take a look at it. Our supplement section is over there." He gestured toward the wall to his right.

"Okay. Thanks."

"And think about getting some insurance for your family," he offered as she walked away.

Yeah, I'll do that, she thought. *Right after I get enough feed for the horses to last the winter, gas for the truck, and a lawyer to get my father out of jail.*

She moved down the aisle next to the wall where the vitamins and minerals were stacked. As she thumbed through the brochure, she heard the door open and close. A woman with bleached-blonde hair, heavy makeup, and a low-cut sweater flounced into the store and headed quickly for the pharmacy, her high heels tapping angrily on the old wooden floor. She opened the door to the druggist's area and barged in.

"Orville!" Tonya heard the woman say. "What's the meaning of this?"

Tonya peered over the shelf and saw her wave a

sheet of paper under the druggist's nose. He looked up at the woman who was at least four inches taller than him, puffing his chest out in an effort to match her aggression. "The meaning," he said sarcastically, "is that you are cut off. The bank will no longer honor your credit. I'm sick of paying your bar bills."

She threw the paper at him. "You've got a lot of nerve."

He slammed his fist on the counter. "I've got a lot of nerve? Me? Let me tell you what nerve is, Myra. Nerve is hanging around with every lowlife that crawls out from under a rock, running up tabs in every bar in town, and expecting me to pay for it."

Tonya was embarrassed for the two and tried not to eavesdrop, but it was impossible to ignore their shouting.

"You little weasel," the woman hissed in disgust. "If you were half a man, you'd—"

"Half a man like your boyfriend. Or should I say ex-boyfriend? He got what he deserved, didn't he? Sooner or later, those guys always do." MacNeil sneered at his wife. "Go home, Myra. I have work to do."

The woman stormed out of the pharmacy area and down the aisle. Her face was flushed, and the cheap necklaces around her neck clattered as she marched toward the door. Tonya jumped as the door banged shut. She glanced back at the pharmacy window and heard the druggist humming as he continued to fill prescriptions.

Tonya left the drug store without buying any of the supplements suggested in the brochure. Maybe the morning sickness pills the doctor had given Lexi would hold out until the end of the first trimester when the nausea was said to usually subside.

She put a few gallons of gas in the truck, drove to the police station, and parked on the street. Just as she was putting coins in the parking meter, she noticed Tissy, the girl from the hair salon, shuffling toward her with her head down, looking preoccupied.

"Hi, Tissy," Tonya called to her.

Tissy looked up warily then smiled as she recognized Tonya. "Oh, hi. Tonya, isn't it?"

"Yes. I really like the haircut you gave me," Tonya said, patting her hair. "You did a nice job."

Tissy seemed genuinely pleased. "Thanks. It does look nice on you."

"Not working today?"

"Oh, I'm just taking a break. I'm going to the coffee shop." She hesitated for a moment. "I don't suppose…"

Tonya had nothing to do until Lexi came out of the station, so she said, "I'd love a cup, if you would like the company."

Tissy nodded with a small, grateful smile. "Okay. Sure."

They walked together to the little coffee and tea shop on the next block. It was an old-fashioned establishment owned by a gray-haired woman who seemed to be trying to replicate an English tea shop. There were lace curtains, flowered wallpaper, and advertisements for scones and PG Tips tea. Pictures of Queen Elizabeth, the Tower of London, and Buckingham Palace adorned the walls.

Once inside, they ordered coffee at the counter. Tonya gestured toward a booth near the window, but Tissy pointed toward a booth in the back of the shop. "Let's sit back here. Less glare from the window."

After ordering, they sat together in silence. Tonya was becoming more and more curious about this strange girl with the nasty scar and the sad, pain-filled eyes.

Tissy pulled a cigarette lighter out of her purse and began flicking it absentmindedly, staring at the flame each time it appeared. She finally spoke up. "So, were you on your way to the police station?"

"I'm waiting for my stepmother. She's visiting my dad." Tonya looked down at her cup, wondering how much of her life to expose to this stranger.

"Oh, is he a cop?"

"No. He's in jail."

Tissy looked up. "Geez, that's tough," she said sympathetically. "What did he do? If it's none of my business, just—"

"He didn't do anything. He's accused of murdering a man. Didn't you read about it?"

"No, I don't look at the papers. Who's he supposed to have killed?"

Tonya sighed and looked out the window at the dusty street. "A guy named Lucas Caine. Ever hear of him?"

Tissy stared across the table, her eyes wide. She swallowed a large gulp of coffee with a shade of unease. "Um, no-o. I don't think so."

They sat in silence for a few moments, then Tissy inquired casually, "So why do they think your father killed this guy?"

"It's all a big mistake. Dad was with the man early in the evening the night he was killed. They had a bit of an argument, and the stupid cops are making more of it than there is. My father is a good man. He would never do that!" Tonya's lip quivered, and she felt hot tears beginning to form. She turned her face away, surprised by the strength of her anger. With all that had happened, she hadn't had time to process the scope of the tragedy that had engulfed her family. She began to tremble slightly and glanced at Tissy in embarrassment. "Sorry," she mumbled, blinking back her tears.

Tissy reached across the table and grasped her arm. "Don't apologize. It's terrible. Just terrible." She chewed her lip and continued flicking the lighter on and off. "I can't believe it. How could they—"

"The cops are making a mistake, that's all. I'm going to find out who's responsible if it's the last thing I do."

Tissy looked skeptical. "How can you? I mean, if the cops can't—"

"I've done it before," Tonya said, lifting her chin. "I found the killer of three people at the racetrack last summer." Tonya related the details of her investigation of Alton Jeffers and his attempt on her life. Tissy seemed mesmerized by the story.

Tonya was suddenly embarrassed to have shared so much with this stranger and decided to change the subject. "Tell me something. If you don't mind me asking. How did you get that scar?"

Tissy's face darkened, and her brow furrowed. She stared at her coffee, swirling it around in the cup. "The usual story," she sighed. "I met the wrong man. He was married, but his wife had left him, and he took it out on me. He liked to knock me around. One night he picked up a knife and did this." She moved her hair aside, turning the scar toward Tonya. "I think he was just trying to scare me and got carried away. I guess I deserved it."

Tonya was shocked. "Nobody deserves that. Nobody."

Tissy shrugged her shoulders. "I must have done something to make him mad."

Tonya realized that the scar on this girl's face was nothing compared to the scars on her mind and heart. She wondered how some women came to the conclusion they were so worthless that they deserve to be abused.

Tissy reached for her wallet. "I'd better be getting back." Tonya started for her purse, but Tissy said, "I'll get this."

Tonya smiled at her. "Thanks, Tissy. That's an interesting name. Is it short for something?"

Tissy looked down and away. "No. Actually, my name's Celeste. I just like the name Tissy."

CHAPTER 7

The mid-January clouds scudded across the morning sky chased by a chilly breeze. Tonya left the house quietly, not wanting to wake Lexi who was sleeping later and later these days. Her morning sickness had subsided somewhat, but a debilitating fatigue had taken its place. Tonya was concerned about her and urged her to go back to the doctor, but Lexi seemed almost too lethargic to care. Tonya wondered how much of the malaise was due to the pregnancy and how much of it was her depression over Royce. Since her visit to the jail a week ago, Lexi had seemed sad and distracted, unlike her normally strong and capable self. Now she seemed to be having a hard time coping with the simplest tasks.

Tonya had engaged a lawyer for Royce, but this too was an area that concerned them all. How were they ever going to pay him? At least the man seemed sympathetic to Royce's plight. He also seemed to be convinced of Royce's innocence.

Crossing the gravel driveway, Tonya glanced at Mike's trailer, surprised to see that no lights were on. Mike was normally up before her and often had most of the chores done by the time she arrived.

Sliding open the heavy barn door, she was soothed by the familiar smells of horses. The calico barn cat peered down from her perch in the rafters, her yellow eyes glowing in the semi-darkness. The barn seemed deserted now that the mares and yearlings were kept out in the pastures. Only Jake and Gus remained in their stalls. Both their heads craned over their half-doors as they watched her. Jake let out a loud, demanding neigh, almost drowning out Gus's friendly nicker.

In the feed room, she loaded the wheelbarrow with hay and two buckets of grain and pushed it down the shed row. She opened Gus's door and slipped in with his grain bucket. As she fastened it to the hook on the wall, Gus rubbed his head on her and pushed her with his nose. Then he plunged his head into the bucket for a mouthful. She left his hay on the floor and closed the door.

By this time, Jake was kicking his door and tossing his head up and down impatiently. After feeding him, Tonya pushed the wheelbarrow out the back door toward the pastures, glancing again at Mike's trailer. Still no sign of life.

The first pasture on the left was home to the six broodmares all lined up along the fence eager for their breakfast. Tonya tossed flakes of hay over the fence at ten foot intervals, and the more aggressive mares naturally lunged at them first, leaving the others to wait their turn.

Once they had sorted themselves out according to the equine pecking order and were all eating, she moved on to the yearlings' pasture. A couple of the stud colts galloped along the fence as she approached, displaying the natural competitive instinct of all Thoroughbreds to outrace one another. Tonya smiled at their antics that reminded her of rowdy little boys at the breakfast table, each one trying to grab the first Eggo. She tossed the flakes of hay over the fence. The four colts jostled and shoved one another until each had a pile of hay to himself, and then they began tearing at it with gusto.

Tonya returned to the mares, parking the empty wheelbarrow near the gate and opening it. Every morning since they had been turned out, either Tonya or Mike had checked each one carefully. She moved from one mare to the next, stroking their necks, checking their eyes for signs of ill health, then leaning down to check the udders. None was due to foal for another six or eight weeks, so their udders were not yet distended. All six seemed healthy and happy in their little band, having established the social structure necessary for harmony with herd animals. The alpha mare, a big bay named Maisie, kept the others in line with nips and pinned ears, while the others gave her a wide berth.

Leaving the pasture, Tonya was annoyed to see no lights on yet in Mike's trailer. *I guess he figures I'll just do it all myself,* she thought. *At least there are only two stalls to clean now. But still, I shouldn't have to do his job and Lexi's too. At least she has an excuse.*

She pushed the wheelbarrow to the door of Jake's stall and grabbed a pitchfork. Tossing the soiled bedding into the barrow while Jake watched her, she tried not to think about her father eating his breakfast alone in jail. Royce, who loved hard work and the outdoors even more than she did, must be feeling terribly claustrophobic. A lump formed in her throat as she pictured him in his tiny cell.

She threw the pitchfork forcefully into the wheelbarrow when she was done, mumbling to herself what she would say to Adam if he was here. How the young cop could believe Royce was a murderer was impossible for her to comprehend. Hadn't he spent enough time with the

Callahans the previous summer to know Royce? He had been like one of the family. She remembered Adam and Royce chatting in the front room of the trailer while she got ready for their dinner date. How handsome Adam had looked in his navy blue jacket and striped tie. How his eyes had shone when she entered the room in her new green dress. Although it was only four months ago, it seemed like another life, another world.

She moved on to Gus's stall and was just opening the door when Mike slipped into the shed row through the back door. His hair was uncombed, and his clothes were wrinkled, as though he had slept in them. As he walked quickly toward her, his expression was a mixture of fatigue and embarrassment.

"Sorry I'm late," he mumbled, running his hand through his hair. "I was up late studying."

Tonya experienced a slight pang of guilt at having neglected Mike's studies lately. Her agreement with Doc Frey and Royce had been that she would help guide Mike through his GED studies while he taught her Spanish. At the time, it seemed like an ideal arrangement. But things had changed, and now she had more than enough to do with the housework Lexi couldn't handle, trying to balance the finances, and taking over Jake's breeding schedule. She spent hours on the computer planning the schedule and communicating with the owners who were bringing their mares to Jake. That meant Mike had to study alone without the computer. *Well, that's tough*, she thought. *We all have to make sacrifices.*

"No problem," she said with a nonchalance she really didn't feel. "It's all done except Gus's stall."

"Let me do that." He reached for the pitchfork. "Did you check the mares?"

"Yep. All healthy as horses." She smiled at her little joke, but Mike seemed preoccupied. She suddenly felt sorry for her callous thoughts and wanted to make it up to him. "Come up to the house when you're done. I'll make us some breakfast."

"That would be great. Thanks. I'll be up in a few minutes."

Tonya left the barn and started up the drive toward the house, wondering what there was in the kitchen to eat. She hadn't been grocery shopping in a week, and she knew Lexi hadn't either. They were pinching every penny, trying to make their meager savings last until spring. Most of their combined winnings from the previous summer's races had been used for the down payment on the farm, and Royce's savings account was nearly empty. She wondered what Mike's financial condition was. How long would his jockey's winnings last?

She opened the front door carefully, trying not to wake Lexi, but found her sitting in Royce's chair near the fireplace, still in her bathrobe, her long hair hanging loosely about her shoulders. Tonya noticed her nearly black hair had a few more gray hairs. Lexi looked haggard, causing Tonya to wonder if thirty-five might be a little late to be having a first baby.

"Hi, Lex," she said with as much cheerfulness as she could muster. "Sleep well?"

"Not too bad. I just don't know how I can sleep for ten hours and still wake up exhausted."

Tonya left her jacket on the couch and stood over Lexi. "What did the doctor say?"

"He said it wasn't unusual, and it would pass after a couple of months. Until then, I'm to sleep as much as I need to." She looked up at Tonya, the dark circles under her eyes pronounced. "But I feel guilty leaving all the work for you to do." She sighed and leaned back in the chair. "I feel so useless."

"Don't even think that way. You can't help how you feel. And there's not as much to do now that the horses are mostly in the pastures. Mike and I can handle it. Stop worrying. Hey, want some breakfast?"

Lexi perked up a little. "I think I could eat something. I just took a nausea pill."

"Okay, I'll see what I can make. Mike's coming in, too." Tonya went into the kitchen only to stop, disgusted at the sight of the sink piled with yesterday's dirty dishes. She opened the refrigerator and realized there were only two eggs and a little milk. She found some stale bread in the freezer and decided French toast was the only option. Thawing the bread in the microwave, she leaned against the counter and surveyed the mess. Housework was never her passion, but even she could see that conditions in the old farmhouse were rapidly deteriorating. She resolved to spend some time cleaning today.

While the French toast was frying, she brought the dishes and condiments into the dining room and set them on the table.

Mike had come in and was standing at the computer in the living room. He looked up at her hopefully. "Maybe we can do some studying today? If you're not too busy, that is."

Tonya bristled. "Maybe," she replied curtly. "Then maybe after I make everyone's breakfast, clean up last night's dishes, do the laundry, and go into town for groceries, I can walk on water." She slammed the silverware down on the table and went back to the kitchen. *Who does he think he is?*

She flipped the French toast onto a platter and took it out to the table. "It's ready," she called, not looking at either of them.

They ate quietly, the atmosphere thick with tension. Tonya watched Mike wolfing down his food. For some reason, it annoyed her. She sighed and played with her food, having lost her appetite.

Finally, Lexi said, "Tonya, I can do the shopping if you like. Or I can clean up the kitchen if you want to go into town."

"Don't be silly, Lexi. You're as weak as a kitten. Just go back to bed. You know what the doctor said."

Mike's deep brown eyes found hers. "Anything I can do?"

She leaned back in her chair. "What I really need is for you to take over what Dad was doing with Jake's breeding schedule. It's all on the computer. On the desk, there's a list of calls I was going to make today to the mare owners."

Mike gazed over at the computer desk, and Tonya wondered if he was thinking about his studies. She knew becoming a veterinarian had become his life's ambition, but she also knew they would probably have to delay his studies, at least until Royce came home.

He stood with his hands in his pockets. "I guess I can do that," he offered with little enthusiasm.

They heard a car's wheels crunching on the gravel driveway.

"Damn," Tonya said, looking out the window. "I forgot all about Doc Frey. He was scheduled to come to-day to check on Gus's leg." She got up and headed for the door, wondering how she was going to pay his bill. Mike followed her, and the two of them greeted the veterinarian as he got out of his truck.

"Hello, you two. Nice morning. How's the patient doing?"

Mike described taking Gus for walks around the property and the way he had dragged the two of them down the track.

The vet nodded. "Sounds like he's on the mend."

They walked toward Gus's stall together and found him playing with the calico cat who was walking along the ledge halfway up the wall. The two had become fast friends. Gus pushed the cat gently with his nose, blowing softly on her fur, while the cat responded by rubbing against the horse's muzzle. They both turned to watch the visitors open the door and come into the stall.

Tonya slipped Gus's halter over his head and stood stroking his face while Mike and the vet examined the leg. Doc Frey's expert hands palpated the tendon, checking for heat or tenderness. When he pinched the tendon with some force, Gus lifted his leg slightly and pinned his ears back. Doc began describing the anatomy of the equine leg to Mike in terms Tonya didn't recognize, but Mike seemed to understand completely what he was saying. Tonya felt a mixture of pride in his accomplishments and guilt at neglecting to help Mike with his studies.

Doc took out his stethoscope and listened to Gus's heart. Then he lifted his top lip to check his gums and teeth. He ran his hand across Gus's glossy side. "He looks great." He put the stethoscope back in his bag. Leaving the stall, he added, "He's recovering, but that tendon will need a couple more months to fully heal. I have to tell you, Tonya, he may never recover completely. Remember this is the second time for this injury. Were you planning on racing him again?"

"That's up to his owner, but Dad said Mr. Brooks wanted to try to get him back to the track next summer. If he does well, the plan is to retire him to stud after that."

Doc rubbed his hand across his chin. "We'll have to see how he progresses over the next month or so. By the way, how is your dad?"

"Well, I guess you heard he was arrested for killing that man who was here Christmas day."

Doc stood next to his truck and gazed off toward the hills. "You know, I thought I recognized him. I've seen him before. He worked at the feed store, didn't he?"

"That's right. Did you know him?"

Doc tossed his bag into the front of his pickup. "Not personally, but I remember seeing him arguing with Leo one day when I was in there. They were really going at it."

Tonya's pulse quickened, and she glanced at Mike. "Really? When was this?"

Doc thought a moment. "About a week before Christmas, I think."

"Did you hear what they were arguing about?"

"Not specifically, but Leo was really hot. He was right in Caine's face. He seemed to be warning Caine about something. He said something about Caine being too greedy. It sounded like Leo was threatening him."

Tonya's mind was whirling. What was it Alec had said about more business than selling hay going on at the store? "Doc," she asked eagerly. "Would you be willing to call Lieutenant Abarca and tell him what you heard?"

The vet seemed reluctant. "I don't know. I mean I couldn't swear that was what I heard." He saw the disappointment on Tonya's face. "I'd like to help your dad, but—"

"I don't think you'd have to swear to anything, Doc," Mike chimed in. "Just tell him what you think you heard and leave it at that. It might be enough to get Royce released, I mean if there's another suspect. At least the cops could look into Jenkins."

Doc regarded the two of them for a moment then said, "Okay. I guess it can't hurt. I'll call him when I get back to the office."

Tonya sighed with relief. "Thanks, Doc. Thanks a

lot." She and Mike stood watching his truck move slowly down the drive. She couldn't contain her joy and turned to Mike who was grinning at her. "Oh, thank God," she said. "Thanks for backing me up." Without thinking, she wrapped her arms around his neck and kissed his cheek.

Mike seemed a bit embarrassed but pleased as well. "*No problema.*"

Tonya was ecstatic. "Wouldn't it be great if Dad could come home? You know he doesn't even know yet that Lexi's going to have a baby?" She started for the house. "I have to tell her." Suddenly she turned back to him. "Hey, let's study tonight," she called as she walked backward toward the house.

Mike stood in the drive watching her, a smile slowly spreading across his face. Without waiting for an answer, she turned and sprinted for the porch.

CHAPTER 8

Tonya pulled up in front of the police station that afternoon, feeling guilty that she hadn't visited Royce more often. Lexi was sleeping when she left, and Tonya didn't disturb her. Besides, Tonya wanted some time alone with her father.

She was greeted by the same young uniformed officer inside the door. He smiled at her. "Here to see your dad?" As he led her to a small room interview room, she glanced toward Adam's office. It was empty. She waited in the interview room until Royce was brought in. His face broke into a wide grin when he saw her. As much as she longed to run to him and give him a huge hug, she was prevented by the officer who stood by the door. Her father sat down opposite her at the table, and she noticed that his red hair had grown grayer in the past weeks. He also looked like he had lost weight.

"How are you, Dad...really?"

"Fine, kiddo. Don't worry about me. The worst part about this is knowing you and Lexi are on your own out there. How is she? She didn't look so good when she came in last time."

Tonya longed to tell him the good news that he was

about to be a father again, but it was Lexi's wish that it be
kept a secret until she could tell him when he got home.

"She's okay," she said. "And we're not totally alone.
Mike is there." She started to say that Lexi missed him,
but thought that would only make him feel worse. So she
told him the mundane details of life on the farm, how the
horses were doing, and their decision to turn the mares
and yearlings out into the pastures. She even told him
about the cats and their antics, trying to sound as upbeat
as possible. Finally, she said, "Dad, we just have to get
you out of here. This is so wrong."

"I know, honey. I know. But there's nothing you can
do."

"We called a lawyer. He said he'd be in touch with
you. Have you heard from him?"

"Yeah. He was here. He didn't seem all that optimis-
tic. Motive, opportunity, evidence. You know the drill."

"Can't he get you out on bail or something?" Tonya
shuddered at the thought of trying to raise bail money,
even if bail was a possibility.

Royce sighed. "They don't usually bail out accused
murderers. I just have to wait for the grand jury to decide
whether to send me to trial."

"When will that be?"

"Sometime after the first of February, I think."

Tonya was disgusted. "I can't believe it. It's so unfair. If only we could figure out who really killed him. Or
at least get Adam thinking about some other suspects.
Doc came out to see Gus this morning, and he told us he
heard Leo Jenkins threatening Caine one day before
Christmas. And that woman that works there, Alec? She
told me there was some kind of funny business going on
at that store. Something besides just selling hay. She told
me Caine was up to his eyeballs in something. Any idea
what she could have meant?"

Royce rubbed his hands over his stubbly chin. "No. I always thought Jenkins was a good guy. He threatened Caine?"

"That's what Doc said. He's going to call Adam to tell him what he heard. Maybe that will get Adam investigating Jenkins. Oh, another thing. Do you know that druggist?"

"MacNeil? Sure. Why?"

"I don't know if it means anything, but I heard him arguing with his wife one day in the drug store."

Royce waved his hand. "Nothing unusual about that. Everyone knows Myra. She's a piece of work."

"MacNeil said something about her boyfriend getting what he deserved. Could he have meant Caine?"

"I don't know. She does have a rep for running around with other men." Royce suddenly brightened. "Hey! That night at the motel he told me to leave because he had a date. It could have been with her."

"So that's two people that could have had a reason to kill him. Jenkins because Caine knew something about what was going on at the store and MacNeil, the jealous husband."

"But we don't even know if she was the one he was meeting. We can't go around accusing innocent people. It's bad enough they've got me in here. Let the police handle it."

Tonya knew he was right. But she was determined to pursue the two possibilities and see where they led. If she had let the police handle the murders at the track, Alton Jeffers would still be free.

They continued to chat until the officer at the door cleared his throat. "Time's up, folks. Sorry."

Tonya and Royce stood up. She looked at her father longingly, sick at the thought of him wasting away in a jail cell, but encouraged that there were two potential killers she could look into.

"Well, so long, kiddo. Keep your chin up and take care of Lexi for me."

"I will, Dad. I love you."

"You, too."

The officer walked Royce out of the room, and Tonya sat down again to think things through. One thing was sure: she needed Adam's help. She sighed. *If only I hadn't called him a bastard*, she thought. *I wonder if he's mad at me.*

Leaving the room, she was glad to see the light on in Adam's office. She smoothed her hair and straightened her sweater a little. She stood in his doorway, forcing herself to flash her brightest smile. "Hi, Adam."

Adam looked up from his computer screen, and his eyes shone in recognition. "Hi. Here to see your dad?"

"Yep. Just finished." She sidled into the office and eyed one of the chairs, hoping he would invite her to sit down.

Instead, he got up and joined her near the door. "I'll walk you out."

Disappointed, she allowed him to take her arm and steer her toward the front door of the station. There he looked down at her. "Look, Tonya," he said quietly. "I know this is hard for you. But you have to understand my position. I had no choice but to arrest your father, not with the evidence I had—have."

His six-foot-three frame towered over her, and his nearness was unnerving. The scent of his aftershave brought back memories of their date. Her knees felt a little weak, and she cursed herself for allowing her feelings for him to rise to the surface.

"Have? You mean there's more?"

Adam looked over his shoulder at the officer at the

front desk who was watching them. "What are you doing tonight? Maybe we could meet for dinner."

Tonya thought about Lexi and Mike waiting at home for her. "I have to go grocery shopping now and cook dinner tonight. Lexi's not feeling too good. Could we meet for coffee after dinner instead?"

"That works, too," he said. "How about seven-thirty at Hanks?"

"Fine. I'll see you then." He opened the door for her, and she brushed against him as she passed. *Damn the man*, she thought. *Why does he have to be so good-looking?*

⁂

Tonya pushed her cart down the aisle of the only grocery store in town, carefully adding up the cost of what she had in the cart, trying to decide what else they could afford. It was a struggle to feed just the three of them. *How do people with large families even survive? If this is what marriage and having a family is all about*, she thought, *I'll pass*.

Turning the corner of one of the aisles, she saw Leo Jenkins coming toward her. He was pushing a cart piled so high with food that he seemed to have trouble negotiating it down the aisles. *That's odd*, she thought. Leo was a bachelor who lived alone in a room above his feed store. What was he doing with all that food? But then again, he did have that huge gut. Maybe he was just stocking up for the month.

"Hi, Leo," she said as he approached.

"Hello, Tonya," he said cheerfully. "I don't see you in here often."

"No, my stepmother usually does the shopping, but

she's not feeling well." She gazed at his cart and the dozens of cans of refried beans, along with piles of tortillas and huge blocks of cheese. "I see you like Mexican food."

Leo looked a little uneasy. "Oh, yeah, I'm addicted. Can't get enough of the stuff. Well, see you around." Then he moved off quickly.

℮↷℮↷

After unpacking the sacks of groceries in the kitchen, the weight of household chores came on Tonya like a heavy burden. She also felt she would burst if she didn't get on a horse soon. She determined to get outside and ride Jake, dinner or no dinner. Taking the stairs two at a time, she raced to her room and tore off her clothes. Both cats were curled up on her bed and were startled out of their afternoon naps. They eyed her for a moment, then Clive curled up and went back to sleep. Henry headbutted her arm as she sat on the bed pulling on her boots. She gave him a quick scratch between the ears before heading for the stairs.

Once outside, she inhaled deeply and felt relieved. Even with the recent events, the farm was still a place of peaceful refuge for her. It had been that way from the first day she and Royce had visited the Warrens who treated them to a tour of the property, followed by Joy's homemade cake and lemonade. Relaxing on the porch that day, savoring the scent of Joy's flowers cascading from the porch roof, Tonya thought she had never experienced anything so lovely and serene. That feeling was still there, only now it was dampened just a bit.

Crossing the driveway, she saw Lexi sitting on the top rail of Jake's paddock fence stroking his neck and talking to him. Tonya's eyes lit up when she saw them

together, remembering the first day Lexi had brought
Jake into her stable at the racetrack. "My very own bad
boy," was how she described him. They soon realized he
wasn't bad at all, just rebelling against the rough handling
by the men who had been in charge of him. The owner
had brought him to a female trainer as a last resort.
"Hey there," Tonya called to her as she approached.
"It's good to see you outside." Jake's long ears pricked
up when he heard Tonya, giving him that tall skinny mule
look that always made her laugh.
Lexi climbed gingerly down from the fence. "Hi. I
was getting cabin fever in the house. Where've you
been?"
"I went into town to see Dad. He said I should take
care of you."
Lexi shook her head, her expression pained. "That's
your father. Always thinking of everyone else. How's he
doing?"
"He seems resigned to his situation. I think we're
more upset about it than he is. Oh, by the way, I'm seeing
Adam tonight after dinner. I want to run some things by
him."
"Like what?"
"Like two people who might actually be Caine's
killer." She filled Lexi in on what she knew about Jenkins
and MacNeil. "We just have to get Dad out of there. The
lawyer says they have to wait until the grand jury decides
whether to send him to trial. If there's evidence pointing
to someone else, maybe there will be enough doubt in
their minds to free Dad. At least that's what I'm hoping."
"So you're going to try to get Adam to help you?
Even after you called him a b—"
"I know, I know." Tonya interrupted with a laugh.
"Are you ever going to let me live that down?"

Lexi grinned impishly. "Nope."

Tonya took Jake's lead rope off the fence and clipped it to his halter. Jake followed her into the barn where they stopped at the tack room. "Here," she said handing the rope to Lexi. "Hold him a minute, would you?" She got Jake's saddle and bridle from the room and started to tack him up. Looking around, she asked, "Where's Mike?"

"In his trailer, I guess. I haven't seen him."

"I guess he's hitting the books again. He sure does love to study, doesn't he?" Tonya thought again about how much she had been neglecting Mike lately, and tonight would be no different. But she just had to see Adam to let him know what she had found out. Mike becoming a vet was important to her, but not nearly as important as getting her father out of jail.

Once Jake was saddled, Tonya turned to Lexi. "Do you want to ride him? You haven't been on him in a while."

Lexi's wrapped her arms around her midsection. "I would love to, but I don't want to take any chances."

Tonya lifted her foot. "Okay. How about a lift?"

Lexi put out her cupped hands and boosted Tonya easily onto Jake's back. "Just like old times," Lexi said wistfully.

"I won't be long," Tonya said as she guided Jake toward the open door. "Just a couple of times around the track."

Lexi responded with a face-splitting yawn. "I think I'll take a nap before dinner. See you later."

eఇeౢ

After dinner that evening, Mike sat down at the computer and watched Tonya taking the dishes into the kitchen. He cleared his throat, seemingly as an effort to hurry her along.

She glanced over at him. "Uh, Mike, I know I said we'd study tonight, but I have to go out."

He narrowed his eyes at her but remained silent. Then he turned back to the computer screen and began pulling up the files they used for the different subjects he studied.

She knew he wasn't happy with her. She only hoped he didn't ask where she was going. She went quickly up the stairs and started to change. Pulling on her best sweater, she decided to leave her hair down instead of in the usual pony tail. Anything to help her cause, she decided, and even applied some makeup, hoping she wasn't being too obvious.

Mike gave her an admiring glance as she came down the stairs. "You look nice. Going somewhere special?"

No sense in lying to him. "I'm meeting Adam for coffee. I want to talk to him about Jenkins and MacNeil. And he has some new evidence he wants to share with me."

Mike was silent, but she could tell from his expression that Adam was a bit of a sore subject for him.

"I won't be late. Why don't you start on the grammar exercises, and I'll check them when I get home?"

Mike grunted a reply, turning his back on her. Lexi nodded toward Mike and raised her eyebrows at Tonya.

She slipped out the door and closed it quietly behind her. Driving to the diner, she reflected again on how much of a mess male/female relationships could be.

Dark thunderclouds were forming over the hills just west of town as she drove quickly toward Hank's. The front parking lot of the diner was full, so Tonya pulled into a space in the back.

Adam was waiting for her in a corner booth. He wore a blue shirt that brought out the deep color in his eyes and a handsome suede jacket.

He stood up as she approached and his affection glowed in his eyes, causing her to feel the old familiar attraction to him. Sliding into the booth, she felt her face growing warm and picked up the menu to try to hide behind it.

Finally, she looked up at him. "Adam, I owe you an apology," she said sincerely. "For calling you a bastard. And for losing my temper. I'm sorry."

"I've been called worse things," he replied with a grin. "Forget it. Watching your father being dragged off to jail can't be pleasant. I hope you know it wasn't my choice. The captain looked at the evidence and issued a warrant. There was nothing I could do."

"I know. I still should have controlled myself better." *There*, she thought, *that should clean the slate.*

The waitress approached, and Tonya recognized Meggie from the day she and Lexi had come in. "Hi again," Tonya said.

Meggie looked at her for a moment as though trying to place her. "Oh, hi. You're the horse-y girl, right?"

"Right." Tonya noticed that the waitress still had that distracted, careworn expression she wore the first time they met.

"We'll just have coffee," Adam said, handing Meggie the menus. "Unless you want something else."

"Not me. I'm still stuffed from dinner."

After Meggie walked away, Tonya and Adam small-talked about the weather and the food at the diner. When the waitress returned with the coffee, Tonya nodded at her name tag. "Meggie. That's an interesting name. Short for Meghan or something like that?"

A guarded look closed up the waitress's face.

"Something like that," she replied curtly. "Anything else you folks want?"

"That will be all, thanks," Adam said.

Tonya watched her walk away. "Did I say something wrong?"

Adam smiled and shook his head. "No. Some people are just touchy."

Tonya took a sip of her coffee and set the cup down. "So what's this new evidence you mentioned? If you can tell me, that is."

Adam's eyes rested on hers with a sympathetic gaze. "Believe it or not, Tonya, I'm on your side. I've been trying to find evidence that will clear your father."

"I do believe it, Adam. If I didn't, I wouldn't be here."

He smiled at her. "And here I was thinking it was my charm and sex appeal." He took out his phone and scrolled through his notes. "I interviewed the diner manager," he said, nodding toward the crusty-looking cook at the window behind the counter. "He remembered Caine being in here that night. But he didn't meet anyone, and he left alone."

"That's what the waitress told me. But Caine told my dad he had a date. Maybe he met her somewhere else?"

"He must have. The manager did say he hung around and flirted with that waitress for quite a while. He also said he looked kind of sick when he left. I asked him if it was something he ate, and he about bit my head off."

Tonya laughed. "So maybe it was really food poisoning that killed him. Death by Hank."

"It wasn't food poisoning, but we got the toxicology report back from the coroner. He did have arsenic in his system. Not enough to kill him, but enough to make him sick."

"So whoever was in the motel room with him gave him arsenic?"

"That's where it gets sticky. There were traces of arsenic in one of the cups in his room. The other cup had your father's fingerprints on it. We also know your dad had bought arsenic from the feed store that same day."

Tonya felt her jaw tighten, but she was determined not to lose her temper. "He told you he was there. Caine made coffee for both of them. And the arsenic he bought was for the rats in the barn."

"I'm just telling you what I have, the same evidence the grand jury will hear."

Tonya sipped her coffee again. "Dad's not the only one with access to arsenic. Leo Jenkins has a store full of it. I remember him saying he was missing some. Anybody could have taken it and used it on Caine. And listen to this, that woman who works there, Alec? She told me there's something fishy going on in that store and that Jenkins threatened Caine about it."

"Did she give any indication what it was?"

"No, but when I talked to Jenkins about giving us more credit, he started griping about how hard it is to make a living in the store. Maybe he's doing something illegal to make money, and Caine found out about it. Maybe he's selling drugs through the store."

"He could be. Or it could be money laundering for a drug dealer. We know the drug cartel is active in the area. Remember Carlos at the track?"

Tonya nodded, recalling one of the murder victims from the previous summer.

Adam made a note on his phone. "I'll have a word with Jenkins."

Tonya gazed out the window at the light rain beginning to fall then turned back to Adam. "Oh, and there's that druggist, MacNeil. My dad said his wife was running around with someone, and I heard him and his wife arguing in the store. He was saying something about her boyfriend getting what he deserved. I think he meant Caine. He would have access to different things with arsenic in them, wouldn't he?"

Adam made another note. "Certainly." Then he reached into his pocket, pulled out a piece of black leather, and placed it on the table. "We found this in Caine's room. We're trying to identify it. Any idea what it is?"

Tonya took it from him. "Sure. It's a popper from a racing bat."

"A what from a what?"

"A popper from a racing bat, a whip. This leather loop is attached to the end of the whips jockeys use. When you hit the horse, it makes a loud popping noise. It's supposed to scare them and make them run faster. I don't know if it really works that way, but most all the whips have them. And look here. It's brand new. No fraying of the leather like a whip that's been used. Why would Caine take the popper off a whip?"

"I don't think he did. I think someone used it on him. The autopsy showed multiple marks on the body from a long thin weapon. Of course, there was so much damage from the fire that it's hard to know whether they were inflicted pre- or post-mortem. We also found an empty alcohol container in the woods behind the motel."

Tonya narrowed her eyes at Adam. "Wait a minute. You're saying someone poisoned him with arsenic, beat him to death with a whip, poured alcohol on him, and then set him on fire?"

"It looks that way, yes."

Tonya's pulse quickened, and her eyes flashed. "And you think my father could have done that?"

Adam sighed. "I keep telling you, Tonya, I'm only

doing my job. Your father had access to arsenic. He had a motive for killing Caine. And don't you have whips in your tack room? Are any of them missing this leather thing?"

Tonya was seething. "How dare you? You sit here pretending to be my friend?" She stood up suddenly, glaring down at him.

He grasped her wrist. "Please, Tonya. Let's not do this again. Sit down and drink your coffee."

"Drop dead." She grabbed her jacket, marched down the aisle, and stormed out of the diner, blinking back tears of rage. Striding quickly to the back parking lot, she was overwhelmed with horror at the violence of Caine's killer and furious at Adam for suspecting Royce, for thinking he was capable of doing such brutal things.

The rain had started in earnest as Tonya reached the dark back parking lot. The smell of rotting garbage emanated from the battered green dumpster, and a mangy orange cat peered at her from underneath it. Lightning flashed and illuminated the eerie scene, followed by a clap of thunder that made Tonya jump.

Fumbling with the key in the lock of the driver's door, she was suddenly jerked backward by something around her neck. She staggered back, her hands instinctively going to her throat. Then she had the sensation of someone behind her holding her close. She felt hot breath on her neck as a raspy voice whispered viciously in her ear. "Stop asking questions. And stop playing detective. Or you and that nice little farm of yours will go up in smoke."

Then she was pushed violently against the door, her head banging hard against the metal. Lights danced before her eyes, and she had the sensation of falling. She slid to the ground face first, gravel grinding into her mouth as blood poured from her nose. Her last sensation was of something sharp striking her across the neck.

CHAPTER 9

Tonya lay in the darkness next to the truck, afraid to move. The teeming rain soaked her hair and ran into her eyes. Slowly she sat up and peered around. No one was there. Leaning against the pickup's door, she wiped the blood from her face on her wet sleeve while her heartbeat returned to normal. Her neck was throbbing. Feeling it with her hand, she sensed a welt beginning to rise on the skin. Suddenly she heard footsteps running toward her, and she began to panic. What if her attacker was returning to finish the job?

She staggered to her feet, searching for her keys. They were lying on the ground at her feet. Could she bend over to get them without passing out?

All of a sudden, Adam was by her side, his arm around her shoulders. "Tonya. What happened? Are you all right?"

Almost against her will, she leaned against him and burst into tears. He held her close, his arms wrapped tenderly around her, apparently not caring that she was bleeding all over his nice jacket. For several minutes, she couldn't speak. Finally, he held her at arms' length and surveyed the damage.

"You need to go to the emergency room. I'll call an ambulance." He took out his cell phone.

"No, Adam, no," she whispered. "I don't need that. I just need to go home." She bent down to retrieve the keys, but when she straightened up, dizziness and nausea overwhelmed her.

Adam looked her over with the practiced eye of a policeman familiar with accidents and injuries. "I'll drive you to the hospital. You might have a concussion."

"No. I'm going home." She started to open the door of the truck, but he closed it firmly.

"I can't let you do that," he said, using his official voice. "If you have no concern for yourself, that's one thing. But you're a danger to other motorists. If you won't go to the ER, at least let me take you home. My car is right over here."

Before she could protest, he steered her toward his cruiser and opened the door for her. Settling into the seat, her mind whirled. Who could have done such a thing? There was no attempt to take her purse or steal her truck, so it must have been personal. And what was it the voice said? Stop asking questions? Who knew she had been asking questions? This must be connected to Caine's murder. Was it the murderer who attacked her? And what was that about the farm going up in smoke?

Adam drove slowly out of the parking lot and down the street, eyeing each person walking along the main street of the town. As they got to the end of the street, he sped up and turned onto the highway leading to the farm. As he drove, he kept glancing over at her uneasily.

When they pulled into the driveway, she saw that Mike's trailer was dark, but the lights blazed from the living room of the farmhouse. *He must still be at the computer, waiting for me*, she thought.

Adam helped her up the porch steps and to the front door. She hoped Lexi had already gone to bed, but when Adam opened the door, she saw her leaning over Mike's shoulder staring at the computer screen. They both looked up in shock at her bloody clothes and rapidly-swelling nose.

"My God," Lexi gasped, rushing toward her. "What happened?"

Mike got up and hurried into the kitchen.

Adam helped her to the couch. "She was attacked in the parking lot at the diner. She wouldn't let me take her to the hospital."

"I don't need a doctor. I'm fine."

"Funny," Lexi said with a smirk, sitting down next to her. "You don't look fine."

Mike returned with a wet cloth and began wiping Tonya's face with a gentle touch while Lexi helped her off with her jacket.

Adam stood awkwardly by the couch and took out his phone. "Tonya, I need to ask you some questions."

Mike glared at him. "Can't it wait?"

Adam sat in the chair opposite Tonya. "Afraid not. Did you get a look at the person who attacked you?"

"No, he grabbed me from behind."

"Did he take anything?"

"No. My purse was on my arm, but he never touched it."

"Did he assault you sexually in any way?"

"No."

"Did he say anything?"

"He said something about not asking questions, not playing detective. And he said something about the farm going up in smoke."

"Would you recognize his voice if you heard it again?"

Tonya furrowed her brow. "I don't think so. It was really a whisper."

"Did you notice anything else? How big he was? What he smelled like?"

Tonya leaned back against the couch, her head spinning as she tried to concentrate. "Bigger than me. Not as big as you, though. Strong. Heavy. No smells that I remember."

"Okay. He warned you to stop playing detective. Who have you told about what happened last summer?"

Mike bristled. "You make it sound like this is her fault. She didn't have to tell anyone about solving those murders. It was in all the papers."

Adam stood up, his six-foot, three-inch frame dwarfing Mike. "I'm not accusing her of anything. I'm just trying to cover all the bases."

Mike's eyes flashed as he glared at Adam.

Lexi stepped in to diffuse the situation. "We know you're just doing your job, Adam. Thank God you were there."

Adam looked down at Mike. "Please move away from her. I need to examine her injuries."

Tonya said, "I'm all right, Adam."

"If you won't go to the hospital, you'll have to put up with me looking at your injuries. For my report."

Mike glared at Adam again but moved out of his way. Adam touched Tonya's lip and nose. Tonya winced a little, and he said, "I'll try not to hurt you." He made more notes on his phone. "Pull your collar away from your neck." He took out a small measuring device and placed it against her neck where the welt had appeared. He made several measurements of the welt and the bruises on her face, making notes on his phone.

Finally, Adam stood up and put away his phone.

"Keep an eye on her tonight," he advised Lexi. "If she shows any unusual symptoms, they could be signs of a concussion, so call an ambulance." He looked down at Tonya. "I'll have someone bring your truck to you in the morning."

Tonya nodded and handed him the keys. "Sorry about your nice jacket," she said with a small smile.

Lexi walked Adam to the door. "Thanks, Adam. For everything."

"Good night, folks."

When she heard Adam's car start and begin moving down the driveway, Tonya suddenly felt vulnerable. She wrapped her arms around herself and trembled. But more than anything, she was bewildered. Who could have done such a thing and why? She slid off the couch and started for the stairs. "I'm going to take a hot bath. I'm starting to ache all over."

"Do you need anything? Aspirin or something?" Lexi asked.

"Better not give her anything until we see whether she has any concussion-like symptoms," Mike advised.

Tonya smiled at him. "Yes, Dr. Torres."

"After your bath, better get into bed. I'll bring you some ice for your face and neck," Lexi said.

In the bathroom, Tonya turned on the taps to fill the tub then looked in the mirror. Her nose and lips were swelling, and there was dried blood and a dirt-filled scrape on her chin. A nasty red welt ran across her neck. She peeled off her bloody clothes and stepped into the tub. Sliding down into the steaming bath water, she tried to forget the ugly incident. But just like after the fall during a race that landed her in the hospital overnight, each time she closed her eyes, it all came back to her. She relived the feeling of being choked from behind and then slammed into the truck. Then the searing pain across her neck. She wondered what happened to those pain pills she had been given at the hospital after the race. *I could use one of those tonight*, she thought.

As she lay in bed later with the ice pack on her face, the two cats watched her with concern. Both seemed to be able to intuitively read her thoughts, each one reacting to her in his own special way. Henry curled by her side trying to comfort her, while Clive sat protectively near her pillow keeping an eye on the window. Not for the first time, she wished she had let Royce teach her to shoot his rifle.

☙❧

Tonya awoke to the touch of Henry's whiskers on her cheek. She opened her eyes and saw his face close to hers, his quizzical expression seeming to ask what she was still doing in bed. She turned over to look at the clock and noticed the dried blood on her pillow. Eight-thirty. She listened to the voices in the living room. Mike seemed to be talking to someone on the phone.

Tonya pulled on a bathrobe and moved gingerly to the top of the stairs.

"Okay, Doc. Thanks." Mike clicked off his phone and started for the door. He stopped when he saw Tonya. "Oh, there you are. Feeling any better?"

"I guess. Were you just talking to Doc Frey?"

"Yeah. It looks like old Maisie may be foaling."

"What? She's not due for at least six more weeks, maybe eight."

Mike ran his hand through his disheveled black hair. "I know. Either she's delivering prematurely, or Mr. Warren's dates were wrong. I'm going out there to wait for Doc."

Tonya watched him leave. Then she moved painfully down the stairs and into the kitchen.

Lexi was at the stove frying bacon and humming to herself. She looked up. "Hey. How are you?"

"Not too bad," Tonya lied.

"You hungry? I was just going to fix some scrambled eggs."

Tonya was grateful that Lexi was finally regaining her appetite. Her eyes were clearer, and she seemed to have more energy this morning. Tonya wished she felt half as good as Lexi. "Thanks, but I'll just have some milk. I want to get out to the barn."

Lexi looked at her skeptically, but she poured her a glass from the milk in the fridge and handed it to her.

Tonya leaned carefully against the counter, drinking the milk and gazing at the bright blue sky. The sunlight caressed the bare trees in the back yard as though trying to coax them out of their winter lethargy. It was hard to believe such a beautiful morning could have followed a night of violence, fear, and pain.

By the time Tonya slowly dressed and limped out to the barn, Mike had brought Maisie in, and he was standing in the corner of her stall. The big bay mare pawed the thickly laid straw. She was sweating, even in the cool January morning, biting at her sides now and then. She lay down and rolled, not an easy task in her heavily pregnant condition. She lay still for a moment, panting and staring at the wall. Then she heaved her bulk up on her feet to start the whole process over again.

Mike leaned against the wall watching her, his brow knit in worry. Every few minutes, he went to her, stroked her neck and talked to her, hoping to ease her distress. But he could do nothing for her. Tonya stood next to him, sharing his concern for the mare.

Doc Frey opened the bottom half of the double door

and slipped quietly into the stall. "How long has she been like this?"

Mike ran his hands through his hair. "I'm not sure. When I fed them this morning, I saw that she was in pain. I thought it was colic, but after I watched her for a while, I realized she might be foaling. I was going to take her out to one of the foaling sheds, but it's warmer in here. By old man Warren's calendar, she's not due until the first of March. But I don't know how accurate that is. His records are kind of a mess."

Doc noticed Tonya standing in the corner. Squinting at her face, he asked, "What the heck happened to you?"

Tonya's hand went to her nose and touched the swelling. "I was mugged last night. In the parking lot of Hank's. Someone tried to choke me. He warned me to stop asking questions about Caine's murder, then he threatened to burn down the farm if I didn't."

The vet shook his head and whistled. "And I always thought this was a quiet, safe little town."

The three of them stood watching helplessly as the mare continued to paw the straw, grunt, and pace around the stall with a worried, pained look in her eyes. A seventeen-year-old mare giving birth was never an easy process. That she was delivering a foal six weeks early made it all the more dangerous. Mike stood with his hands in his pockets, watching the mare. Every now and then, she looked over at her visitors as if to say, "Well, don't just stand there! Help me out here."

"Poor old girl," Mike said. "I hope she survives this. The foal will probably be stillborn, but it would be a shame to lose her too. She's produced some great horses in the past. I know Royce was hoping to breed her to Jake and get one more out of her. But this doesn't look good."

After a while, Doc said, "I think maybe she's settling

down." The mare had lost her distracted look and was munching on some hay, a sure sign her pain was abating. "Let's hope it's just false labor."

Mike left the stall, came back with a bucket of fresh water, and exchanged it for the one in the stall, clipping it securely to the wall. He went to the mare and stroked her neck again. "Maybe it's just a false alarm. I read where this kind of thing can just be the foal repositioning itself. It can be painful for the mare, and she shows signs of labor when it happens."

"That's right," Doc agreed, nodding.

"Why don't we go up to the house for some breakfast?" Tonya said. They left the stall together, crossed the yard to the huge wooden porch, and rubbed the bottoms of their boots across the scraper attached to the porch floor.

In the house, Lexi was setting the table. She had made a fire in the fireplace, giving the old farmhouse a warm and comfortable atmosphere after the chilly barn. "I knew you'd all be hungry. Morning, Doc. Good to see you." Tonya marveled at Lexi's ability to bounce back from any number of difficulties. She was pregnant, her husband was in jail accused of murder, they were broke, and Tonya had been attacked the night before. But getting rid of the morning sickness seemed to have changed her whole outlook on life, a testament to her strong, resilient character.

Tonya sat quietly, trying to find a way to put food between her swollen lips with as little pain as possible. Her jaw ached as she tried to chew, and she finally gave up and just stared out the window at the rain-washed yard.

Mike and Doc chatted about Maisie and pregnant mares in general as they ate. Tonya suddenly remembered that there was no money to pay Doc for his visit today. Listening to Doc talk to Mike about veterinary medicine, she realized how valuable his knowledge was, how long it had taken him to learn all he knew, and how unfair it was to expect him to work for free. She started to feel sick to her stomach.

The conversation soon turned to Royce and the prospect of his being released.

"I don't think that's going to happen anytime soon," Lexi said, stirring her coffee. "The lawyer says they don't usually grant bail to an accused murderer."

Tonya winced at the word "murderer." Royce Callahan—the kindest, most honorable man she had ever known, one of the few racehorse trainers who refused to dope his horses to increase his chances of winning, a loving husband and father—an accused murderer. It was monstrous. "We've just got to find the real murderer," she said. "At least give the grand jury somebody else to suspect. Doc, do you know MacNeil, the druggist."

"Sure. I get lots of supplies from him. Why?"

Tonya wasn't sure she should cast suspicion on a potentially innocent man, but she was desperate. "There's a possibility there was something going on between Caine and MacNeil's wife. More than a possibility. I overheard them arguing about him in the store one day. At least I think it was Caine they were talking about. MacNeil said he got what he deserved."

Doc stared at his plate. "I don't like to speak ill of anyone. But his marital problems are no secret in this town. His wife has quite a reputation."

"That's what Dad said," Tonya replied, becoming more interested. "The jealous husband always has a motive for murder."

"Careful, Tonya," Doc warned. "Presumed innocent, remember?"

"I know, Doc, but my father's in jail. And he's innocent."

Doc sighed and gazed kindly at her. "From all I know of him, MacNeil is a harmless little man, although..."

Tonya narrowed her eyes. "Although what?"

"Well, there was an incident once involving them. At least that's what I heard." He hesitated.

"What happened?" Doc's reluctance to speak was maddening.

"MacNeil supposedly, and I emphasize *supposedly*, stormed into a bar one night and dragged his wife out by the hair. Literally."

"No," Lexi breathed, looking from Tonya to Mike.

"Then what happened?" Tonya asked.

"I don't know for sure. But Myra wasn't seen for a couple of weeks. When she surfaced, she had a limp and some bruises on her face. And her hair was really, really short."

"*Ay, caramba*," Mike whispered.

"I knew it," Tonya nearly shouted. "I knew he was violent. I bet he found out about Caine and his wife, and he followed them to the motel. Caine told Dad he had a date that night. It must have been with MacNeil's wife. Besides, MacNeil would have access to any number of poisons. Wouldn't he?"

"You have no proof of anything. You don't want to ruin the reputation of an innocent man."

Tonya thought how ironic it was that she should have to be concerned about the reputation of a wife beater.

"I'd better be going. I have two more stops to make this morning." Doc stood up and thanked Lexi for breakfast. "Call me," he said to Mike, "if anything changes with the mare. Hopefully, she'll settle down."

"I'll walk you out, Doc," Tonya said. She followed

him and closed the door behind them. They stood on the porch together. "Um, Doc, thanks a lot for coming out today," she began, "but I don't know how we're going to..." She was suddenly overwhelmed with shame and burst into tears.

Doc put his arm around her shoulders, and his kind gray eyes found hers. "How you're going to pay my bill?" he said.

She nodded dumbly, embarrassed at their financial condition and ashamed at having to beg people for credit.

"Tonya, I hope you know you and your family are more than just clients to me," he said sympathetically. "I also know you're going through a rough patch right now. You have more things to worry about than my bill. You'll get caught up one of these days. I have no doubt. Please don't worry about it." He patted her shoulder.

She looked up at him gratefully. "Thanks," she mumbled. "We won't forget it." She watched him get into his truck and move slowly down the drive, marveling at how so much decency and so much evil could exist side by side in one small town.

CHAPTER 10

The next morning, Tonya awoke to voices downstairs and the sound of the front door opening and
closing. She rolled over and looked out the window. The sky was gray, the morning sunshine barely able
to break through the clouds.

Henry got up from his place at her side, stretched and
strolled up to her pillow. He rubbed on Tonya's face, his
whiskers tickling her nose. She stroked his sleek fur, her
mind going back to the day she almost lost him. Alton
Jeffers had broken into their mobile home at the track and
tried to strangle the cat with a wire, but Mike had saved
his life. That was the beginning of a new friendship between her and Mike, one she never thought would come
about after their relationship's rocky start. She smiled as
she remembered once calling him a macho jerk.

Lexi's voice called up the stairs. "Hey up there! Are
you going to sleep all day? Come and see the new baby."

Tonya stared at the ceiling for a moment, wondering
what new baby her stepmother was talking about. Maisie!
She started to jump out of bed but was pulled up short by
her aching muscles, still sore from the mugging. She
pulled on a robe and opened her bedroom door, coming

halfway down the stairs just as Lexi was on her way out the door with Mike. "Hey! Did Maisie foal?"

"She sure did," Lexi answered.

She wore a puffy jacket, jeans, and boots, and her long dark hair was pulled back into the pony tail she usually wore. She seemed healthier than ever, her eyes bright and her complexion clear.

"Is it a filly or a colt? Is it okay? Is Maisie okay?"

Mike and Lexi both looked a little uncomfortable. "It's a colt. They're both alive," Mike answered. "She must have foaled after I last checked her last night. She's exhausted, and the little guy's going to have a rough go of it. Doc Frey's with them now. Let's wait and see what he says."

A colt! The first one born at Hibernia. Tonya hurried back up the stairs and dressed as quickly as she could. She glanced in the mirror as she pulled her boots on. Her face was still swollen and sore, the ugly welt on her neck still red and brutal looking, but it wasn't quite as bad as yesterday.

When she got to the barn, she found Maisie lying down on her side with her eyes closed. A tiny bay colt with a white star on his forehead curled in the corner of the stall. He seemed too weak to stand and just lay there looking bewildered. What was this strange world he had been forced into after spending ten months in the warm, comfortable womb? Tonya knew that most foals stand within a half hour of birth, compelled by nature to look for their first meal. But even if this little guy had the strength to get up, he would find no nourishment from his prostrate mother.

Doc Frey was in the stall with the mare. "Let's try to get her up on her feet. Mike, give me a hand, will you?" The two men stood behind the mare as she lay on the straw, talking to her and stroking her. The vet clipped a lead rope to her halter and said, "Lexi, if you and Tonya will pull on the rope as we push her, we may be able to get her to stand."

The two women grasped the rope. As the vet pushed the mare's head up, they held it there with the rope, not allowing her to lie back down. Doc and Mike stood behind the mare, one at her shoulder and the other at her hip. "Ready?" the vet said. "One, two three." The men heaved the thousand-pound horse onto her stomach as the women hauled on the halter rope.

Maisie seemed to understand they were trying to help her. She put her front legs out in front of her, made one herculean effort, and lurched unsteadily to her feet. The four people encouraged and praised her as she stood trembling with fatigue.

After a moment, she noticed the foal in the corner and her ears pricked up, showing the first sign of interest in her surroundings. She staggered slowly over to him and began to lick him. The weak foal closed his eyes as his mother's rough tongue stimulated his skin, clearly enjoying the sensation.

"We'd better get him up to the milk bar," Doc Frey said. He lifted the tiny foal and arranged his long, thin legs under him. Then he moved the colt around to the mare's udder and directed his nose to the teats. He seemed almost too weak to suckle, but hunger eventually overrode his fatigue, and he began to drink the life-sustaining first colostrum, his tiny tail flapping with ecstasy.

Lexi beamed at the colt. "Look at that. He might make it after all."

"If he keeps drinking and the mare stays on her feet, they should have a chance," the vet said to Mike as he moved toward the stall door. "But you'll have to keep an eye on them. If she goes down or he won't nurse, call me right away. I've given her a shot of vitamins to help her along, but it will be touch and go for a couple of days."

"But you're staying for breakfast, aren't you, Doc?" Tonya asked.

If they couldn't pay him, the least they could do was feed him.

"I'd like to, but I have another call to make." They all walked out of the barn and headed back toward the house. The vet tossed his bag into the front seat of his pickup and got in. "Let me know how they get on," he said to Mike and waved as he started down the driveway.

"What are you doing today?" Lexi asked Tonya as they watched him.

"I'm not sure. Why?"

"I was hoping to visit your dad. Can I have the truck?"

Tonya considered going with her to see Royce but thought better of it. She knew he needed some time alone with his wife. "Tell you what. I'll go into town with you. You can visit Dad, and I'll see Adam. Maybe he's found out something about whoever attacked me."

At the mention of Adam's name, Mike's face clouded over. "If he's found out anything, wouldn't he call you?"

"Maybe. But I'm going to check with him anyway."

Lexi said, "Let's have some breakfast first. Mike, come and eat something."

"No, thanks. I want to stay with the mare." He gave Tonya one last look and headed back to the barn, his shoulders hunched and his hands in his pockets.

Tonya watched him go. "What's with him?"

Lexi regarded her sideways. "Pretty obvious, isn't it? He's jealous."

ᘓᘓᘓ

The police station was quiet when they arrived. Lexi was shown into the interview room to wait for Royce, while Tonya headed for Adam's office. He was on the phone, so she stood outside the door waiting for him. Finally, he called, "Come in, Tonya." He leaned back in his chair as she sat down, his eyes assessing her. "How are you doing? Your face looks better."

Her hand went self-consciously to her nose and felt the swelling. "It's okay."

"No concussion symptoms?"

"Nothing."

"You were lucky. Do you know that? It could have been—"

"Please, Adam," she sighed. "No lectures."

He grinned in his boyish way at her and her annoyance with him melted. "Okay. No lectures."

"Lexi is visiting Dad, so I thought I'd see if there's anything new in the investigation."

He leaned forward and opened a folder. "As a matter of fact, I was going to call you. I interviewed our friend the druggist yesterday. He got huffy with me when I called him in. Claimed I was harassing him and said he was going to call his lawyer." Adam chuckled. "He calmed right down when I told him the motel manager became suspicious and took down his license plate. It seems MacNeil was parked nearby watching the motel."

"I knew it," Tonya mumbled.

"The motel manager has seen his car parked there before. He didn't think much of it until Caine's body was found. MacNeil admitted watching the motel because he suspected his wife was having an affair with Caine. The night Caine was killed, MacNeil sat in his car until he saw Caine go into his room with a woman. But it wasn't Myra."

"Who was it?"

"He said he wasn't close enough to get a good look at her, but he knew it wasn't his wife, so he drove off. Apparently, the woman was shorter and stockier than his wife."

"He could be lying. It could have been his wife. He could have come back later or waited until his wife left and then killed Caine."

"Maybe. But I don't think so. His wife was home when he got there. At least that's what they both say. She says she was with a friend that evening and got home around nine. I verified her alibi with the friend. It checks out."

"They could all be lying," Tonya said, grasping at straws.

"Why would they? It doesn't fit."

Tonya sighed. She had been so sure it was MacNeil. "Okay, so where does that leave us?"

His eyes bored in on her. "It leaves us with someone dangerous, Tonya. Someone who warned you not to get involved. Please leave the police work to me. I'm doing everything I can to find the killer."

Tonya's hand went to her nose and lip. "I know you are," she said quietly. "But I can't just sit back and do nothing while my dad is in jail. I have to do something."

Adam sighed, and his gaze became less intense. "Look, let me fill you in on some ideas I have. For one thing, I want to check on people who moved into town around the same time as Caine. He hasn't been here long enough to make that many enemies. Suppose whoever killed him followed him here from the East."

"But he's been here since September. Why not kill

him and leave town months ago? Why hang around for this long and take the chance of getting caught?"

"I don't know. And another thing. That clerk at the feed store. Why did she tell me she heard your father and Caine arguing that night? Your father insists they didn't start arguing until they got to the motel room."

"Dad said Caine seemed happy to see him," Tonya recalled, "at least at first."

"If that's true, why would she lie to me? And why would she try to implicate your father? They hardly knew each other."

Tonya thought about Alec's telling her to mind her own business. Maybe the feed store was the key to all this. Caine worked there, he and Jenkins were involved in something together, and Alec knew more than she was saying.

Adam consulted his notes again. "I also want to look into Jenkins's finances. I can't get a warrant to check his bank account, but I can get at Caine's records. If Jenkins and Caine were into something together, there might be deposits from him to Caine's bank account."

"Unless they were dealing in cash."

"There was no cash in the motel room. But we did find this on the body." He took a key ring from his desk drawer. There was one key on it, badly burned and bearing the number twelve. Adam fingered it thoughtfully. "Caine didn't have a car. And his motel room door opened with a key card. So what does this key open?"

Tonya peered at the key. This was becoming more confusing by the minute.

Adam hesitated a moment. "Then there's this. I wasn't sure I should show it to you, but..." He pulled a piece of paper out of his drawer and set it before Tonya. She read it out loud.

You have the wrong man in jail. He didn't kill Caine. We did. The Furious.

Adam watched her face carefully. She looked up at him, her brow furrowed. "Where did you find this?"

"It was sent to the station. Came in the morning mail."

Tonya scanned the note again and looked up at Adam. "Doesn't this tell you something? That my dad is innocent?"

Adam cleared his throat and stared intently into Tonya's eyes. "Unless you or Lexi sent it."

Tonya's jaw tightened, and she glared at him. Desperate to control her temper, she laid the note carefully back on the desk. "No," she said through clenched teeth, "we did not."

Adam put the note back into his drawer. "I believe you."

Tonya exhaled slowly. "If the note is real, we know there is more than one killer. Don't we?"

"Maybe. Or it could be the killer just saying 'we' to confuse us. But here's what I don't understand. Wouldn't the killer or killers be happy that someone else was being blamed for what they did? I mean, why try to get him exonerated? It makes no sense."

"Maybe whoever it is has a conscience. Or maybe they're feeling guilty."

"Maybe. But that doesn't fit the profile of most killers. And another thing. The note is signed 'The Furious.' Not just 'furious,' as in 'we killed him out of anger.' The Furious. Doesn't that seem odd?"

"Yeah. It's like he, or they, have given themselves a nickname or something. Maybe it's a gang?"

Adam shook his head. "I have no idea." He stood up. "I'm going to look into this key. There are only so many places in this town where things can be locked up. And I want to talk to the feed store clerk. I'll let you know what I find out, if anything. In the meantime, be careful. Don't go anywhere by yourself, especially at night. Okay?"

Tonya got up and gave a mock salute. "Yes, Lieutenant."

Lexi was waiting for her in the hallway, and they left the station together. "How about a cup of tea before we go home?" Lexi asked.

"Sure. Why not?" They walked along the dusty tree-lined street toward the tea shop. The bare tree limbs protruded starkly from their trunks as though waiting patiently for the first buds to appear. All around her, Tonya had the sensation of a world in anticipation.

"How's Dad doing?"

"He's his usual self, trying to be upbeat so I won't worry about him." She shook her head. "But I know he's having a hard time in there. I wish I could tell him about the baby. That would cheer him up."

"Did you tell him about Maisie?"

"Yeah. He perked up when I told him about the little guy struggling to get up and nurse. I think it gave him hope for the future."

They entered the tea shop and found a booth near the window. After sitting down and ordering tea and scones, Tonya told Lexi all she had learned from Adam.

"Well," Lexi said, "at least he's trying to find out who really killed Lucas. That means he knows Royce is innocent."

"Then why doesn't he just release him and let him come home?"

"I don't think he can. He has a boss to answer to. Like he says, he's just doing his job."

"Yeah, he's doing his job all right."

"Don't be sarcastic. Considering that you called him

a bastard and told him to drop dead, it's a miracle he even talks to you, much less tells you about the investigation. He has every right to boot you out of his office."

Tonya knew Lexi was right. She had treated Adam badly, yet he never retaliated. She determined to be nicer to him in the future. She gazed around the shop and noticed Tissy sitting alone in the back booth. She was flicking her cigarette lighter on and off, staring at the flame. She seemed lost in thought.

"There's Tissy," Tonya said. "Let's invite her over." Without waiting for Lexi's answer, Tonya got up and moved toward the back booth. "Hey," she said.

Tissy looked up suddenly, appearing startled and wary. Then she smiled at Tonya. "Oh, hi. You're here again."

"Yeah. I'm with Lexi. Come and join us, why don't you?"

"Okay, sure. Thanks." She tossed the lighter into her purse, picked up her coffee cup, and followed Tonya.

Tissy greeted Lexi and sat down across the table from her while Tonya slid into the seat next to Lexi. She couldn't help noticing Tissy's unkempt look. Her hair was unwashed, and she wore no makeup, unusual for someone who worked in a beauty salon.

"How's your dad doing?" Tissy said, her brow furrowed with apparently genuine concern. "Is he still in jail?"

"Yeah. We've just been at the police station again," Tonya said. "Lexi was visiting him, and I was talking to the lieutenant. He has some interesting theories about whoever killed Lucas Caine."

"Like what?" Tissy asked.

"I can't really get into it," Tonya replied. "But I'm sure he knows my father is innocent."

Tissy's eyes were sorrowful. "You must really miss him," she said to Lexi. "I can't imagine what it's like."

Lexi just nodded and sipped her tea.

"I mean you two have to do all the work out there, don't you?"

"Most of it," Lexi admitted. "And there will be more and more as spring comes on."

"Yeah," Tonya added. "Mares foaling, yearlings to get ready for auction. We had one mare foal just last night."

Tissy perked up. "Really? A baby? I'd love to see it. I just love little foals."

"He's little all right," Tonya said. "Six weeks premature."

"Oh, I wish I could see him."

Tonya saw the excitement in the girl's eyes. "Ever been around horses?"

"Yes," Tissy replied without explanation.

"Ever done any grooming?"

"Yes," she said again.

Lexi looked at Tonya quizzically.

Tonya took a bite of her scone. "Why don't you come out and spend a day at the farm? We have some yearlings we need to start grooming to get them ready for the sale. They're out in the pasture now, and they all look pretty scruffy. If you can give us a hand with them, it would be a big help. And you can see the baby while you're there."

Lexi chimed in. "We'll introduce you to Jake, our stallion. He's quite a character."

Tissy looked pleased. "Sunday's my day off. Can I come over then?"

"Sure. That would be great," Tonya was feeling sorry for this strange, enigmatic girl and had a sudden urge to find out more about her.

"Well, I better get back to the salon. I'll see you Sunday. And thanks. Thanks a lot."

After she left, Lexi said, "That's one ugly scar on her face, isn't it?"

"Yeah. I never told you, but she got it from a former boyfriend who abused her."

Lexi put her coffee cup down. "Oh no," she said sadly, gazing out the window at Tissy heading down the street. "Not another one."

CHAPTER 11

Returning from town, Lexi said she had decided to tackle the housework, so Tonya wandered over to the barn to see the foal. Jake and Gus were outside in their pastures, so the barn was very quiet. She opened Maisie's stall door and slipped in. The mare was standing over the little colt while he snoozed in the straw. She was dozing, too, her eyes half closed. She had one hind leg cocked at the ankle and resting on the straw. She looked up as Tonya entered the stall. She still seemed fatigued, but her eyes and general demeanor were somewhat improved since the morning. At least she was on her feet. She had tiny wisps of hay protruding from her muzzle, a good indication that she had been eating.

Tonya went to her and stroked her neck, making sure the mare understood that she was a friend and posed no threat to her baby. Then Tonya knelt down and peered at the little colt, marveling at his tiny hooves that were still soft. His eyes half opened as he gazed at her without fear.

"Hello, little one," she crooned softly to him. "How are you doing?" She reached slowly toward him, and he raised his nose to meet her hand. When he started sucking on her fingers, relief flooded over her. It looked like he was going to make it, after all. She withdrew her fingers from his toothless little mouth and helped the colt struggle to his feet and totter over to his mother. The mare nickered encouragement to him as he reached for her udder and began to suckle.

Tonya sat quietly in the straw, a lump forming in her throat. The beauty and wonder of horses, of life and of creation, never failed to move her.

Leaving the stall after a few minutes, she found Mike sitting on a hay bale near the tack room reading what looked like a letter. She wondered who was writing to him. He looked up as she approached and folded the letter carefully. His shoulders drooped, and his eyes had a faraway look.

"Hi," she said, sitting next to him on the bale. "I was just checking on the baby. He's nursing again. That's a good sign, right?"

"Yeah."

"Is anything wrong? Did you get a letter from someone?"

Mike exhaled slowly, giving Tonya the impression he was wrestling with himself about something. Finally, he said, "It's from my sister in Guadalajara."

"Oh, that's nice. How is she?"

"Maria's fine. It's my mother. She's been sick a lot. Maria says she's seen the doctor, but..." He shrugged his shoulders and looked away.

Tonya put her hand on his shoulder. "That's too bad. I'm sorry. Really."

Mike nodded, self-consciously brushing a tear from his cheek.

Tonya's heart ached for him. "How long has it been since you've seen your family?"

"About eight years. Since I came here to find work."

Tonya was shocked. She had no idea he had been separated from his family so long. The idea of not seeing Royce for eight years was unthinkable to her.

Mike got up. "I'm going to give Gus his exercise. Are you going to ride Jake?"

Clearly, Mike wanted to end the conversation, but Tonya said, "If there's anything I can do..."

He gave her a sad smile. "You don't happen to have a couple of thousand dollars lying around, do you?"

"No, I don't. But if I did, it would be yours. You know that."

He nodded and walked away.

Later, in the house, Tonya told Lexi about Mike's letter and his family situation.

Lexi said, "Remember when he was riding races? He was sending most of his money to his family. You know how he would do anything to win as much as he could."

Tonya nodded, recalling Mike's reputation with the other jockeys and trainers.

Lexi continued, "Now he's doing what he loves, studying to be a vet, but he's not making any money. He's living on the little he saved from his winnings, just like we are. But I doubt he has much to send to his family. Now with his mother sick, he's feeling the pinch."

"I wish we could give him a big salary," Tonya said wistfully.

"So do I. Maybe after the mares start arriving for Jake and the yearlings are sold, we can do something for him. But now, with your father in jail and the lawyer to pay, I don't know how we're going to make ends meet ourselves."

Tonya sighed. "Why does it always come down to money? It's just not fair."

eɔeɔ

Sunday dawned clear and cool with a strong breeze blowing from the West. It rattled the windows in the old house and whooshed down the chimney, scattering ashes from the fireplace on the floor until Lexi closed the flue. After feeding the horses and cleaning the stalls, Mike and Tonya sat at the breakfast table with Lexi, who had regained her energy and seemed upbeat, even though Royce remained in jail.

"I'm going into town to see Royce," she said. "Is there anything you need?"

Tonya shook her head.

"How about you, Mike? Anything I can pick up for you? Mike?"

"Huh? What? Sorry, I wasn't listening."

Tonya thought Mike seemed especially moody since he had received that letter from his sister. He was beginning to remind her of the old Mike she knew at the track the previous summer. "Lexi wants to know if you need anything from town."

He pushed his plate away and sat back. The dark circles under his eyes spoke to long hours without sleep. Was he just studying a lot or was there something else keeping him awake?

"No. Nothing." He got up and took his plate to the kitchen. Then, without a word, he headed for the door, his eyes downcast and his hands in his pockets.

After the door closed, Lexi whistled low. "That is one unhappy young man. I've never seen him like this," she said. "Have you?"

Tonya chewed the last of her toast. "Once. Last summer." She thought of Mike's confessing to her his frustration at having to keep riding in races to support his family instead of being able to pursue a career in veterinary medicine. "I'll be a jockey until I'm too old to ride anymore," was the way he had expressed it, his eyes smoldering with bitterness at his situation.

Lexi got up from the table. "I need to get some stuff together for your father. Books, magazines, toiletries, stuff like that. I'll probably be in town most of the day. Should I pick up some cat food?"

"Yeah, we're almost out." Tonya reached down to pet Clive who was pacing back and forth beneath her chair, rubbing his long white tail against her leg.

"What are you going to do today?"

"Tissy is coming out today, remember? I'm going to get her to help me with the yearlings. They need grooming and some work in the round corral."

Lexi laughed. "Sure, put her to work. She'll be sorry she ever asked to come."

e∕೨e∕೨

But Tissy was far from sorry to be at Hibernia. From the moment she pulled into the driveway, Tonya could see a difference in her demeanor. Her eyes ranged joyfully over the barns, the mares and yearlings in their pastures, and Gus and Jake in their paddocks, her face aglow with awe and pleasure. She was like a child who had been released early from a dreary classroom to find the schoolyard magically transformed into an amusement park.

"Welcome to Hibernia," Tonya called from the porch. "Come on in for a while."

Tissy could hardly tear her eyes away from the property, turning on the porch to gaze at the horses again as though afraid they would disappear if she lost sight of them. "Thanks for inviting me," she said shyly as she came in. "This is really a treat. It seems a long time since..." She gazed around the living room. "What a lovely old house."

"You should see the place in the summer when the grass and trees are green, and the flowers are everywhere. It's beautiful."

Tissy strolled around the living room, stopping in front of the huge brick fireplace that was now cold and dark. "I bet this puts out a lot of heat," she said, running her hand over the oak mantelpiece. "I just love a nice hot fire in the winter."

Clive and Henry stood in the doorway of the kitchen, curious at the sound of a strange voice. Henry came to the two women, looking for affection. He rubbed on Tonya's legs and meowed his welcome to Tissy, who bent down and stroked him while he arched his back and purred.

"What a beautiful kitty," she murmured as she admired his white fur and blue eyes.

"Yes, he is," Tonya said. "And to think I almost lost him a few months ago."

"Oh?"

"Remember that murderer I told you about, the one that killed those two men and my friend, Alana? Well, he tried to kill Henry by putting a wire around his neck."

She looked up at Tonya, her face reflecting her horror. "That's terrible! How can anyone hurt an animal?"

"He was a sicko."

"What happened to him?"

"He's in an asylum somewhere. I try not to think about him."

Tissy noticed Clive still standing in the doorway to the kitchen. "Oh, there's another one!"

"That's Clive. They're brothers." Tonya bent down and called to Clive, but the cat turned and disappeared back into the kitchen. "I guess he's getting shy in his old age."

"I'm not crazy about strangers either," Tissy said as she continued to stroke Henry.

"Well," Tonya said, standing up, "are you ready to see the horses?"

"I can't wait."

"Let me just grab a few carrots, and we'll go."

They left the house and strolled across the yard while Tonya explained their plans for the farm. She pointed to the outbuildings, the foaling sheds, and the training track with the starting gate off in the distance. As they approached the paddocks, Gus and Jake trotted toward them. Tonya handed Tissy a couple of carrots. "Here. Give them these, and they'll be your friends for life."

They stood stroking the two horses and feeding them the carrots while the barn cat sauntered along the top of the fence separating the two paddocks with the ease of a circus tightrope walker. Her yellow eyes and sleek calico coat shone with good health and general bonhomie. She came to Tissy and rubbed on her. Tissy sighed, and Tonya thought she had never seen this fragile girl seem so peacefully content. What was it about the farm that had that effect on people?

"Those are the yearlings we are going to work with today," Tonya said, nodding to the large pasture next to Jake's paddock. The four yearlings, two bays and two chestnuts, stood at the fence watching. Suddenly, a gust of wind caused one of them to take off and bolt down the hill, the others following him. They bucked and nipped at one another as they ran, racing along the fence line. They circled the huge pasture once and skidded to a stop in the same place, snorting and prancing as though unable to contain their youthful exuberance.

"Just like little boys," Tonya said, smiling at their antics. "Let's get a couple of halters and bring them into the barn for grooming."

Tissy followed her into the barn and down the shed row. They stopped at Maisie's stall, and Tonya peered over the half door. The foal was nursing again, and he looked up when he heard them approach. His fuzzy little ears pricked up at them, milk dribbling off his tiny muzzle.

"Oh, how beautiful," Tissy whispered.

"That's our newest baby, the first one born at the farm. Six weeks premature. He's tiny, but he's a fighter."

Tissy continued to stare at the foal, her eyes misty.

Tonya brought a grooming box and two halters from the tack room and gave one halter to Tissy. They went back to the pasture where the yearlings were waiting near the gate. Tonya opened it and turned to Tissy. "Are you sure you can handle one of these guys? They can be pretty rambunctious."

Tissy smiled. "I'm sure."

They brought the two chestnut colts into the barn and cross-tied them in the aisle facing each other. The yearlings settled down quickly, enjoying the sensations as they were curried and brushed for the first time in months. The girls combed the burrs out of their manes and tails and chatted easily as they worked.

Tonya watched Tissy out of the corner of her eye to be sure she knew what she was doing and was impressed with her techniques. She used the equipment correctly, always brushed in the direction that the hair grew, and kept carefully out of the way of possible kicks from the young horses.

"Where did you learn how to groom horses?" Tonya asked after a while.

Tissy's face darkened, and Tonya thought she was

going to shut down, but Tissy said, "Remember that man I told you about, the one that gave me this scar?"

"Yes."

"Well, he was a horse trainer. I met him at the track near home. That was before I came here. He gave me a job walking the horses. He's the one who taught me how to groom."

Tonya was silent, hoping that Tissy would open up more.

Tissy stroked her colt's neck absentmindedly, gazing off into space, lost in her memories.

"Oh, he was so charming. I totally fell for him. I felt sorry for him when he told me his wife had left him. He would go off now and then to look for her, but he never found her. And when he came back, he was always in a foul mood and would take it out on me."

"Why did you put up with it?"

"I don't know," she sighed. "Why does any woman stay with a man that abuses her?"

"I've wondered that myself. How did you get away from him?"

"I didn't. He left on one of his searches and never came back." She looked sorrowfully at Tonya. "Not long after that, I moved here."

"What made you pick Centerville? Didn't you say you came from Ohio?"

Tissy shrugged her shoulders. They brushed the horses in silence, then Tissy said, "By the way, how is your father?"

"He's doing okay, considering where he is. I just wish they'd hurry up and find the real killer so he can come home. I miss him like crazy. He doesn't even know his wife is pregnant."

"Geez, that's tough. Are they any closer to finding out what really happened?"

"There are some leads. I think whoever did it was the one who attacked me in Hank's parking lot. Did I tell you about that?"

"No," Tissy said, her brow furrowing. "What happened?"

"Someone grabbed me from behind and told me to stop asking questions about Caine's murder. Then he hit me with some kind of stick or something. Right here." She pulled aside her turtleneck to show Tissy the red mark still prominent on her neck.

Tissy stared at her in horror, clutching the brush to her chest as if to smother a pain, or a feeling there as sharp as pain.

Tonya failed to notice her expression and kept talking as she combed the colt's mane. "He even threatened to burn down the farm. Can you believe it?"

"How do you know it was a man?"

Tonya paused a moment and saw Tissy's wide eyes. "I...I don't really. I just assumed. The voice was really more like a whisper."

Tissy suddenly dropped the brush in the box. "I think I need to be going." She started toward the door.

Tonya couldn't believe it. "But you just got here! I thought you were going to spend the day."

Tissy turned back to her. "Thanks for letting me come," she said stiffly. "I had a nice time." Then she left the barn and strode quickly to her car.

Tonya watched her go, astonished at what just happened. "Well, I'll be damned," she said.

CHAPTER 12

By the time Lexi returned from town, Tonya had groomed all four yearlings and was working with one in the round corral. The largest of the colts was trotting quietly around the fence of the small corral while Tonya stood in the middle of the ring with a long whip urging him forward. After a few minutes, she said, "Whoa" and used the whip to turn him in the other direction. He trotted around for a while then broke into a canter. He had a nice long, fluid stride, and Tonya thought he might make a good racehorse if he remained healthy and sound. Hopefully, the buyers at the yearling sale in March would see his potential.

She was just bringing him back to the pasture when she saw Mike sitting on the step outside his trailer talking on his cell phone. Tonya didn't know who he could be talking to, but his body language told her he was dispirited.

As she turned the colt out and closed the gate, she heard Mike say, "Okay, Shorty. Thanks. I'll wait to hear from you." He put his phone in his pocket and went back into the trailer.

Tonya put the colt's halter back in the tack room and

headed for the house. As she helped unload the few bags of groceries and unpack them in the kitchen, she told Lexi about Tissy's sudden and strange departure.

"Huh," Lexi said. "I wonder what that was all about. Did you say something that offended her?"

"I don't think so. We were talking about me getting mugged in the parking lot. I showed her the mark on my neck. What was really weird is that she asked me if I was sure it was a man who attacked me."

Lexi thought a moment. "Well, are you sure? Could it have been a woman?"

Tonya shrugged. "All I know is that the person is strong, has a raspy voice, and wants me to stop asking questions about Caine's murder."

Lexi shook her head. "I don't know. It's all a muddle to me."

They puttered in the kitchen silently for a while, then Tonya said, "I heard Mike on the phone just now. He was talking to someone named Shorty."

"The only Shorty I know is Shorty Ashman. He's a jockey's agent. In fact, he was Mike's agent, wasn't he?"

"I remember him. Tall, skinny guy. He must miss Mike and that ten percent agent's fee he was pulling in."

Tonya gazed out the kitchen window at the trees whipping in the wind. Dirt and dead leaves eddied around them like crazed dancers in some kind of whirling ritual, reminding her of her own confused thoughts.

Why was Mike in touch with his agent again? Why had Tissy left so suddenly? Was it the talk about being attacked? Could that have brought back distressing memories of her own experiences?

Or was there something else? And why would she ask about the attacker being a woman? Did she have someone in mind?

⊘℺⊘

The evening shadows were lengthening across the pastures the next evening as Tonya, Mike, and Lexi ate a silent meal together, all lost in their own thoughts. Mike ate very little, just a piece of beef and some vegetables. When Lexi asked him about dessert, he just shook his head and left the table.

He sat at the computer, pulling his books out of his backpack.

"I'll be right with you," Tonya assured him. "As soon as I help Lexi with the dishes."

"Don't bother with the dishes," Lexi said quietly once they were in the kitchen. "I can manage. And Mike needs you."

Tonya nodded, aware that she had been neglecting him lately. She left the kitchen and pulled a chair up to the computer. "What's on the schedule tonight?" she asked.

"English grammar. It's killing me."

Tonya laughed.

"I don't know why English has so many words that mean the same thing. Spanish isn't like that. We have a different word for everything."

"Like what?"

"Everything. Take this book. In English, *book* can be this thing with pages. It can also mean to make a reservation, like 'book a room.' Or describe the guy who takes bets, the bookie. It's *loco*."

"I guess I never thought about it. It does seem just about every word has more than one meaning."

Mike shook his head. "No wonder so many Chicanos have a hard time making a living here and mostly just work in the fields."

"It can't be easy learning a new language. Not to

mention a new culture. But you're way ahead of me, Mike. I can only speak one language."

Mike grunted in a noncommittal way.

"And just think," she continued. "Once you're a vet, you'll have an advantage over guys who can only speak English, especially in this area. You'll get all the clients."

That seemed to perk him a bit. "Maybe. But first, I have to pass the English part of the GED test."

"Okay," she said. "Let's do this exercise. Do you know the difference between these three words?" She pointed to the screen where the words *there*, *their*, and *they're* were printed.

"I'm not sure."

"Well, *they're* is the easy one. It means—" Her cell phone rang and cut her off.

"Hello? Oh, hi Adam."

Mike scowled and turned back to the screen. Tonya got up and went into the kitchen. Adam's voice made her pulse increase ever so slightly.

"What are you up to?" he said.

"Just helping Mike with some grammar exercises. How about you?"

"Not much. I was wondering if you're busy tomorrow night. If you're not doing anything, would you like to have dinner with me?"

Tonya hesitated a moment. "Do you have some more information about the case?" Lexi looked up at her, her eyes hopeful.

Adam exhaled slowly. "No. But not everything has to be about the case. I just want to see you." When she hesitated again, he said, "Nothing special. Just a meal at Hank's. Not going to the country club again or anything fancy."

Tonya shook her head at Lexi who turned back to the

dishes in the sink. Tonya was torn between wanting to see Adam again and not wanting to upset Mike.

"Okay," she said quietly. "But don't come out here. I'll meet you there. About six-thirty?"

"I look forward to it." She hung up, and Lexi smiled at her.

"Where are you meeting him at six-thirty?"

"At Hank's tomorrow night. He says it's not about the case. He just wants to see me."

"Hmm," Lexi said and left it at that. She dried her hands on a towel. "I'm going to call my mom. She's worried about me."

"How long has it been since you visited her?"

"Years. I never wanted to take the chance of running into Lucas back there. I wish I could go back for a visit," she said wistfully. "But that's impossible now. Maybe after Royce gets out."

"Why don't you invite her to come here?"

Lexi thought a moment. "Well, she's getting on, and her health isn't the best. But maybe if her brother came with her—"

"Sure! We've got plenty of room. There's the two empty bedrooms upstairs. Do it, Lex. Call her and invite them tonight."

Lexi's face lit up with delight. "Okay, I will!" She hugged Tonya and left the kitchen.

Tonya went back to the computer. Mike was struggling through the grammar exercise, and she corrected a couple of his mistakes. "Here's how to pick the right one. If it doesn't mean 'they are,' and it doesn't mean 'belongs to them,' then it's 'there.' See?"

Mike frowned. "In Spanish, it's either *son* or *pertenece a ellos*. Why the same word in English?"

Tonya sighed. "I don't know. Maybe we're just too lazy to think of different words for things."

She wondered why he was suddenly so grumpy.

"So was that the sheriff on the phone?" he growled. "Still saving the world, is he?"

"He's a lieutenant, not a sheriff," she said stiffly. *What is it with men? Does everything have to be a competition?*

"Humph."

Tonya had had just about enough. "Look, what I do and who I see is my business. I don't belong to anyone."

His jaw clenched. "Me either. I don't belong to you or your father or Doc Frey or this farm." He stood up and started putting his books in his backpack. "I'm going back to the trailer." He left without saying another word.

Tonya watched him close the front door behind him, not sure if she felt sad or relieved.

Lexi came down the stairs, still talking on her phone. "Okay, Mom, see you next week. Love you. Bye." Her face was beaming. "They're coming. Next week she and my uncle Jack are flying down. She's so excited about the baby. She always wanted to be a grandmother. Wouldn't it be wonderful if Royce was home by then?"

"That's great, Lex."

"Where did Mike go?"

"He left. I guess he's in a huff about me going out with Adam. And he said something about not belonging to us or Doc Frey or this farm."

"What does that mean?"

Tonya shrugged her shoulders and got up from the computer. "I don't know what's eating him, but he's getting on my nerves."

ᔕᓍᔕ

By the time Tonya got to the barn the next morning,

Mike had already fed the horses and was just finishing with the stalls. His *"Buenos dias"* was a bit cool, but Tonya decided to ignore it, and she gave him as bright a smile as she could.

She stopped at each of the stalls to greet the horses. She broke Gus's morning carrot into pieces and dropped them into his feed bucket with his grain. He looked up at her with his liquid brown fawn-like eyes as if to thank her for the treat then plunged his nose back into the bucket. She ran her hand down his left foreleg. It was cool and showed no signs of swelling. She gave him a final pat on the neck and left the stall.

Jake's reception wasn't quite as cheerful. He watched her come into his stall with his usual haughty expression, much like an imperious monarch allowing a commoner into his presence.

"Oh, don't give me that look," she said, slapping him playfully on the rump. "I know you're king of the hill around here, but don't let it go to your head."

The big horse pricked his long ears up at her, listening to her voice. She dropped a carrot into his bucket. He picked it up by the end and held it in his teeth, letting it dangle from his mouth. She couldn't help laughing at his comical expression.

She stopped at Maisie's stall next, marveling at how the foal had grown and filled out in just a few days. He stood next to his mother, rubbing his head on her side as she ate from her feed bucket. Tonya slipped into the stall and squatted down next to the wall, waiting for the colt's curiosity to get the better of him. He watched her with the wide eyes of an innocent young creature for whom the world was still a safe and pleasant place. Sure enough, in a few minutes, he moved closer to her, his little eyes and ears trained on her.

She held out her hand to him. "Come on, baby," she crooned. "Come and visit me."

He walked boldly to her and began to sniff her hand then her face and hair. He seemed to sense she presented nothing fearsome and was just a rather large toy brought in for his amusement. The closer he got, eventually trying to step into her lap, the more she giggled.

"You're too big to sit on me," she protested with a laugh and pushed him away. But he seemed to be enjoying the game and continued to rub on her and chew her hair.

Mike appeared, scowling at her from the door of the stall. "You're teaching him bad habits."

"He's had a rough start in life. There's nothing wrong with giving him some love."

"He's not one of your cats."

"Thank you, Dr. Torres, but I do know the difference between a horse and a cat." *Two can play that game.*

"Humph," he said.

Tonya ignored him and continued playing with the foal. If he wanted to be cranky, fine. But she wasn't going to humor him.

ℰ✄ℰ✄

Late that afternoon, Tonya sat on her bed reading a racing magazine. The cats had taken up their usual positions, Henry curled up by her side and Clive sitting on the end of the bed watching her with curious eyes. She scratched Henry's ears absentmindedly, smiling as his booming purr filled the room.

She looked out the window at the setting sun casting long, dark shadows on the driveway. She thought back to the happy days on the track in the little trailer she shared with Royce. He would putter around in the kitchen trying to come up with something edible for dinner while she insisted she wasn't hungry and that he shouldn't bother. It was a regular ritual for them, Royce fussing at her for not eating enough and her trying to keep her weight at a steady 103 pounds, ideal for a jockey. Suddenly, she felt his absence so keenly that it hurt. If he didn't get out of jail soon, she might get used to him not being around, and that thought brought tears to her eyes.

She got up and went to the closet, wondering what to wear for her dinner with Adam. She finally chose slacks and a sweater. She brushed her thick auburn hair and decided to wear it down tonight. She applied a little makeup and tied the gold chain with the tiny gold horseshoe that Lexi had given her around her neck. She studied her image in the mirror. "Where is this going?" she asked herself. "Are you seeing Adam because he can help you find Caine's killer? Is that the only reason?"

Her reflection stared back at her, no answer forthcoming. Just exactly what was Adam to her? He was handsome, strong, intelligent, and capable, and he surely had feelings for her. But what were her feelings toward him? She didn't know and couldn't understand why not. Maybe she would find out tonight.

She came down the stairs, half expecting to see Mike at the computer, but the living room was dark. Lexi sat at the table in the kitchen preparing a shopping list. She looked up when Tonya came into the room. "You look nice. Ready to go?"

"Yeah. Was Mike here for dinner?"

"Nope. Haven't seen him."

Tonya sat down next to her. "Lexi, can I ask you something?"

"Shoot."

"When did you know you were in love with Dad?"

Lexi looked up in surprise, half expecting Tonya to make a joke, but she could see the seriousness in Tonya's deep green eyes.

Lexi leaned against the back of the chair. "Well, I think it was the day Jake took a bite out of his butt. Remember that?"

Tonya giggled. "I sure do. I thought I would bust a gut trying not to laugh."

"That was the day we realized how much Jake hated men. About that same time, it came to me that your father was the one for me. Ever since then, he's been like a part of me."

Tonya sighed. "Maybe I should just invite Adam over, have him and Mike go into Jake's stall, and let Jake make the decision for me."

"So whoever he bites is the one for you?"

Tonya shrugged.

"Maybe neither one is the one for you. Ever think of that?" Lexi watched her for a moment. "What brought all this on?"

"I don't know. It's silly. Just ignore me." She got up and started for the door. "See you later."

"Have fun."

Driving to the diner, Tonya reflected on the changes that had come into her life in less than a year. Last spring, all she wanted was to get her jockey's license and compete in a male-dominated sport. Then there were the three murders on the backstretch, the attempt on her life by Alton Jeffers, her father's marriage, and their move to the farm. Now here she was only a few months later trying to analyze her feelings for two men, one she hated then and one she hadn't even met yet. Where was that passion she once felt about riding in races? How had it all changed? Was Lucas Caine to blame? She stared at the white line in the tarmac that disappeared into the darkness beyond her headlights and wondered what that darkness held for her.

CHAPTER 13

Tonya pulled into the parking lot at the back of the diner. She shut off the engine, and a queasy feeling came over her as she peered into the darkness and remembered the last time she was here. Angry at herself for letting the past spook her, she got out of the truck and slammed the door as if to frighten off anyone intent on harming her.

Adam was seated at the end of the counter, his jacket over the stool next to him. He grinned at her as she came toward him, making Tonya wish again that he wasn't so handsome. His looks made it hard to be objective about him and about her feelings toward him. He stood up and picked up his jacket. "Hi. Pretty crowded in here. Is this okay or would you rather wait for a booth?"

"This is fine," she said, sliding onto the stool. As he sat down next to her, his long legs were scrunched against the wall of the counter, while her feet barely touched the floor. She thought about gazing into Mike's eyes as he stood in front of her, only a couple of inches taller than her. Maybe that was part of Adam's mystery. He was so tall she couldn't really see into the depth of his eyes.

He handed her a menu, and Tonya saw Meggie staring at them with narrowed eyes from the other end of the counter. When she came up to them, her pad in hand, she had an especially haggard look about her, and Tonya realized there was only one other waitress besides her working that night.

"Hi, folks," she said, painting a smile on her face. "Ready to order? Or do you need more time?"

"A few minutes more, please," Adam replied. "But I'll have an iced tea."

"Me, too," Tonya said, noticing the dark roots contrasting with Meggie's bleached blonde hair.

"Coming right up." She went to the window in response to the bell rung by the cook. "Order up," the man growled. Meggie retrieved several plates and put them on a tray. Then she hurried with them to a booth near the door.

Tonya and Adam studied their menus for a few minutes. Then Adam laid his down and turned to Tonya. "What have you been up to?"

"Nothing much. Working with the horses, trying to keep up with it all. It's hard without my dad."

Adam nodded. "I can imagine. If it helps at all, I do check on him every day. He's okay. Some people don't do well cooped up in a cell. But he seems to be pretty tough."

"He is tough. But nobody likes being accused of something he didn't do. Any more leads in the case?"

Adam shifted uncomfortably on his stool. "Not really. Could we not talk about the case? Just for tonight? I'd like this evening to be about us. Okay?"

Tonya wasn't sure what "about us" meant, but she shrugged and said, "Okay."

The waitress brought the two iced teas and set them down on the counter. "Decided yet?"

"I'll have the pork loin platter," Adam said. Tonya handed her the menu. "I guess the chef's salad. With blue cheese dressing on the side." Meggie looked around. "We're swamped, so it might be a bit longer than usual." "No problem," Adam assured her. "We have plenty of time." She hurried away, and Adam cleared his throat. "Can I ask you something?"

"Sure."

"That jockey that lives on the farm, Mike? What is he to you? If you don't mind my asking." Tonya was silent. "I mean if it's none of my business, just say so. But he seemed a little possessive of you that night I brought you home after the attack."

"Possessive? What do you mean?"

"Well, maybe it was nothing. It's just that he got a little touchy when I tried to question you."

Tonya gave a noncommittal shrug. "We're just friends," she replied, not really knowing whether that was true. "As for his being possessive, I don't belong to him. Or anyone." She sipped her iced tea, wanting to pursue a different line of conversation. "So tell me, how did you get interested in police work?"

"Okay. I get it. It's none of my business. Well, I've always liked puzzles. Crime is just another type of puzzle. But with serious consequences to the community. Figuring out who committed a crime, why they did it, how they did it, and how to protect other people from them. That's the job."

"Do you enjoy it?"

"I really do. When I can get a bad guy off the street so people can live their lives in peace and safety, that's very satisfying."

Tonya nearly said something about how he felt

knowing he had taken an innocent man off the street, but she restrained herself. Tonight wasn't supposed to be about the case.

"How about you?" he continued. "What brought you to the life you're living now?"

"Growing up on the racetrack, horses and horse racing are all I've ever known. My mom died when I was little."

"That must have been tough for you."

"I was too young to remember her. Dad and I got along fine. We've always been very close. And the backstretch is kinda like a family. Jockeys, exercise riders, grooms, trainers—you're never lonely. Of course, there was Luis. You remember him, Dad's assistant. He was like another father to me."

"Oh, yeah. What happened to him?"

"He took the whole outfit to Arizona for the racing there. Dad made him the boss over the Callahan racing stable. I miss him. I miss hearing him call me *mija*. It means 'my daughter' in Spanish."

He gazed at her as though fascinated by her. "When did you know you wanted to be a jockey?"

"I can't remember a time I didn't want it. I'd watch them riding the races and afterwards ask them questions about what they did and why." She laughed. "Now that I think about it, I must have been a terrible pest."

They sat and talked for another twenty minutes, easy and comfortable with one another. Tonya finished her iced tea and excused herself. As she walked through the diner on her way to the ladies' room, she passed the druggist and his wife, Myra, seated at a booth near the door.

MacNeil was pointing his finger in his wife's face, and she was glaring at him sulkily, her arms crossed in front of her. Tonya heard him say, "You will regret this,

Myra. It's the last time—" He broke off as Tonya passed, glancing up at her with narrowed eyes.

In the ladies' room, Tonya locked the door of the stall and began to unbuckle her belt. Suddenly the ladies' room door opened with a bang, and two women entered. They were arguing. Tonya recognized Tissy's voice, high-pitched and nearly hysterical. "But she was attacked! Because of what I told you. It's my fault!"

"Shh. Keep your voice down," the other woman said. Tonya thought she recognized the voice, but couldn't place it. "What do you want," she continued, "for her to find out about us? Like she did that guy last summer?"

Tonya peered through the crack between the door and the wall trying to see them, but they were out of sight to her left, near the sinks.

Tissy seemed frantic, on the verge of tears. "But her father is in jail," she wailed. "Suppose they—"

"Suppose they what? Convict him? So what? Stop your whining and get a grip. There's a cop out there, and he might not be as stupid as he looks."

Tissy's voice was becoming more frantic. "But that wasn't the plan."

"You took an oath. We all did. Say it."

"No."

"Say it, Celeste!"

Tissy began to recite something in a trembling, muffled voice. Tonya could only hear a few words and phrases. "By the power of...for the sake of our sisters...let us never—Ow, you're hurting me!"

"I'll do worse than hurt you if you screw this up. Now get out."

The door banged again, and Tonya peeked out of the stall at the empty bathroom. If only she could have seen who the other woman was.

When she sat back down next to Adam, she peered around the crowded diner. She spotted Tissy sitting at the end of the counter. She was alone. What had just happened in there? Who was the other woman, and what was that oath all about? Whatever it was, it was clear that Tissy knew who had attacked Tonya in the parking lot.

Adam broke into her thoughts. "Looking for someone?"

"What? Oh, yeah. I just heard the strangest conversation in the bathroom. You know Tissy, the hairdresser?"

He nodded toward the end of the counter. "She's sitting right down there."

"Well, she was in the ladies' room with another woman, and it sounded like they were talking about my attack."

Meggie set their plates down in front of them, staring at Tonya with wide eyes and raised eyebrows. But she plastered over her expression with a fake smile. "Here you are. Sorry for the wait." She took Tonya's empty glass. "I'll refill that for you. Let me know if you need anything else." She picked up the glass and hurried through the swinging doors into the kitchen.

Adam started cutting into his pork.

Tonya grabbed Adam's sleeve. "Did you hear me?"

"Yes. I heard you. What else did they say?"

"Something about making a pledge or...an oath. That's what it was. An oath. The other woman made Tissy recite it. It was weird, like a chant." Adam chewed thoughtfully, and Tonya thought he seemed maddeningly calm. "Adam! You have to do something. Did you see who came out of the hallway with Tissy?"

"Keep your voice down," he said quietly. "It won't do to let her hear you. We can talk about it later. And no one came out of the hallway. She was alone. Eat your salad."

Meggie came back with the iced tea, and Tonya took a large gulp of it, trying to remain calm and keep from panicking. Tissy! The girl who styled her hair, who came to the farm and loved on the cats and horses. Involved in something evil? No, it couldn't be. She must have misheard them or misinterpreted what she did hear. But who was that other woman, and where did she disappear to?

Tonya picked at her salad, not really interested in eating. Suddenly Tissy was beside her on the next stool. "Hi," she said with a bright smile. "Enjoying your dinner?"

Tonya could only stare at her, trying not to reveal her shock. "Hi," she finally stammered. "How are you?"

"Oh, I'm fine."

"You here alone?"

"Yep. I just stopped in for a quick bite. Then I have to get back to the shop. Me and Michelle are doing some serious cleaning tonight."

Tonya stared at her in disbelief then said, "Oh, this is Adam. This is my friend, Tissy."

Tissy stuck out her hand and shook Adam's. "Nice to meet you. Well, I won't interrupt you." As she brought her hand back, she knocked over Tonya's iced tea, and it spilled all over the counter. "Oops," Tissy said.

Meggie seemed to appear from nowhere, a rag in her hand. She began to wipe up the tea, glaring at Tissy.

"Sorry. Have a nice evening, you two," Tissy said. As she slid off the stool, she leaned toward Tonya. "Don't drink anything else," she whispered in her ear. Then she walked quickly out of the diner.

Meggie watched her go, her eyes blazing. Then that plastered smile appeared again. "No harm done," she said to Tonya. "I'll get you some more tea."

Through the window, Tonya watched Tissy walk

quickly across the parking lot. Meggie came back with another glass of tea and set it on the counter. Tonya just stared at it. As she waited for Adam to finish, Tonya's stomach was churning and her heart pounding. She couldn't wait to leave. Adam laid his credit card on the check the waitress put in front of him then leaned back and patted his stomach. "Very good," he said.

Meggie's smile was so forced that it gave her face a grotesque quality. "Glad you liked it. Be sure to come back and see us again."

Adam was maddeningly slow in signing for the bill and placing the receipt in his wallet. They got up, and he ushered Tonya out the door, guiding her toward his cruiser in the front parking lot. They got in, and Adam turned to her, his arm across the back of her seat. "Okay. Tell me everything you can remember. Word for word."

Tonya repeated as much as she could recall. "The other woman was threatening Tissy. Like I told you, she said something about an oath, and she said they all had taken it. She made Tissy repeat it, but Tissy didn't want to."

"What was it?"

"I only caught a few words. It was something about the power of something that sounded like 'Pyrenees.'"

"Like the mountains?"

"Yeah, but it wasn't Pyrenees, just something that sounded like it."

Adam made notes on his phone. "Anything else?"

Tonya was growing more and more frustrated with Adam's calm demeanor. "Yeah, she knew you were a cop and said you might not be as stupid as you look." *That ought to get a rise out of him.*

But Adam simply made another note. "How about this woman's voice? Anything distinctive? An accent? Did she sound like she was from Texas?"

"I'm not sure. No, she didn't have a Texas accent."

He looked kindly at her, but there was urgency in his eyes. "Think, Tonya. Your memory of it will never be as good as it is right now. So concentrate."

Tonya took a deep breath. "I think that's all I heard. No, wait. She said I was attacked because of what Tissy said I told her."

"What was it you told her?"

"I don't know. We talked mostly about the horses. The day we had coffee she seemed upset about my father being in jail. I said I was going to find out who the real killer is and that I'd done it before. Then I told her about Jeffers."

"Whoever attacked you warned you to stop asking questions, right?" Tonya nodded. Adam sighed. "He must have been talking to Tissy."

"He or she."

Adam stared at her. "Could it have been a woman who attacked you?"

"That's what Tissy asked me. Maybe. I honestly don't know."

He rubbed his hand across his chin. "Someone must have seen the other woman in the bathroom. I'll talk to the cook tomorrow. In the meantime, keep a low profile. And if Tissy tries to contact you, let me know right away." He gazed out the window. "I'll talk to the woman who runs the hair salon where she works. Maybe she knows who Tissy hangs out with." He turned back to Tonya. "Could it have been her you heard? Michelle?"

Tonya frowned, trying to remember the sound of Michelle's voice. "I'm not sure. I thought I recognized the voice from somewhere. It could have been her. Adam, could Tissy be involved in Caine's murder? Could that be the plan they were talking about?"

"Like I said, I'll look into it. Come on. I'll walk you to your truck. Then I'll go to the office and see if I can find anything in their DMV records."

Adam came around to her side of the car and opened the door. As she slid out, a sudden pain in her stomach took her breath away and made her wince. "Oh," she gasped.

"What is it?"

"Nothing. Just a little cramp."

He walked her to the back parking lot, looking carefully around as they turned each corner.

She handed him the keys, and he unlocked the door for her. He looked down at her and laid his hand on her shoulder. "Be careful," he said. "Call me right away if you see anything or hear from Tissy."

Tonya nodded and slipped behind the wheel. *Some date this turned out to be.* "Please let me know what you find out."

"I will."

"Adam, isn't this enough to release my father?"

"It's all hearsay right now, but it does give me something to go on. Don't worry. Your father will be home before you know it."

"Thanks. And thanks for the dinner."

"You're welcome. Maybe next time will be less dramatic."

He closed the door and walked away. Tonya started the truck and drove slowly out of the parking lot. Her mind was whirling. Tissy had something to do with the attack on Tonya! Tissy, that fragile, pathetic girl who looked like she'd be blown over by a strong breeze. It was unfathomable.

As she drove along the dark highway, passing hardly any cars, she suddenly felt a fierce pain, like something was ripping her insides apart. She gasped and groaned, gripping her middle with her free arm. Waves of nausea washed over her and took her breath away. She doubled over and sensed the truck leaving the highway, bumping through the brush on the side of the road, the tires sending dirt and gravel everywhere. Tonya gasped again and wrenched the steering wheel, but it was too late. She couldn't steer back onto the road. In spite of the searing pain in her stomach, she tromped on the brake as hard as she could. The truck skidded, coming to rest next to a barbed wire fence, just inches from an oak tree.

CHAPTER 14

Tonya sat in the cab of the truck holding her stomach and groaning. She had been sick with the flu before, had terrible cramps, and even had a touch of food poisoning once from some potato salad they had left out too long. But this was different. The pain washed over her, causing her to double over. She thought of calling Lexi, but since there was no other vehicle at the farm, Lexi would be powerless to help. Maybe calling Adam was the best thing to do. No, he would overreact and want to take her to the hospital. If she waited a few minutes, surely it would pass.

Suddenly, Tissy's words, "Don't drink anything else," echoed in her ears. What did she mean? Did she know something about what was being served at the diner? Was Adam sick, too? How did Tissy know what she had been drinking?

She opened the window of the cab and gulped in the clear cool air, breathing deeply to try to clear her head. The road was dark, the trees casting black shadows in her headlights. She thought she heard rustling off the right side of the truck. Then it stopped. She peered into the darkness, her eyes trying to adjust. She turned off the headlights, hoping there was enough moonlight to help her see. There was another rustling as though someone was moving through the brush. Tonya's pulse raced, and her breath quickened. She looked around frantically for some place to hide, but knowing she was safer in the pickup, she locked her door.

Something moved closer to the truck, just on the other side of the barbed wire fence. Then a loud "moo-o-o" shattered the stillness, and Tonya saw two white-faced cows staring over the fence at her, their large liquid eyes reflecting the moonlight. Several others joined them, all looking curiously at this intrusion into their peaceful pasture life.

Tonya nearly laughed out loud in relief. The adrenaline rush had quelled the pain in her midsection somewhat, and she decided to try to make it home. She started the engine and pulled slowly off the grass onto the blacktop. There were no headlights coming in either direction. If only she could make it home without another spasm, if only she could get into the house where Lexi would take care of her. She kept breathing deeply as she drove, trying to keep the pain at bay.

"Oh, thank God," she whispered as the lights of the farmhouse shone through the darkness. She pulled off the highway and down the long driveway, noticing the yearlings and mares in their pastures, their ears forward, gazing at her curiously as she passed.

She parked the truck in front of the house and got out. Moving caused the pain to increase, but by walking doubled over, she managed to get to the door. Through the window, she could see Lexi sitting in Royce's chair near the fireplace reading a book. Clive and Henry kept their usual vigil on the back of the couch waiting for her to come home. They spotted her through the window then hopped off the couch and came to the door. Tonya heard one of them meow, causing Lexi to look up.

She unlocked the door and staggered into the living room. Lexi gasped and jumped off the chair. "What's wrong? You look awful! What happened?" She grabbed Tonya's arm as she nearly fell onto the couch.

"I'm sick," she said, holding her stomach and lying against the back of the couch.

"Did you get sick at the diner?"

"No. On the way home."

"Do you think it's the flu? There's always something going around this time of year."

Tonya groaned again. "I don't know."

"Should I call a doctor? Or take you to the ER?"

"No. It's not as bad as it was. Let me just sit here for a minute."

Lexi went to the kitchen, and the two cats jumped back up on the couch. They both sat close to Tonya, staring at her with wide eyes. She reached out and stroked Henry's head.

"Here. Put this on your forehead," Lexi said, returning from the kitchen with a wet cloth. Lexi continued to watch her with alarm. The cats snuggled up to Tonya and seemed to feel her distress.

After a while, the pain began to subside. Tonya took a deep breath and removed the cloth from her forehead. "Thanks. I feel better. At least the pain isn't so bad."

"Let's get you up to bed," Lexi said, helping Tonya to get up.

"You're going to make a wonderful mother," Tonya said. "Your baby is very lucky."

Lexi's pleasure glowed in her eyes. "Here, lean on me." She helped Tonya up the stairs, the cats following closely behind.

Once in her room, Tonya collapsed on the bed. "I

don't think I'll get undressed. Let me just lay here for a while." Drained, confused, and more than a little frightened, she reviewed what had just happened. Even more than after the attack in the parking lot, Tonya suspected that she was involved in something truly sinister, something that could take her life. Whoever killed Lucas Caine would have no qualms about killing her. Of that she was sure. Not even Adam could protect her all the time. And with her father in jail, she was more vulnerable than ever before.

"Okay," Lexi said, covering her with a blanket. "I'll leave the door open. Call me if you need anything."

"Thanks." The pain was subsiding, and she was no longer nauseous. Exhausted and thankful to be alive, she fell asleep.

 intstyle

It took two days for Tonya to recover. During that time, Lexi fussed over her like a mother hen. Tonya spent most of those two days in bed with intermittent cramps and sweating, while Clive and Henry watched her anxiously. She tried to convince herself that it was a bout with the flu, but Tissy's warning kept repeating in her mind. '*Don't drink anything else.*' Had someone really tried to poison her? If so, who? And was that what happened to Caine?

On the third day, Tonya decided to get up, but, still, she felt weak. She came slowly down the stairs and into the kitchen, stopping every few steps to catch her breath.

Lexi was at the table drinking coffee and looked up. "There you are. Feeling any better?" Tonya nodded. "Are you sure you should be up?" Lexi asked. "I can bring you something on a tray."

"I'm tired of being in bed. It feels good to be up."
She sat at the table and felt her stomach growling. Lexi
put some scrambled eggs and toast in front of her, and
eating it made her feel much better. She thought about
not being able to get out to the barn since coming home
sick. "How's Mike?"

"He asked about you a couple of times," Lexi said.
"He's been doing all the barn work and told me not to
bother you with it."

"That's nice of him."

"Yeah. He hasn't been in to use the computer either.
And he never eats here anymore. I swear he's lost ten
pounds in the past two weeks. I keep asking him to come
in for a meal, but he always says no."

"That's not like him. I'll have a talk with him. Maybe he's upset about something. Did he get any more letters from his family?"

"I don't know. Why?"

"It seems he's been moodier than normal since that
last letter from his sister." Just then, Tonya's cell phone
rang. "Hello? Oh, hi, Adam. Fine. How about you?"

Lexi whispered, "Didn't you tell him you were
sick?"

Tonya shook her head at Lexi and got up from the
table.

"I've found out a few things you might be interested
in," Adam said. "For one thing, that welt on your neck is
the same dimensions as those marks on Caine's body."

Tonya sat on the couch and looked out the window.
She stroked the cats as they sat perched on the back of the
couch. "Oh? That means whoever killed him hit me behind the diner."

"Well, maybe. But at least we think it was the same
weapon. And Tonya, the dimensions are the same as a lot
of the whips jockeys use."

Tonya was silent, her mind whirling at the idea a jockey could be involved. But the only jockey she knew in the area was Mike, and whoever attacked her was bigger than Mike. Besides, Mike would never do such a thing.

Adam continued, "That explains the leather thing-y we found in the room."

"The popper."

"Yeah. Also, I've been to see Jenkins. I had quite a talk with him. He told me someone had stolen a whip from his store. Along with some arsenic."

"I remember him saying that."

"He denied there was anything going on between him and Caine. He said if they were seen arguing, it was probably about Caine showing up late or not doing his job. He showed me Caine's employment record, so I have his social security number. Now I can do a background check on him."

"That's good." Tonya hesitated, not wanting Adam to think she was being overly dramatic. But he had to know everything she knew if they were to work together to free Royce. "Adam, when I left the diner that night, I got really sick on the way home. Almost drove off the road."

"What? Are you okay?"

"I've been sick for a couple of days, but I'm fine now. But the thing is…"

"Go on."

"You remember the girl I introduced you to, Tissy? Just as we were leaving, she whispered to me to not drink anything else. I think that's why she spilled my iced tea."

She heard Adam exhale. "But we both had iced tea."

"Yes, but mine was refilled, remember? That waitress took the glass and came back with more tea."

"You're telling me you think the waitress put something in your tea?"

Tonya felt very foolish. "No. Maybe it really was just the flu or something. But why the warning about not drinking anything else?"

"I don't know. You said yourself that girl is strange. Who knows what goes through people's minds? Still, it can't be a coincidence. And that conversation you overheard in the bathroom has me stumped. If only we knew who the other woman was."

Tonya sighed, suddenly feeling she was in the middle of another nightmare. She longed to get away from it and lose herself in just caring for the horses. But she shook the feeling, knowing that until her father was back home again, this nightmare wouldn't end.

Adam continued, "I'm going to check on that waitress, too. But the diner is owned by a conglomerate out of Amarillo. It may take some time. I'll let you know if I find out anything."

"Thanks."

"And Tonya? Be careful."

Tonya hung up and sat for a moment petting Henry who purred and head-butted her hand. Clive stared out the window at some movement near the barn, and Tonya saw Mike leading Jake to his paddock. She went upstairs and changed into her barn clothes, determined to find out what Mike was up to and apologize for ignoring him lately.

By the time she crossed the drive, Mike had turned Gus out and was just closing the gate to his paddock. Gus trotted over to Jake, and the two horses nuzzled each other over the fence as Tonya approached. Mike turned and gave her a small, sad smile. "Hi," he said. "Feeling better?"

"A lot better." They stood together watching the horses.

Mike said, "I was just thinking. Once the mares start arriving, you may want to separate Jake and Gus. Jake is not going to want another stud around his harem, even if Gus is only three years old."

Tonya smiled at the thought of Jake protecting his mares, but she knew it was typical herd behavior. In the wild, stallions always drove out the young males as soon as they reached maturity.

"We'll let you take care of that when the time comes."

Mike shifted uncomfortably and looked at her sadly. "You won't be able to count on me. I won't be here."

Tonya froze, staring at him in disbelief. "What?"

"Come inside, and I'll explain," he said, ushering her toward the trailer.

Mike held the door open for her. Once inside, she looked around at what had been her home for so many years. It brought a wave of nostalgia and a desperate longing for her father.

She sat at the small table that had seen so many events over the years. It was at that table that Tonya first told Royce she wanted to be a jockey. Alana sat here with her the day after the accident that put her in the hospital overnight, watching Royce and Lexi cooking dinner together. And she was sitting at that table the morning Royce and Adam came to break the terrible news of Alana's murder. She had the feeling that this little table was going to be the scene of another major event in her life, and it didn't feel like it would be a good one.

"Can I get you anything?" Mike asked.

"No, thanks. What did you mean just now? About not being here."

"I got in touch with Shorty Ashman. My agent?"

"I know who he is."

"I asked him to get me some races. He called this morning. He can get me in with some trainers at Golden Gate Fields in San Francisco. They have winter racing there."

Tonya couldn't believe what she was hearing. "You're going back to riding? After all this time?"

He nodded and looked down, as though trying to avoid eye contact.

"But why? What about your studies? Don't you want to be a vet anymore? I thought you were sick of riding. You're going to just leave us? With Dad in jail? How can you?" Tonya raised her voice, her disbelief verging on anger.

Mike pulled a folded paper out of his pocket. "I got another letter from my sister. My mother is getting worse. They are broke. My sister works in a little tourist shop in Guadalajara, but that doesn't cover the doctor's bills."

Tonya stared at the letter. "But—"

"I'm sorry. I have to go. I have to make enough money to support them, the same as I did before." He put the letter away. "Nothing has changed and nothing ever will," he said bitterly.

Tonya looked at his protruding cheekbones and understood why he had been eating so little. He was trying to get back to riding weight. Her anger subsided, and she felt terribly sorry for him, but at the same time, a panicky feeling started to wash over her. How on earth could she and Lexi manage, especially with the upcoming yearling auction and Jake's breeding schedule about to begin? She swallowed, almost afraid to ask the question. "When will you be leaving?"

"Next week. I have to be there by February first."

She leaned forward, her elbows on the table and her head in her hands. "I can't believe it."

He reached across and laid his hand on her arm. "I hate to leave you like this. Royce in jail, Lexi pregnant. It will all fall on you, I know. If only there was some other way. But there isn't. I'm so sorry."

Tonya didn't know what to say. The future seemed black and dismal. Her eyes met his, and she wondered if hers looked half as sad as his. She got up to leave, and he rose with her. Suddenly, they were in each other's arms. Tonya laid her head on his shoulder, and he tenderly stroked her hair. There were no words between them. Without looking at him again, she left the trailer and closed the door quietly behind her. As she walked across the drive, her hot tears flowed freely.

CHAPTER 15

As Tonya entered the house quietly, she heard Lexi
in the kitchen. She tiptoed up the stairs to her
room to change. The last thing she needed was to
have to explain her red eyes. But Lexi, who had the hom-
ing ability of a radar installation, called out as Tonya was
trying to slip back down the stairs. "Tonya?" She came
out of the kitchen carrying a coffee cup. "Are you going
somewhere?"

Tonya stopped at the door but kept her eyes averted.
"Into town. Need anything?"

"I never did get those prenatal vitamins. Maybe you
could stop at the drugstore?"

"Sure. See you later."

Driving into town, she felt bad about not telling Lexi
she was going to visit Royce, but she wanted his advice
about Mike before she burdened Lexi with it. With Lexi's
mother and uncle coming to visit, the work would all fall
on Tonya, and she knew that would only make Lexi feel
guilty.

As she passed the spot where she had driven off the
road several nights ago, she noticed the white-faced cows
still grazing near the fence. She decided not to tell Royce

about what had happened at the diner either. One crisis at a time, and Mike's leaving was enough for today.

She passed Adam's office on her way to the interview room, but he wasn't there. She felt a mixture of disappointment and relief that she wouldn't have to try to explain her swollen red eyes to him.

As soon as Royce came into the room, accompanied by the officer who stood by the door, his searching eyes told Tonya he knew something wasn't right. *I never could keep anything from him*, she thought.

He slid into the chair opposite her. "What's wrong, kiddo? Is it Lexi?"

"No. Lexi's fine. It's Mike. He's leaving. Going to Golden Gate Fields to ride again."

Royce didn't seem surprised. "I was afraid of that. Is it his family?"

Tonya explained Mike's situation, trying to hold back the tears as she recalled the sadness in his eyes and their last embrace. "What are we going to do, Dad?" She hated to burden Royce with something he had no power over, but she couldn't see anything but bleakness ahead of her and desperately needed the comfort of his advice.

Royce rubbed his hand across his stubbly chin and stared at the wall. Finally, he said, "Honey, all you can do is just take it one day at a time. Is there enough feed for the horses?"

She nodded. "I think Leo felt sorry for me. He gave us enough to last a couple of months."

"That's one thing we don't have to worry about. How about Jake? Are you on time with his schedule?"

"Mike has been calling the mare owners. I think he has that pretty well in hand." She started to relax a little. Royce was always so organized, and his calm objectivity gave her confidence.

"How is Lexi doing? I mean really? She's always upbeat when she comes to see me, but I know she doesn't want to worry me."

"She's fine. Really. Oh, guess what. Her mother and uncle are coming from Ohio for a visit."

"That's great. She hasn't seen them in years." He looked down and frowned. "I wish I could be there."

Tonya eyed her father's face, her lip quivering. *Don't start crying again*, she warned herself. "You will be, Dad. Adam has several leads he's following up on. He'll find the real killer soon, and we can all be together again. Keep the faith."

Royce looked up and gave her a sad smile. "I will, honey. Don't worry about me." His eyes focused on the dusty light fixture in the ceiling. "You know, I might have an idea."

"What?"

He waved his hand as though chasing a fly away. "It may not work out. I'll tell you when I know for sure."

Tonya couldn't imagine what he was thinking, but there was no sense in pressing him.

When their time was up, Tonya left the room, passing Adam's empty office again. She walked over to the drug store to get Lexi's vitamins. Entering the store, she noticed Leo Jenkins standing at the pharmacy window talking to the druggist. *This must be my lucky day,* she thought. *The two suspects together.* The two men were arguing about something and didn't notice her. She moved quietly to the side of the store and hid behind the standing shelves, creeping as close to the window as she could without being seen.

"Come on, Orville," Leo was saying. "What harm can it do?"

MacNeil replied sulkily, "I could lose my license. It's not worth it."

"But no one will ever know. And I'll pay double."

"Not without a prescription. I told you. What you're doing is illegal, and I want no part of it."

Jenkins used his most ingratiating, wheedling voice. "Now, Orville, you know I can't take them to a doctor. And they're only here a couple more days anyway. The kid's got an infected foot. He's really miserable. Come on, have a heart."

Tonya heard the druggist sigh. She peeked over the top of the shelves and saw him pour some pills into an envelope and hand it to Jenkins. "I'm not writing anything on the envelope, so make sure they understand it's only for him. One every four hours. And I will *not* be responsible if he has an allergic reaction or anything else goes wrong, I'll deny you were even in here. Got it?"

"Got it. Don't worry. Nothing will go wrong. Thanks, Orville."

Jenkins took the envelope and walked quickly down the main aisle and out the door. Tonya continued looking for the prenatal vitamins, wondering what kid they were talking about. Jenkins was a bachelor with no children. None that Tonya knew about, as least. And whoever the kid with the infected foot was, why couldn't he be taken to a doctor?

The door opened, and Myra MacNeil came into the store. Her appearance was much different from the first time Tonya had seen the druggist's wife. She wore sweat pants and an old shirt. Her bleached blonde hair was pulled back into a pony tail, showing dark roots at least a half inch long. She wore no makeup, and her manner was uncharacteristically subdued. She walked gingerly to the pharmacy window as though walking generated some kind of pain. She stood for a moment then cleared her throat.

The druggist looked up. "What is it, Myra?" he said in a slightly annoyed tone.

She mumbled something Tonya couldn't hear, and her husband replied, "No. I told you before. No more money."

"Was that Jenkins I just saw leaving the store?"

"None of your business. Now go home. I'm busy."

The woman hesitated a moment then slunk toward the door. Tonya had never seen anyone look quite so defeated. She waited until the door closed then took her bottle of vitamins to the counter. MacNeil seemed surprised to see her. "Hello, Tonya. I didn't see you." He wrinkled his brow and looked sideways at her. "How long have you been here?"

Long enough to know you are into something you shouldn't be, she thought. "Just a few minutes. I came in to get these for my stepmother."

He looked at her somewhat suspiciously, and Tonya flashed her most innocent smile at him. He rang up the purchase, and she paid with the last few dollars in her wallet. "Thanks," she said and turned toward the door. As she left the store, she could almost feel his eyes boring into her back.

As she left the drug store, a fire truck raced down Main Street past her, its siren blaring. Peering in the direction the truck was traveling, she saw a billow of black smoke a few blocks away. People were rushing along the sidewalk in the direction of the smoke, and Tonya decided to follow them. She turned the corner and saw the source of the smoke. An old warehouse on the edge of town, abandoned and empty for years, was ablaze.

Tonya watched the firemen hook up their hoses to the hydrant and point the water toward the roof of the building. Their movements were choreographed, each one knowing exactly what his job was, the whole group working together in rhythm.

The heat from the fire was powerful, causing the crowd that had gathered to move back as the fire's intensity grew. Black smoke filled the air, and ashes rained down on the street. The wind carried burning embers in all directions. Tonya scanned the crowd and saw the druggist's wife standing by herself near the fire engine. She also noticed Tissy standing with Michelle watching the spectacle. Michelle's salon was only a block away, so they must have just come from there. Tonya thought this was a good time to try to get an explanation from Tissy for her strange and sudden departure from the barn. She wouldn't tell her about overhearing her and the other woman in the bathroom at the diner, preferring instead to just try to reestablish a friendship with her.

The two women were arguing as she approached from behind. Although she couldn't hear what they were saying, it was clear that Michelle wasn't happy with Tissy. Tonya tried to listen closely to Michelle's voice. Was this the voice she heard in the diner's bathroom? She couldn't decide.

"Hi," Tonya said.

Michelle turned and said hello, but Tissy couldn't seem to take her eyes off the fire, watching it with an eager, enthralled look on her face.

"How did the fire start?" Tonya asked.

"No one seems to know," Michelle replied.

Tissy remained transfixed by the sight before her with an excitement that seemed almost manic.

Michelle said, "I'd better get back to the salon. Are you coming, Tissy?"

"In a minute," she replied. "I want to watch for a few minutes more."

Michelle walked away, and Tonya stepped closer to Tissy. "I haven't seen you since you came to the farm. How have you been?" Tissy was silent. Tonya cleared her throat. "You left so suddenly that day," she said. "I hope I didn't say anything to upset you."

Tissy turned to her as though seeing her for the first time. "What? Oh. No, you didn't say anything." She looked around uncomfortably. "I better get back to the salon. See you."

Tonya watched her walk away, thinking that she had never met anyone as strange as this fragile-looking girl. She felt sorry for her and at the same time a little afraid of her. Surely she was involved with whoever attacked Tonya, but it seemed impossible that this pathetic creature could harm anyone. Tonya determined to probe deeper into the mysterious Tissy.

ლოლ

Tonya returned home to see Mike standing at the fence of the yearlings' pasture, his head on his arms folded on the top railing. One of the colts was nuzzling his hair. He reached up and scratched the colt's cheek. Tonya watched him for a moment. He looked so small and alone. She decided not to interrupt him, but his situation couldn't be kept from Lexi any longer. She deserved to know the worst.

In the house, she called to Lexi and heard her in her bedroom off the living room. Tonya opened the door and found her lying on the bed reading a brochure, both cats curled up next to her. Tonya felt just a little jealous that Clive and Henry seemed to be nearly as fond of Lexi as they were of her.

"Hi," Lexi said, looking up. "I'm just trying to plan what to do with my mom and uncle when they get here.

This isn't exactly a tourist's paradise, is it?"

Tonya plopped down on the bed, and the cats got up to greet her. She stroked them and scratched their heads. "I guess not. Are they the sightseeing type?"

Lexi tossed the brochure aside. "Not really."

"Then why not just let them hang out with you? After all this time, they will probably be happy just doing that."

"Did you get the vitamins?"

"Yeah," Tonya said, taking the bottle out of her pocket and handing it to Lexi. "Listen to this. I saw Leo Jenkins in the drug store. He was trying to get MacNeil to give him something without a prescription. Claimed it was for a kid with an infected foot that couldn't be taken to a doctor."

"What kid?"

"No idea. But MacNeil said he knew Jenkins was doing something illegal. Maybe that's what Caine knew, and that's what got him killed."

"You think Leo Jenkins killed Caine?" Lexi asked, her eyes wide.

Tonya thought about Leo's generosity in giving them credit. She couldn't imagine him as a killer. "It doesn't seem possible, does it? But remember Jeffers? We all thought he was just a harmless, silly man."

Lexi chewed her lip.

"Lex, I need to tell you something. Mike is leaving."

"Leaving? Where's he going?"

Tonya explained about his plan to ride in California and the letters he had received from his sister.

Lexi's eyes misted up. "Poor Mike," she said. "What a rotten thing to happen to him. When's he going?"

"He has to be there February first. So I guess he'll be going in a couple of days."

"How are we ever going to manage?" Lexi whispered.

Tonya squared her shoulders. "One day at a time, that's what Dad said."

"Did you see him today?"

Tonya told her about visiting Royce. "Maybe once the mares start coming, and the yearlings are sold, we'll be able to hire someone to help out. Until then, it will be just the two of us. If you take care of the meals and the house, I'll see to the horses. We'll just have to hang on a while longer. Adam is working hard to find Caine's killer, and when he does, Dad will be home again."

Lexi said, "You're right. We can do it."

Tonya gazed out the window at the pale afternoon sun in the slightly overcast sky. The bare tree limbs seemed sad and lonely, but at the same time, hopeful of the promise of the new spring buds just waiting to emerge. It gave her a comforting sense of the certainty of nature and the creation, constantly renewing itself in spite of harsh winters, droughts, and natural disasters. "I'd better get started. Jake needs exercise, and the yearlings need attention."

Lexi yawned. "Okay, I think I'll take a nap and then get dinner started. Ask Mike to come and eat with us."

Tonya got up, and the cats hopped off the bed. "I'll ask, but I doubt he'll want to eat." She opened the door for the cats, and both scooted out. She turned back to Lexi. "Oh, there was a fire in town. That old warehouse on South Main."

"About time that eyesore went up. Anything else burn?"

"No. But I saw Tissy and Michelle there. I was going to try to find out what made Tissy spook that day she was here, but she took off before I could ask."

"Hmm. She's a weird bird, isn't she?"

"Have a nice nap." Tonya closed the door quietly and went upstairs to change. The cats padded after her, meowing for attention. As she sat on the bed, Henry rubbed on her arm, and Clive kneaded her leg with his front paws.

"Have you guys missed me?" she murmured to them, stroking both their heads. "I haven't been around much, have I?" She spent a few more minutes, giving them the attention they needed, then changed into her barn clothes. As she left the room, she looked back at their two little faces, peering at her with wide eyes, and felt guilty at having to leave them again.

She entered the empty barn and took Jake's tack and brushes out of the tack room. She went out the back door to his paddock. Mike wasn't around, for which she was grateful. She didn't think she could cope with another emotional scene.

Jake trotted up to the gate and put his head into his halter, eager to break his daily routine to do something different. Gus whinnied as she led Jake out of the paddock toward the barn. *I'll have to do something with him, too*, she thought. *Then I'll groom and lunge the yearlings, and by then it will be time for the evening feeding.* She was already feeling the burden of the work ahead of her, but she determined to put her head down and keep at it, just as she did on the track when she had to work for weeks honing her skills in order to compete with the older, more experienced jockeys. There were times she thought it was an insurmountable task, but the hard work paid off, and, by the end of the summer, she was not only competing, but winning.

She gave Jake a quick grooming, pushing his nose away each time he tried to nip at her playfully. She saddled him and led him to the mounting block where she slid onto his back. As she jogged him toward the training track, she glanced at the rise under the elm tree where the Warrens' stallion was buried. The wrinkled faces of the old couple rose up before her and seemed to inspire her with their courage. For forty years they had worked together on this farm, doing many of the same things the Callahans were planning—breeding, training and racing Thoroughbreds. And they did it mostly by themselves, raising children and grandchildren at the same time. They had what she desperately needed now, determination, a willingness to work hard, and a strong sense of what was right.

After Jake was cooled out and returned to his paddock, she took Gus for his walk around the property for an hour then turned him out again and watched him roll in the dirt, scratching his back. Then she took the yearlings out, one by one, worked them in the round corral, and afterward, groomed each of them. But the time she finished with them, the sun was setting, and her stomach was growling. Mike hadn't emerged from his trailer all day, and she was torn between disappointment and relief.

When she returned to the barn to prepare for the evening feeding, she stopped at Maisie's stall to check her and her baby. She peered over the half door and watched the colt following the barn cat as she did her tightrope walk along the ledge halfway up the wall. The colt was too little to reach the calico with his nose, but he trailed along after her, determined to keep up. The colt had had a rough start in life, and the odds were against him. But here he was, not only surviving, but thriving. If he could defy the odds and make it, so could she. This wasn't the first time she derived immense comfort and inspiration from the horses.

CHAPTER 16

The last day of January dawned cool and dry, the winter skies a dreary gray. Little rain had fallen since early December, and the fire danger was high. There had been a couple of suspicious fires near town since the warehouse went up in a blaze, causing the townspeople to watch the skies anxiously. Many of them were old enough to remember the fire of the early nineties, when a teenager, angry at his girlfriend, had set fire to some dry brush near the Texas/Oklahoma border and burned thousands of acres, torching over 300 homes and barns. Two people had died, trying to outrun the flames.

Tonya's thoughts were far from the fire danger when she entered the barn that morning. The calico cat met her at the door, meowing for her breakfast. Lexi had warned that feeding her regular cat food would curb her desire to hunt for food and make her fat and lazy, but Tonya couldn't resist the cat's pleading amber eyes. The calico trotted at her heels as she opened the feed room door.

Jake, Gus, and Maisie watched her, their heads craned over their wooden half doors, their ears pricked up. She could hear the mares and yearlings in their pas-

tures whinnying and stomping as they gathered near their
gates in watchful anticipation.

Tonya worked quickly, loading the wheelbarrow
with hay and grain and wheeling it down the shed row
toward the back door. She stopped at Maisie's stall and
peered over the door to see her colt capering around the
stall, bucking and playing. He danced in circles around
his mother. Then he lost his balance, bumped into her,
and sat down hard, his long spindly legs splayed out in
front of him. His mother patiently tolerated his antics.
Then he hopped up, gave a high-pitched whinny, and resumed his play. Tonya wondered when she could turn
them both out with the other mares. She had no doubt
that, as Maisie was the dominant mare in the herd, none
of the others would dare to come near her baby in a
threatening manner. They would simply sniff at him jeal-
ously until their own foals started arriving in a month or
two.

After the barn horses were fed, Tonya wheeled the
barrow out the back door, trying not to look at Mike's
dark, deserted trailer. He had left for San Francisco several days earlier. Tonya had dreaded the goodbye scene,
knowing she would not be able to hold back her tears.
Perhaps Mike knew that, because he had simply left the
key to the trailer in the feed room, along with a brief note
thanking the Callahans for their kindness. The lump in
her throat each time she thought of him leaving caught
her by surprise again as she tossed the hay over the fence
to the mares and yearlings.

After checking each of the mares, she returned to the
house. In about an hour, she would go back to the barn,
turn Jake and Gus out into their paddocks, and clean the
stalls.

In the kitchen, Lexi was scrambling eggs and frying
bacon. Clive and Henry sat at attention at her feet, their

whiskers quivering as they sniffed the delicious bacon smell. Their tails were wrapped demurely around their front legs, and they gazed up at Lexi with hopeful eyes.

"Oh, don't give me that look," Lexi admonished them. "You've had your breakfast."

Tonya sat down at the round kitchen table and poured some milk from the pitcher. "They know you're a pushover and that you'll eventually give in."

"I know, but I like to keep them in suspense," Lexi said, leaning down to pat their heads. Lexi had never owned a cat before she married Royce, but she had grown to love Henry and Clive as much as Tonya did.

"Lex, what do you think about turning Maisie and the foal out with the mares? He's two weeks old and growing like a weed. He must have put on fifty pounds since he was born. Do you think we can chance it?"

Lexi scraped the eggs onto the two plates and sat down. "Hmm. I don't know. The weather is sure mild enough. Maybe you should call Doc and ask him what he thinks."

Tonya sighed. "I'm afraid he'll want to come out and see him. We already owe him more than we can pay."

Lexi watched Tonya eat. "I hate to see you working so hard. You're doing the work of three people out there."

"That was the deal. You cook and do the housework. I take care of the horses. It's not so bad. Staying busy keeps my mind off...stuff."

They ate in silence for several minutes, then Lexi said, "Hey. Why don't we go into town? I could visit your Dad, and you could see Adam. I mean, if you want to."

Tonya thought a moment. She hadn't talked to Adam in over a week. Surely he had found out something about the people he was checking on. Maybe seeing him again would help her get a handle on her feelings for him, now that Mike was gone. "Okay. I'll turn Jake and Gus out, and we can go. The stalls can wait."

❧❧❧

As they drove down Centerville's main street, Tonya pointed to the blackened ruins of the warehouse. The smell of burned wood still lingered in the air.

Lexi wrinkled her nose. "I hope they catch whoever is setting those fires."

Pulling up in front of the police station, Tonya noticed that Adam's cruiser wasn't there. She fed the parking meter and turned to Lexi. "I'm going over to Jenkins's while you see Dad."

Lexi looked at Tonya sideways. "You're not going to ask Leo for more credit, are you?"

Tonya laughed. "No. He'd probably kick me out. I'm just going to poke around and see what I can see over there. There's something about that store that has to do with Caine's murder. I'm sure of it."

"Okay, but you know how Adam hates it when you poke."

"What he doesn't know, he can't hate. I won't be long. Give Dad my love."

Lexi rolled her eyes. "I wish I could hug him. It's so stupid that we can't have any physical contact with prisoners. Maybe you could talk to Adam about that."

"Adam is anal about the rules. But I can ask."

Tonya watched Lexi go into the station and turned toward the feed store. The small town lay quietly under the vast Texas sky, hiding its secrets under a languid exterior. Someone in this town had brutally killed a man and someone—perhaps the same person—was setting fires.

She passed Michelle's salon and glanced in the window. Michelle was cutting a woman's hair while Tissy sat in the chair near her. Tissy looked up as Tonya passed by, no recognition registering on her blank face. *There's another mystery*, Tonya thought, recalling the conversation she overheard in the ladies' room of the diner.

As she approached Jenkins Feed and Tack, she could just see the back of the store from the sidewalk and noticed the same white van she had seen there before. Several young men and boys, all in laborers' clothes, scooted out the door and climbed quickly into the van. One of the boys was limping. The side door of the van slammed shut, and the van pulled slowly out of the parking lot. As it passed her, the driver, a dark-haired, dark-skinned man wearing sunglasses, stared at her for a moment. She couldn't see into the van's exterior. Its heavily tinted windows were impenetrable.

She stood on the sidewalk, deciding it was too much of a coincidence that she had seen the same van at the store three times. She moved along the side of the building to the back door and pulled it open. There was no one around. The back room was packed with supplies and bags of feed. Bales of alfalfa hay were piled nearly to the ceiling. She could hear Leo Jenkins talking to a customer through the curtained doorway to the store. She looked around and noticed another door slightly ajar. Sidling over to it, she opened it just enough to hear whispering. The door opened onto a rickety staircase descending into darkness. She listened carefully and thought she heard at least three different voices, all male and all speaking Spanish. She silently cursed herself for not studying her Spanish lessons more while Mike was here. What was

Leo Jenkins doing with people in his basement, and what did that white van have to do with them?

Tonya crept quietly to the curtained doorway just in time to hear Jenkins saying to Alec, "Stay out of the cellar. I've told you before. You have no business there."

Alec's voice dripped with sarcasm. "Whatever you say, Mr. J."

"Watch your step, buster!" the parrot squawked.

Tonya slipped silently out the back door and hurried to the police station. She was pleased to see Adam's cruiser now parked in its usual spot. Dashing into the station, she headed for his office. He looked up in surprise as she barged in and plopped into a chair facing his desk.

"Adam," she said, catching her breath. "I was just at Jenkins's store, and wait till you hear what I saw."

"What?"

"First, there was this white van that I've seen there before. A bunch of laborer types got into the van, and it pulled away. Then I heard some guys whispering in the cellar in Spanish. And I heard Jenkins tell Alec, the clerk, to stay away from the cellar."

Adam raised one eyebrow. "What were you doing in the back of his store?"

Tonya ground her teeth. "What difference does it make?" she nearly shouted. "Didn't you hear what I said?"

"It would make a great deal of difference if he had caught you and charged you with breaking and entering."

Tonya struggled to keep her temper under control. "I didn't break into the store. The back door was open. Look, I think he's smuggling illegals. The van, the Spanish speakers in the cellar—it all adds up. Another thing, I saw him in the market with a shopping basket full of Mexican food, enough for twenty people. I'll bet Jenkins is involved with the coyotes. They're bringing illegal laborers across the border, and he's helping them."

Adam tapped his pencil on the desk and stared into space. "You may be right. The coyotes have been working in the area. He may very well be involved."

"If Caine found out about it, he might have started helping him."

Adam leaned forward and opened a folder. His slow, deliberate manner was maddening to her. "Caine may have been doing more than helping. I found out what that key opens. A locker at the bus station. Know what we found?"

"What?"

"Two thousand in cash. All small bills."

"So Caine was involved with the smuggling."

"Maybe. It's also possible he was blackmailing Jenkins, and Jenkins was paying him to keep his mouth shut."

Tonya sat back and exhaled loudly. So that was it. Leo got tired of paying Caine and finally killed him. She knitted her brow. Could Jenkins really be a killer? He seemed so innocuous. But then again, so did Alton Jeffers. Tonya had learned from that experience not to judge someone by their outward appearance.

Adam stood up. "I'm going to have a little talk with Jenkins."

"Can I come?"

"Absolutely not. This is police business. Stay here and wait for Lexi. If anything comes of it, I'll let you know."

Tonya frowned.

"Now don't start pouting," Adam said, pulling on his jacket and taking his pistol and handcuffs out of the desk drawer. She stuck her lower lip out at him, and he smirked.

He left the station, got into his cruiser, and drove toward the store. Tonya sat, drumming her fingers on the desk. Did she dare walk to the store and go in the back door again? No, that would be foolish. She couldn't risk irritating Adam with her snooping.

It wasn't long before Adam came back to the station escorting Leo in handcuffs. Adam handed Jenkins to a uniformed officer who ushered him to an interview room.

Coming into the office, he put his weapon back into the drawer. "You were right. He's harboring illegals in the cellar. He's running a safe house. The coyotes bring the illegals across the border, hide them in a series of safe houses then parcel them out to farmers and ranchers from here to Canada. Each of the safe house owners takes his cut from the coyotes or the cartels that employ them. Quite a sophisticated operation." He headed for the door again. "I'm going to question him now."

"Adam. Please let me listen to the interview. I won't say a word. I promise." She pleaded with her eyes and saw him hesitate.

"It's against procedure, but I guess it can't do any harm. Unless he lawyers up and the lawyer forbids it. But you'll have to listen from behind the two-way glass in the next room."

Tonya was so grateful she nearly kissed him. Now maybe there would be enough evidence to free her father.

Adam took her to the viewing room and turned on the speaker next to the window. She saw Leo sitting at the table, his head in his hands. "He can't see or hear you."

She touched his arm gratefully. "Thanks, Adam."

He reached down and moved a strand of hair away from her eye. "You're welcome."

Tonya watched through the window as Adam entered the room with a folder and sat at the table opposite Leo.

Adam began paging through his notes. Leo looked like a boy caught smoking behind the barn, frightened and not at all like a criminal.

Adam cleared his throat. "Mr. Jenkins, you are in some serious trouble. Do you know the penalty for smuggling illegals? It's a felony, punishable by a fine and up to ten years in prison. The courts don't look kindly on anyone making a profit out of the misery of others."

Jenkins shifted uncomfortably in his chair. "Look, Lieutenant, I'm doing those folks a favor."

"A favor. How so?"

He leaned forward, his eyes searching Adam's face. "Do you have any idea what those poor people go through to get here? Do you know there are thousands who have died in the desert trying to reach the border? Some of them walk for days in temperatures over a hundred degrees. They run out of what little water they bring with them. Then they wander around in shock until they die from thirst, unless they're lucky enough to be found by the Border Patrol. Some of them drown crossing the river. Others are bitten by rattlesnakes or die of heart attacks. They get hit by trains or cars on the interstate. They have found the bodies of pregnant women, kids, old men rotting where they fell. And their families never know what happened to them."

His voice broke, and his eyes became misty. "Then there are the coyotes who will take their money, lead them into the wilderness, and abandon them to die in the sweltering heat. At least the guys I work with aren't like that. I had a kid here yesterday who had walked for miles in sandals. He had cactus needles in his foot. It was infected and stinking. What would have happened to him if I hadn't helped? All I do is give them a place to stay that's safe. I feed them and help them. So what if I make a few bucks?"

"It's illegal. You're breaking the law and helping them to do the same."

"I'm helping them to stay alive. They come up here and do jobs Americans won't do. All they want is to make a living and send money back to Mexico to help their families. I'm not sorry."

Tonya was moved listening to him and thought about Mike's family in Guadalajara.

Adam stared at Leo. "Tell me, Mr. Jenkins, what part did Lucas Caine have in the operation? We found the money he was stashing at the bus station."

Before Leo could answer, the door opened, and a man in a suit carrying a briefcase stepped in. "The interview is over," the man said to Adam. "I need to confer with my client."

Adam closed his folder and left the room. He came back to the room where Tonya was waiting and turned off the speaker. "You'll have to leave now. You can't overhear his conversation with his lawyer."

Adam walked her to the front door of the station where Lexi was waiting for her. As he opened the door for them, Tonya asked, "What will happen to Leo?"

"He'll probably get out on bail. But his little smuggling operation will be closed down."

"What will happen to the people in his cellar?"

"I have to call the Border Patrol. They'll probably be deported."

Tonya nodded. She wasn't sure who she felt sorrier for, Leo or the illegals. One thing she felt sure of, though. Leo Jenkins was no murderer.

CHAPTER 17

The next day, Tonya awoke to Henry tickling her face with his whiskers. She pushed him away and sat up. The sky was still gray, the sun not quite over the horizon yet. The house was quiet as Tonya glanced at the clock. Five-thirty. She lay back down, hoping for another half hour of sleep. She squeezed her eyes shut, but she could feel the cats staring at her. She opened one eye and saw four blue eyes boring into her from two white furry faces, one on either side of her head. She sighed. "Okay, okay. I'm getting up."

She flung back the blankets, cursing herself for being so soft-hearted with those two. The cats hopped off the bed and paced by the door, meowing for their breakfast. Tonya pulled on her barn clothes, made a quick trip to the bathroom, and tiptoed down the stairs, not wanting to wake Lexi. Her mother and uncle were due to arrive today, and Tonya knew Lexi would be busy cooking for them and trying to make their stay as memorable as possible.

She fed the cats, drank some milk, and stood by the kitchen counter, gazing out the window at the Eastern sky streaked in pink and purple. The sky grew lighter and lighter until the sun popped up suddenly from below the horizon like a giant yellow beach ball that had been held under water.

Tonya left the house, quietly closing the door behind her. She tiptoed across the wooden porch before she realized that the horses whinnying for their breakfast would probably wake Lexi anyway. She crossed the drive and opened the barn door to the usual neighing and stomping of the three horses, accompanied now by the high-pitched whinny of Maisie's colt.

As she went through the morning routine, the thoughts she had been trying to sort out crowded each other like the yearlings near the pasture gate, each one trying to muscle the others out of the way. No sooner would she start on one train of thought than another would pop up like a Whack-a-Mole to take its place. Images of Tissy's face at the fire, the illegals in the van, Leo in handcuffs, her last goodbye with Mike, and her father in the orange county jail jumpsuit flooded through her brain until she stopped the wheelbarrow and dug her fists into her eyes. *I have to stop this*, she thought, *or I'll drive myself crazy.*

While the horses ate their breakfast, she cleaned the stalls, tossing forkfuls of manure into the wheelbarrow with as much force as she could, hoping to wear herself out and prevent her imagination from running away with her. At one point, she thought she heard a car in the driveway, but decided it was far too early for visitors.

She left Jake's stall and moved on to Gus's, parking the wheelbarrow in front of his open door. She stood for a moment, stroking his gleaming chestnut neck while he wolfed down his grain. He didn't bother searching her pockets for carrots anymore. In the past month, she had completely forgotten about their morning carrot routine, and that made her feel sad.

"The little one, he is well?" a voice at the door said.

Tonya turned to the door, startled. "Luis!" she shouted. "Luis!" She ran to the little man standing in the aisle and hugged him tightly. All she could say was, "Luis, Luis."

He laughed and returned the hug. Then he held her at arm's length and said, "Yes, *mija*. It is Luis. How are you?"

Tonya was so overjoyed to see him that she was speechless. She could only hug him again as a feeling of inexpressible relief flooded over her. This wonderful man who had always been a second father to her, who had taught her so much, who had encouraged her in her down times, who had left for Arizona months ago to train Royce's horses at the track there, was standing before her. She could hardly believe it. He was exactly as she remembered him, his black hair streaked with gray, his brown eyes twinkling, a huge smile nearly splitting his face in two. Even the smell of his pipe tobacco lingering on his clothes was the same as she remembered.

Finally, she gasped, "I'm so glad to see you. But what are you doing here?"

"Your papa, he did not tell you?"

"Dad? No."

"He called Luis last week and told me what happened. I was so sorry to hear it, *mija*. How could he be in jail?"

"It's true. He was arrested the day after Christmas. Of course, it's all a mistake."

"He told me about Mike leaving and you and Lexi working the farm by yourselves. He asked if Luis could come and help out for a while."

"But what about the horses at the track?"

"Rafael can take care of things for a while. Once

your papa is home, I will return to Arizona."

Tonya had so many questions, but she knew they would have to wait. She was sure Luis needed to get answers first, and there was so much to tell him.

"Come in the house. Lexi will be so surprised."

Luis picked up his battered suitcase and followed her.

"How did you get here?" she asked as they walked across the drive.

"The bus from Phoenix arrived last night. I stayed in a motel and took a cab here."

"Well, no more motels. You must stay here with us." She thought about the two empty bedrooms that Lexi had prepared for her mother and uncle. But there was always the trailer.

The smells of coffee and bacon greeted them as they opened the front door.

Tonya called toward the kitchen. "Lexi! Look who's here."

"Not already! Mom?" Lexi peered out of the kitchen. Then she stopped as she saw Luis, her jaw dropping. "Luis! Oh, my goodness." She came quickly to them and hugged Luis. "I'm delighted to see you, but what—how?"

"Dad called him and told him we need help," Tonya said, relieving Luis of his bag.

"Did he? Wonderful! Have you eaten? Come into the kitchen and have some breakfast."

Sitting at the kitchen table, they ate and talked and laughed, but soon the conversation turned to the murder of Lucas Caine. Lexi hesitantly related the story of her marriage to Caine, his abuse, and her flight away from him. Luis nodded sympathetically, his warm and gracious manner putting Lexi at ease.

They asked about the horses he was training. He updated them on Sable, the black filly, and Howitzer,

Royce's steady Appaloosa lead pony, and Tonya felt a wave of nostalgia for the racetrack. Would she ever get back to racing, to the world she loved? It seemed like a distant dream that had faded in the harsh light of the events of the past six weeks.

They finished their coffee, and Luis leaned back. "Now, *mija,* tell Luis. What can I do to help?"

"First, let's get you settled in the trailer. Then you can see the mares and yearlings. Did you see the colt? He's in the barn, but we're thinking he and his mama should go out with the rest of the mares. The yearlings need to be exercised and groomed for the sale. Jake and Gus need their workouts every day. Then we have to get the barn ready for the mares that will be coming to be bred to Jake. The foaling sheds behind the barn need some repairs. Let's see, what else?"

Lexi laughed. "Sounds like that's plenty for a start."

Luis nodded. "I am ready."

Tonya put her hand on his arm. "We're so glad to see you, Luis. You have no idea."

✍✍✍

The rest of the morning flew by as Tonya showed Luis around the property and introduced him to the horses. He studied each one with the expert eye of a horseman and decided the yearlings alone would bring the farm into solvency once they were sold. Luis looked over each of the five pregnant mares and pronounced them all fit and healthy.

Tonya showed him Maisie's colt, and Luis seemed impressed with him as well. "Now that we have him, we will have to find another name for Gus. He is no longer 'the little one.'"

"As long as it's not 'runt,' I don't care what you call him," she said, reminding him of Mike's name for Gus.

"You have heard from Miguel since he left?"

"No. He said he would write, but..." She shrugged her shoulders. "I guess he's busy getting back into riding." She looked away from him, hoping he wouldn't notice the disappointment in her eyes.

After a tour of the property, Tonya unlocked the trailer and showed Luis inside. It had a dark and lonely feeling about it that couldn't be accounted for simply by its emptiness. The small table in the front room brought back the memory of Mike's last goodbye, and it nearly took her breath away. She moved around, opening the windows and allowing the fresh air to clear both the atmosphere in the room and her thoughts.

"I'm sure you'll be comfortable here," she said. "Dad and I lived in this place for so many years. It always feels like home." She took his suitcase into what used to be Royce's room and tossed it on the bed.

"I can unpack later. I would like to start with the yearlings now," Luis said, turning toward the door.

"Okay. I'll take Jake out and come back for Gus. Then maybe we can turn Maisie and her colt out to see how the other mares react." She was glad to leave the trailer with all its memories.

They spent the rest of the day doing all the chores that made up life on the farm, stopping only for a quick lunch in the farmhouse kitchen. Luis was as skilled as ever with horses, and he seemed to especially relish working with the yearlings. Tonya loved listening to his cheerful, tuneless humming as he groomed each one. Just like her, Luis seemed to find a kind of peaceful joy working around horses.

Once Jake and Gus and the yearlings were exercised and back in their paddocks, Tonya led Maisie and her baby out of their stall toward the mares' pasture. Maisie seemed delighted to be out of the confined stall after two weeks, but she nickered nervously to her baby as he trotted along close to her side.

Once at the gate, Luis said, "I will hold the others back until we see how they act." He opened the gate and shooed the mares away until Maisie and the colt were inside. Then Tonya closed the gate and stood holding Maisie by her halter.

The mares watched the proceedings with curiosity, especially when the colt came toward them, his ears pricked up and his nostrils quivering.

In no time, the mares lost interest in the colt and wandered as a group toward the oak tree in the middle of the pasture where they spent much of the day dozing. "They will be fine," Luis said.

Tonya removed Maisie's halter and turned her loose. The mare immediately lay down for a nice itch-relieving roll in the dirt, while the colt exhibited his fearless nature by exploring along the fence. *If only everything in life was this easy,* Tonya thought with a sigh.

As they stood watching Maisie saunter over to join the band of mares, Tonya heard Lexi calling from the porch. She was holding her cell phone and gesturing to Tonya to come to the house.

"They're here," she said breathlessly when Tonya got to the porch. "My mother and Uncle Jack. They just got off the bus from the airport. They're at Hank's, and they want us to join them there for dinner."

"I thought you were making dinner for them here."

"I was, but they insisted. I told them we would be there as quick as we can, so get changed."

"What about Luis?"

"Tell him to help himself to whatever is in the kitchen. We can take him food shopping tomorrow. Now hurry!"

"Okay, okay," Tonya said, laughing. "Keep calm. They won't disappear."

Lexi rolled her eyes. "I know I'm being silly, but it's been so long since I've seen my mom."

෨෬෨෬

Lexi's mother was a petite, spunky woman with tightly curled iron gray hair, clear blue eyes, and a dazzling smile. She and her brother, Jack, were sitting on a bench in front of Hank's diner. As they pulled up, Lexi jumped out of the truck almost before it came to a stop and grasped her mother, tears in both of their eyes.

Tonya stayed in the truck for a few minutes, busying herself in order to give them a few minutes alone. Lexi, her mother, and uncle were locked in a three-way embrace, and as Tonya watched them, she realized what she was missing by having no siblings or aunts and uncles. It made her miss her father even more.

Lexi motioned to Tonya to join them. She got out of the pickup and shook hands with both.

"So you're my girl's stepdaughter," her mother said. "Glad to meet you. This is my brother, Jack. He's a psychologist," she said proudly.

Tonya shook hands with Jack, a tall, thin man in his fifties with a shock of graying brown hair. He wore thick glasses that gave his eyes an owlish, intellectual look. He had a reserved, somewhat formal manner, a complete contrast to Lexi's mother who apparently had never met someone she wasn't instantly comfortable with.

"I'm happy to meet you both, Mrs....er." Tonya almost called her Mrs. Parr until she remembered that Lexi's real name was Diana Wilkins.

"Just call me Sylvia, honey."

"Nice to meet you, Sylvia," Tonya said gratefully.

"Let's eat," Sylvia said. "Is the food here any good?" She peered into the diner.

Lexi took her mother's arm. "Not bad, considering it's about the only place in town."

They trooped into the diner and found a booth near the door. It was still early for the dinner crowd, so the diner was nearly empty. As they settled into their seats, Meggie came out from behind the counter with menus. She came to the booth, her usual fake welcoming smile plastered on her face. She set the menus down and started to greet them. But as her eyes met Jack's, they widened, and her mouth dropped open.

"Oh, my gosh," she exclaimed.

Jack looked up at the waitress, his face registering his surprise. "Hello, Erin. Fancy meeting you here."

Meggie stood riveted to the spot, seemingly unable to speak. Her jaw worked nervously, but no words came out. Finally, she cleared her throat and said, "Yeah, hi."

"Small world, isn't it?" Jack said to her kindly, trying to diffuse what was obviously an uncomfortable situation.

Tonya glanced from the waitress to Lexi's uncle, wondering why he called her Erin, but not at all surprised to discover that there were unknown facets to the enigmatic Meggie.

"Yeah, small world," Meggie said, recovering her composure. "Can I get you folks something to drink?"

Tonya's mind drifted back to the incident of the spilled iced tea and Tissy's warning to her not to drink anything else that night.

"Just bring us four waters," Sylvia said.

"Fine. I'll be back to take your order."

As she walked away, Tonya turned to Jack. "How do you know her?"

"She was one of my patients," he said. "She was part of a grief support group I ran back in Ohio." He gazed after Meggie thoughtfully. "Imagine her winding up here."

CHAPTER 18

All through dinner, Tonya's mind was whirling. She was dying to pump Jack for more information about Meggie, but she hesitated. The waitress continued to watch them as they ate, although whenever Tonya looked directly at her, she looked away. When she did come to the table with that phony smile on her face, she made sure to keep the conversation light. She asked if they needed anything else, if they would like dessert, how the food was, and the usual waitress chit-chat. But she was never far from the table and seemed to be trying to overhear their conversation.

Although Tonya was eager to find out more about Meggie, she knew that, as a psychologist, Jack would be reluctant to disclose anything confidential about her. But Meggie was the last person to see Caine alive, next to the murderer, and Tonya was sure she was hiding something.

They finally finished dinner, and Jack called Meggie over and asked for the check. He reached for his wallet. "My treat."

Tonya and Lexi exchanged grateful glances, both breathing a sigh of relief that their slim finances wouldn't have to take another hit.

"Ready?" Lexi asked.

They slid out of the booth and started for the door. Tonya looked back at the waitress and was startled to see her talking to Tissy who was sitting at the end of the counter. How long had she been here? And how did she get into the diner without Tonya seeing her? They both glanced up at Tonya as Jack held the door open for her. Meggie's expression was one of hostility, while Tissy appeared anxious and hunted, like a rabbit being pursued by hounds closing in for the kill.

As they drove home, all squashed into the cab of the pickup, Tonya waited for a lull in the conversation, not easy to do in the company of the loquacious Sylvia who had babbled away all through dinner. Sylvia asked questions about the farms and ranches they passed along the highway, what it was like living in Centerville, the plans for the training farm, and whatever else came to mind. Lexi accommodated her, answering questions and telling stories about Jake and their success with him the previous summer. It was as though no one wanted to mention the fact that Lexi's former husband was dead, and Royce was in jail for a murder he didn't commit.

As they pulled into the driveway, Tonya noticed the lights on in the trailer and was glad to see that Luis had settled in. Once in the house, Lexi showed Sylvia and Jack to their rooms while Tonya went to the kitchen to make coffee. At one point, Tonya heard Sylvia loudly exclaim from upstairs, "Ohhh, kittycats! I just love kitties." Clearly, Clive and Henry had made a positive impression.

Jack strolled into the kitchen, sat down, and said, "Whew. I forgot how much my sister can talk."

Tonya smiled. "She's just excited to be here. I'm sure she appreciates your coming here with her. It's been so long since she and Lexi, I mean Diana, have seen each other." She poured the coffee and invited him to sit down. "We have some cookies here, I think," she said, rummaging through the cabinet.

"Just coffee for me, thanks."

She sat down across from him and sipped her coffee. "So. You're a psychologist," she began nonchalantly. "That must be fascinating."

"It is."

"I think you mentioned a grief group of some kind? What happens in a grief group?" She held her breath, hoping she could bring the conversation around to Meggie.

"It's a support group for people who have had a loss in their lives, usually the death of a loved one. They can also be grieving over a lost career or a bad relationship or a terminal illness. All kinds of things can cause grief in our lives."

"And you help them learn to deal with it?"

"I try. Many times just being with others who have suffered is therapeutic in itself. Sometimes members of those groups can form very tight bonds with one another."

Tonya decided to plunge in and see how much she could get out of him. "Really funny finding one of your group members here, huh?" Before he could answer, she continued, "When we first met Meggie, she told us about her sister who died from a drug overdose. I guess that must have been why she was in the group." She stopped, hoping Jack would offer more information.

He shifted in his chair a bit uncomfortably. "I can't usually talk about my patients, but since you already know, yes. Jacque, her sister, had a very bad drug experience and lost the baby she was carrying. Erin, or Meggie as she calls herself now, came into the group full of rage.

Not uncommon with that kind of loss. It's one of the steps of mourning. Denial, anger, bargaining, depression, and finally acceptance. She was deep in the anger stage and couldn't seem to get past it."

"Was she ever able to accept her sister's death?"

"I think she did. Especially after she developed strong bonds with some of the other group members. They would meet after the sessions. Quite often, actually."

"Others with similar stories?"

"Others who were having difficulty coming to grips with their losses. There was one woman…" He glanced up at Tonya then down at his cup. "Well, let's just say they had a lot in common."

"Are the others still in your group?"

"No, actually. One by one, they've all left. Moved out of the area. I offered to give them referrals to someone wherever they were moving, but they all declined. I don't even know where they are. Except for Erin, that is. I wonder what brought her here. She's lived in Ohio her whole life."

Tonya stared out the window at the darkened sky, trying to put together all she knew about Meggie. What Jack had shared only deepened the mystery. What had brought her here? She didn't seem to know anyone in town. Why choose this small, out of the way place to settle down? Could it be that she just needed a complete change of scenery? Or was there more to it?

Tonya remembered that Meggie wasn't the only one who had changed her name. Tissy's real name, she had admitted, was Celeste. "Jack," she said, "let me ask you something. Why do people change their names? I don't mean officially or when they're running from something. I mean when they just start calling themselves by a different name."

"Lots of reasons. Sometimes they just don't like the name they were given. Often they are trying to forge new identities, new personalities."

"Kind of start a new life, you mean."

"Exactly. In Erin's case, I suspect she's just trying to put her past with its sorrows behind her and start a new life. Changing her name may be helping her to do that. I hope so."

Tonya couldn't help wondering again why anyone would want to start a new life in a small Texas town in the middle of nowhere.

Jack seemed to be warming to his subject. "Sometimes people choose names that make a statement or that tell the world something about them. This farm, for instance. Why did you name it Hibernia?"

"That's easy. Hibernia is the ancient name for Ireland. We're Irish, so Dad thought it would be a way to honor the old country. They say Ireland never loses its grip on the Irishman."

Lexi and her mother came into the kitchen. Sylvia was carrying Henry on her shoulder, and Henry was purring and kneading her with his paws, loving the attention.

"I see you've made a new friend," Tonya said.

"He's a lover boy, aren't you?" Sylvia said, stroking Henry's sleek white fur. "I may just have to take him home with me."

"Don't get too attached, Mom," Lexi said. "Tonya would part with an arm before she'd part with one of those cats."

Sylvia strolled around the kitchen, looking out the windows and admiring the décor. "This is such a lovely old house. I can't wait to see the rest of the property."

Lexi said, "I'll give you the full tour tomorrow. How about a cup of coffee?"

"I'd better not, dear, or I'll be up all night. In fact, I think I'll turn in. It's been a long day."

"Okay, Mom," Lexi said as she gave her mother a hug. "See you in the morning."

"Good night, Syl," Jack said.

Tonya was sorry that her conversation with Jack had been interrupted, but she thought it best to give Lexi and her uncle some time to catch up on family affairs. She excused herself and went to her room.

As she lay in bed later that night, she decided that, as interesting as the mysterious Meggie might be, Tonya's main focus had to be on finding Caine's killer so her father would be released. She would call Adam in the morning to find out if he had any more information about Leo Jenkins and his smuggling operation. She had decided that Leo was too soft-hearted to kill anyone, but maybe Lucas Caine got himself mixed up with the coyotes, or maybe he tried to extort money from them to keep quiet. The more she learned about Caine, the more she realized he could have been involved with just about anything. Whatever it was that got him killed, Tonya was determined to discover it.

∽ఎ∾ఎ

The next morning, Tonya and Luis breezed through the feeding and stall cleaning in no time. She invited Luis to join the family for breakfast, but he declined.

"Why don't we go into town?" she asked as they stood watching the mares. "I have some errands to run, and you can stop at the grocery store. Then I'll take you to visit Dad. He'll be so glad to know that you're here."

Luis's eyes lit up when she mentioned her father. The two men had been like brothers for so many years, and she knew it pained him to think of Royce in jail.

"You will not want to be with your family today?"

"They're not my family. They're Lexi's. She's going to give them a tour of the farm and show them the horses. That should keep them busy."

"Then we will go," Luis said.

Tonya went to the house, changed clothes quickly, and came back downstairs. She heard laughter coming from the kitchen. "Tonya?" she heard Lexi say. "Come and have some breakfast."

"No, thanks. I'm not hungry," Tonya called from the living room. "I'm taking Luis into town so he can buy some food. We won't be long. See you all later." She slipped out the front door before there was any more discussion about food. Lexi was a firm believer in a hearty breakfast and always frowned at Tonya when she started her day with nothing more than the usual glass of milk.

Luis was waiting by the pickup. He stood gazing at the horses in their pastures, and Tonya felt immediately at peace when she saw him. Luis was one of those people who were never in a hurry, never ruffled by anything. His calm, thoughtful manner had been a refuge for Tonya many times when she was overwhelmed with life's challenges, especially those she couldn't share with her father.

Tonya thought back to the day Luis had found her crying in the barn at the track, frustrated because the trainers wouldn't give her a chance to prove herself as a jockey. He had calmly analyzed the situation and put it in perspective. His advice to try again and keep on trying had encouraged her and shored up her sagging spirits. As usual with Luis's advice, it proved to be right. She had persevered at becoming a better rider, continued to impress the trainers with her work ethic, and finally succeeded in getting mounts in races.

They drove in silence for a while, then Luis said, "Senor Royce, he will be a papa again soon, yes?"

"Did Lexi tell you?"

"No."

Tonya gasped. "But how did you know?"

Luis smiled at her and shrugged his shoulders.

"Yes. She's due in July. But please don't mention it to Dad. He doesn't know yet."

"Ah, Luis will keep the secret."

Tonya shook her head. Once again, Luis managed to surprise her with his uncanny intuition. It was what made him a good judge of both horses and people. She wondered if he might be able to help her solve the mystery of Caine's killer.

They pulled up in front of the police station just in time to see Orville MacNeil, the druggist, being escorted into the station in handcuffs. His wife, Myra, followed, holding a wad of bloody tissue to her face. *So the rumors about MacNeil abusing his wife are true.* Tonya's heart went out to Myra and for any woman who had to endure that life.

They waited for the MacNeils to enter the station. Then they went in, and she introduced Luis to the duty officer. She glanced at the MacNeils who averted their eyes from her. She called to Luis as the officer led him toward the interview room. "I'll be out here when you're finished talking to Dad. Give him my love."

"I will, *mija.*"

Tonya saw Adam on the phone in his office. He glanced up and mouthed "wait," so she sat on a bench in the hallway. In a moment, she heard her father's voice as the officer escorted him into the interview room. "Luis! *Mi amigo!* You're here!"

Tonya grinned as she imagined the two old friends together and her father's beaming face. One day soon, they would all be together again and would give him the huge hugs they were prevented from giving him now.

"Come in, Tonya," Adam called from his office. She got up and unconsciously smoothed her hair. He stood up as she entered the office. *Always the gentleman*, she thought.

"I was just going to call you," he said, gesturing to a chair.

"Oh?"

He handed her an envelope. "Yes, look at this."

She opened it to find a note similar to the first one he had received. She read, *Tell your girlfriend to be careful. The Furious Three are dangerous. They killed once. They can kill again.*

"The Furious Three?"

Adam nodded. "Any idea who or what that means?"

"Not a clue. This is really getting weird. So I guess I'm the girlfriend?"

"Apparently." He raised an eyebrow. "Have you been snooping again? Asking questions where you shouldn't?"

She didn't answer but turned the envelope over. "There's no stamp on it."

"It was on the windshield of my car this morning."

"Someone knows your car? And where you live?" Tonya stared at the note again, trying to make sense of the information. "So if we put the two notes together, someone is telling you that my father is innocent. They claim to have killed Caine. They are warning me to be careful. And there are three of them. Is that about it?"

"Except that we don't know for sure there are three of them. It could be one person trying to lead us off into the weeds. In fact, we don't even know for sure whoever sent the two notes is really responsible." He took the note back from her. "It wouldn't be the first time someone confessed to something they had nothing to do with. It happens all the time." He narrowed his eyes at her. "You're sure you haven't been snooping."

She decided there was no sense in trying to keep anything from Adam. She told him about Lexi's uncle, their visit to the diner the previous evening, how he had recognized Meggie, and all she had learned from him about the waitress. "Isn't that bizarre? What are the chances Lexi's uncle would see one of his patients from Ohio here in Centerville?"

Adam listened to her. Then he pulled out a folder, opened it, and read from his notes. "Erin Venino. Forty years old. Born in Cleveland. Both parents deceased. One sibling, a sister named Jacque, also deceased. Erin moved to Centerville last November. Works at Hank's Diner. No criminal record."

Tonya gasped. "You knew all the time."

"No, I didn't know about the grief support group. That's new information. But it makes sense. She's had a lot of loss in her life. The question is why did she change her name to Meggie? And what is she doing here?"

"I asked Jack the same question. He said sometimes people just want to take on new names to go along with the new life they're trying to build." Tonya leaned back and looked at the ceiling. "The first time we met her at the diner, she told me and Lexi that her sister worked at a racetrack once. She had some kind of bad experience and turned to drugs. Sometime after that, she died of an over-dose."

"Racetrack, huh? That's interesting. Listen to this." He opened another folder and read. "Celeste Lacey. Twenty-six years old. Born and raised in Cincinnati. Only child. Attended beauty school there."

"Tissy!"

Adam nodded and continued reading. "Worked at a hair salon then at a racetrack near her home. No criminal record. Moved to Centerville in—"

"Let me guess. November."

"Bingo."

Tonya stared at him, her mind reeling. "Two women. Both from Ohio. Both with connections to horse racing. Both moved here in November. Both changed their names." She stood up and started pacing. "Lexi is from Ohio. And so was Caine. And he was a horse trainer! That's how Lexi met him." She stopped, looking eagerly at Adam. "Could the two women have followed Caine here? Followed him to kill him?" Without waiting for an answer, she paced again, talking to herself. "Tissy was in some kind of abusive relationship. That's how she got that scar on her face. And Meggie said her sister had some kind of bad experience and turned to drugs." She stopped and nearly shouted at Adam. "The support group! That's where they met. I'd bet my life on it." She headed for the door. "I have to talk to—"

Adam jumped up and blocked the doorway. "You aren't going to talk to anyone."

She tried to push past him, but he stopped her.

Both hands gripping her shoulders, he glared down at her. "Do you hear me? Talk to no one. The closer you get to the truth, the more danger you're in. Someone is trying to warn you by sending that note. Take the hint."

She scowled at him. "I can't just sit back and do nothing."

"You'll have to. You were attacked once, remember? And possibly poisoned once? How many more hints do you think you'll be given before it's too late? What good would it do to exonerate your father, only to have him come out of jail to find you dead?"

"That was a low blow," she said sulkily.

"I know. Now, please. Leave the police work to me. Your father doesn't want to lose you." He tilted her chin up to him. "Neither do I."

CHAPTER 19

After a quick trip to the grocery store, Tonya and Luis drove home. She was quiet, going over what she had learned about Meggie and Tissy. They both had been in some kind of tragic relationship with a man connected to horse racing. And that man was very likely Lucas Caine. It certainly fit with Lexi's description of Caine as an abuser of women. Hadn't Tissy told her the man who gave her that scar used to take regular trips away looking for his wife? And she said that the last time, he didn't return. If the man was Lucas Caine, that would explain his not returning. He had found the wife he was looking for. Lexi.

But Caine had been in the area since September while Meggie and Tissy only came here in November. Besides, how did they know he was here? Were they having him followed, maybe by a private detective? Did they follow him here to kill him? She could almost see Meggie as a murderer, but Tissy? It hardly seemed possible.

Those two notes to Adam were also confusing. If there really were three people who killed Caine, and Meggie and Tissy were two of them, who was the third? Could it have been Leo Jenkins? If Caine was cutting in on his territory, Leo certainly had motive. If Leo was as protective of the illegals as he seemed to be, and Caine was threatening them somehow, that would also give Leo a motive. Could it have been Leo who attacked Tonya in the parking lot that night? Whoever it was said something about the farm going up in smoke. Was the third person the same one setting fires around town?

"You are so quiet, *mija,*" Luis said, interrupting her mental questions. "Can Luis help?"

"I don't think so, Luis. I'm just trying to figure out who killed Lucas Caine." She pounded her fist on the steering wheel. "God, how I wish I had never heard that name. He's been a damned nuisance, dead and alive. Whoever killed him did the world a favor."

"All things happen for a reason, *mija,*" he said softly. "Luis knows this is true."

Tonya glanced over at him, and his dark hair and brown skin reminded her of the people hiding in Leo Jenkins's cellar. "Luis, can I ask you something?"

"*Si.*"

"You came across the border illegally, didn't you?"

"*Si,* many years ago."

"I'm wondering about those guys that bring illegal immigrants across the border."

"Coyotes."

"Yeah. How does that work?"

Luis sighed, and Tonya wondered if she was digging too deeply into Luis's personal life. But he seemed open to talking about it.

"The coyotes work for the cartels who pay them to guide groups of workers across."

"But it's dangerous, isn't it?"

"*Si.* Especially for the poor. They can walk hundreds of miles across the desert. Those who can afford to pay more are given rides. The cartels are businessmen, selling a service. That is the way they see it."

"Leo Jenkins was helping bring illegals across. His feed store was a kind of safe house, a stop along the way."

Luis nodded. "There are many of those."

"And everyone makes a buck." Tonya thought about the money in Caine's locker at the bus station. Maybe either Jenkins or the coyotes were paying Lucas Caine to keep quiet about the safe house. Tonya shook her head, wondering how people could be so cruel as to profit from the misery and desperation of others.

They pulled into the driveway and watched the yearlings chasing each other around their pasture, while Jake and Gus trotted along the fence between them. The mares were gathered under the elm tree in the middle of their pasture, Maisie standing apart from them, guarding her baby sleeping peacefully at her feet. The idyllic scene soothed Tonya's nerves and provided temporary respite from the ugliness of the world.

She parked near the trailer while Luis unloaded his groceries from the bed of the truck. Tonya's stomach was growling, and she hoped there were leftovers from lunch. "Come up to the house for some lunch, Luis."

He smiled at her. "No, *gracias, mija.* Luis has plenty of food here."

"Okay. I'll come down later and help with the horses."

Lexi, Sylvia, and Jack were sitting in the living room when Tonya entered the house. Lexi hopped up as soon as the door opened. "There you are! Have a nice time in town?"

"Yeah, we did. Dad was glad to see Luis." She was reluctant to share what she knew about Tissy and Meggie and the support group, especially with Jack sitting there. But she suspected the key to unlocking the mystery of Meggie and Tissy lay with the psychologist and what he knew about them.

"That's great," Lexi said. "Are you going to be home the rest of the day?"

"I think so, why?"

"I'd like to take Mom and Uncle Jack over to the track. It's probably closed now, but I'd like them to see where your father and I met. Can we take the pickup?"

Tonya handed Lexi the keys. "Sure. I need to exercise Jake and Gus anyway. I'll probably be in the barn all day helping Luis."

After the three of them left, Tonya went to the kitchen and found some leftover chili in the fridge. As she was heating it in the microwave, Clive and Henry strolled into the kitchen, meowing their greetings to her. She bent down to stroke their soft white fur while they arched their backs under her hands.

After a quick lunch and a change of clothes, Tonya hurried toward the barn. The wind had picked up, blowing dust and dead leaves across the driveway. The air was especially dry, increasing the fire danger. She found Luis grooming one of the yearlings, a tall, well-proportioned bay colt with a white stripe on his face and two white socks. *He may never be a racehorse*, she thought, *but he sure is a looker. Maybe he has a future as a hunter/jumper or event horse.*

"I'm going to take Jake out," she said as she went to get Jake's gear out of the tack room. Luis nodded and continued brushing the colt, humming as he worked.

Once on Jake's back, Tonya had the sensation of being at home, of being right where she was meant to be. She gazed down at Jake's long thin neck, smiled at his long ears flopping as he walked, and felt his rhythmic breathing beneath her. Never was she more at peace than on the back of a horse. Since coming to the farm, she had spent less time riding and more time working in the barn. She had thought this was the life she wanted, but each time she rode Jake, she felt the old longing for the race-track welling up within her. As much as she wanted to be angry at Mike for leaving to go back to riding races, she had to admit she envied him. She shook her head at the irony. Each of them was longing to be where the other one was.

Jake pricked up his ears and walked faster as they approached the training track at the back of the property. The half-mile oval was surrounded by trees in the remot-est part of the farm. She let Jake jog down the back-stretch, standing high in the stirrups as he broke into a slow gallop. They made three circuits of the track, and Tonya was about to push him a little faster for the last quarter mile when she felt his body stiffen and slow down. His ears were forward, and he seemed to be staring at a clump of trees near the far turn at the back of the property. She chirped to him and moved her hands on his neck, trying to get his mind back on his workout, but he continued to focus on the trees. She couldn't see anything that might be spooking him, but as they passed by the ar-ea, she had the strangest sensation of being watched. She experienced a feeling of relief that this was their last lap around the track. As she walked Jake along the path back to the barn, Adam's words came back to her: "The closer you get to the truth, the more danger you're in." How much danger was she really in?

c∽c∽

Later that evening, Tonya and Lexi were in the

kitchen cleaning up after dinner. Lexi watched Tonya gazing out the window as she dried the dishes. The sun was setting behind the hills to the west, leaving streaks of brilliant color across the whole sky. The wind had died down, and the air was very still, as though the country-side was holding its breath.

"Everything okay, Tonya? You're pretty quiet to-night."

"I'm fine. Just thinking. How was your trip to the track?"

"Kind of sad, really. It was all closed up and desert-ed. But at least they got to see where I met you and your father. What did you do today?"

"The usual. Grooming, exercising, cleaning stalls." She hesitated a moment. "I went to see Adam today while Luis was visiting Dad. He showed me another note. He found it on the windshield of his car this morning."

Lexi stopped what she was doing and stared at To-nya, her eyes expressing her fear. "From the killer?"

"I think so. This one was signed The Furious Three. Does that mean anything to you?"

"Three people who are mad about something? Mad at Lucas? Mad enough to kill him?"

"Does that seem possible? I mean, you knew Caine better than anyone." Tonya hated to bring up the subject of Lexi's cruel ex-husband, but she was convinced what-ever happened to Caine had its origin in Ohio, possibly in her uncle's grief support group.

Lexi folded and unfolded the dish towel, and Tonya was sorry she had made her uncomfortable.

"Well, I wasn't really angry with him, certainly not enough to want him dead. I was mostly mad at myself for getting involved with him in the first place. But people have different reactions to that kind of person. All I ever wanted was to get as far away from him as possible and forget he even existed."

"So you never had thoughts of revenge because of what he did to you?"

She shrugged and shook her head. "No. Like I said, I just wanted to escape from him and be somewhere safe. I thought I had found that when I married your father. I guess you never know, do you?"

Tonya put her arm around Lexi's shoulders. "You're safe here, and Dad will be home soon so we can all get on with our lives. And like Luis says, everything happens for a reason."

Lexi smiled at Tonya. "Do you know something? I was worried that you would resent me when I married your dad. I was afraid you would see me as the wicked stepmother taking your father away from you."

Tonya laughed. "Come on."

"No, really. I never thought we would become such good friends. The truth is I wouldn't have gotten through these last weeks without you."

Tonya was deeply touched. Lexi hadn't shared her inner feelings before. The lump in her throat kept her from telling Lexi how much she meant to her and how glad she was that Royce had found love with her.

They were interrupted by Sylvia who came bustling into the kitchen. "How about making some coffee, dear? Jack is about to fall asleep on that comfortable couch out there." Without waiting for an answer, she began ransacking the cabinets. "Okay, where are you hiding the coffee?"

Tonya couldn't help thinking that the last thing this petite dynamo of a woman needed was caffeine.

Lexi guided her mother toward the door. "I'll get it, Mom. You and Tonya go keep Jack awake."

Tonya settled herself on the couch next to Jack, hoping that she would be able to get him to talk about the grief support group sometime that evening. They small-talked about the trip to the track and their experiences the previous summer.

"So, Tonya," Jack said, "my niece tells me you had a hand in solving a murder last summer. That's amazing."

"Three murders, actually, all by the same person. But I didn't do it alone. Lexi helped me identify him. I don't suppose she mentioned that she was the one who finally stopped   him."

"No, she didn't," he said, raising his eyebrows at Lexi who had entered from the kitchen with the coffee pot and cups on a tray.

Lexi seemed a bit embarrassed by the attention. "I only happened to come in at the right time. And it was just luck that mirror was there."

"Mirror?" Jack said.

Tonya related the story of Lexi smashing the heavy mirror from the locker room wall over the head of Alton Jeffers just as he was trying to strangle Tonya. Jack listened in amazement.

"I had no idea," Sylvia chimed in. "What happened after that?"

Lexi sat down in the chair opposite the couch, her coffee cup in hand. "The cops took him away, and then Tonya rode Jake to a twenty-length victory and a new track record. Just an average day on the racetrack," she said with a grin.

"It's hard to believe that you can both be so blasé about it," Jack said. "That kind of experience can leave scars on victims for years."

Tonya sensed an opening. "Like the people in your grief support group? Did they all have experiences like the one Meggie, I mean Erin, had?"

Jack said, "Yes, some quite similar to hers. Some very different. But all of them were suffering in some way from something they couldn't get past."

"Were they all women?" Tonya asked.

"In that particular group, yes. But I've had other groups with just men and some with both."

Tonya was determined to keep him talking. "Do women react differently from men to grief?"

Jack leaned back, his hands clasped behind his head. "Women tend to react more emotionally, so it's their emotions that become damaged. Men tend to react to difficult experiences with frustration because of their inability to fix things. At the same time, women are often better able to talk through their issues than men, who just want to take action. Of course, that's a generalization. Some women want to act, too."

"This group Meggie—Erin—was in," Tonya said, "were there other women whose emotions were damaged by their experiences?" She was desperate to find out if Tissy had been in the group.

"Yes," he said. "Most people are damaged in some way by grief. It's important that they work through the stages of grief so they can come out on the other side whole human beings."

"And if they don't? What happens then?"

"All kinds of things can happen. Ongoing problems with depression, inability to form relationships, escapes into fantasy worlds, even suicide."

Tonya hesitated then decided to take a chance. "Jack, I need to know something. Was there a woman in that group with a long scar on her left cheek?"

He said nothing, but his reaction told her all she needed to know. He gaped at her, his mouth open and shock written all over his face. He cleared his throat. "I can't really—"

Tonya leaned back. "No, no. Of course, you can't. I'm sorry I asked." But she had her answer. Tissy had been part of the group, and that's where she met Meggie. Now if only Tonya could figure out who the third person was, if there really was a third person. Could that person have been part of the support group, too? Were they drawn together by similar experiences, perhaps with Lucas Caine? If so, how could that be proven?

They sipped their coffee in silence. Then Tonya said, "Can I ask you another question?"

Jack looked at her warily. "I guess."

"Not about the group this time. Just in general. What makes people set fires?"

Jack seemed to relax a bit. "Well, there are arsonists and pyromaniacs."

"Is there a difference?"

"Clinically, yes. Arsonists are those who set fires for personal or monetary gain. Like the guy who sets fire to his failing business to collect the insurance. Pyromania is different. It's an impulse control disorder like kleptomania. The pyromaniac sets fires as a way to relieve unbearable tension due to an emotional stress they can't relieve any other way. Sometimes there is sexual gratification involved. Invariably there are guilt feelings afterward which lead to more stress, and the cycle continues."

"Interesting. We may have a pyromaniac in town. There have been several fires of suspicious origin lately."

"Could be. There's really no way to know the psychology until the person is caught."

"Well," Sylvia said, putting down her cup. "I have to say all this talk is depressing. I'm going to bed."

"Sorry, Mom," Lexi said. "Let me walk you up." They said good night and climbed the stairs together.

Tonya remained seated, stroking Clive who had taken up his usual position on the back of the couch. Henry was curled up between her and Jack.

"I should be going up, too," Jack said.

Tonya nodded. "One more question before you go. I know you are bound by professional ethics where your patients are concerned. But suppose there was a situation where someone's life was in danger, and you knew something about one of your patients that could save that life, could you break the confidence?"

He shifted his position on the couch uncomfortably. "Yes, in very specific circumstances. Why do you ask?"

"Just curious. Good night, Jack. Sleep well."

"Night."

Left alone on the couch with the cats, Tonya stroked Henry thoughtfully and reviewed all she had learned today.

Clive lay on the back of the couch, his eyes half closed. Suddenly he rose into a half crouch and stared out the window, the pupils of his eyes suddenly enlarged and his whiskers twitching.

Tonya stared in the direction he was looking. "What's wrong, Clivey?" she said. A low growling sound came from the cat's throat as he continued to look intently into the darkness, his eyes fixed on the barn area. *Maybe Luis is making a final check on the horses*, she thought. *Or maybe the barn cat is coming too close to the house, and Clive is defending his territory.*

After a few minutes, Clive settled down and began to lick his paw, but Tonya had the same sensation she had that afternoon while riding Jake. And Adam's warning came back to her again along with the words of the second note: *They killed once. They can kill again.*

She stood up and checked to be sure the front door

was securely locked, turned off the lights, and ascended the stairs to her room, the two cats padding after her. For the first time in her life, she wished she owned a dog. A Rottweiler.

CHAPTER 20

The next morning, Tonya and Luis fed the horses and cleaned the stalls. They checked the mares in the pasture together, and Luis pointed to one small dapple gray. "This one will foal first."

"I'll take your word for it." She knew the mare wasn't scheduled to foal first, but she also knew better than to question Luis where horses were concerned. She had no doubt his intuition would prove more accurate than old Mr. Warren's notes.

They strolled together along the fence, admiring the yearlings. The colts were blossoming under the care they had been receiving lately. Their coats were shining, and the exercise they had been doing in the round corral was building muscle tone. Tonya had no doubt they would bring top dollar at the yearling sale. If only the family finances would hold out until then.

She started for the house, wondering what Lexi had prepared for breakfast. "Come join us for breakfast, Luis," she called to him as he swept the aisle in front of the stalls.

"No, *gracias, mija*," he said with a smile. "I have already eaten."

"You know you're always welcome to eat with us. Anytime. You don't even need to ask. When Mike lived here, he ate dinner with us most nights."

He smiled at her and headed back to his trailer, humming to himself. Tonya thought about Luis as she walked toward the house. His calm, peaceful manner in all circumstances amazed her. He had told her once that his desire was to be his own boss and have a training stable like the one her father owned. Yet here he was cleaning stalls and doing menial barn work, and he still seemed perfectly content. She wondered what his secret was. Maybe it was believing, as he had told her, that all things happen for a reason. Unlike Luis, Tonya could only take comfort from that if she actually knew what the reason was.

She left her boots on the porch and entered the house. The smell of coffee, bacon, and cinnamon met her and caused her stomach to growl. Lexi was making her delicious cinnamon pancakes. Tonya washed her hands in the kitchen sink and laughed to see that the cats had taken up their usual begging position at Lexi's feet, sitting with their tails wrapped demurely around their feet and watching her with eager eyes. They knew she would give in eventually and toss them bits of bacon.

Sylvia and Jack were already at the dining room table, and they greeted Tonya as she sat down. "You were up early, Tonya," Sylvia observed.

"That's life on a farm," Tonya replied. "The horses start making a fuss as soon as it gets light, and they can get pretty loud, banging on their doors and demanding their breakfast."

Lexi came in with the plates of pancakes and bacon and set them on the table. She reached into the pocket of her apron. "Tonya, I completely forgot to give you this. It came in yesterday's mail."

The San Francisco postmark on the letter told her it must be from Mike. It had been ten days since he left, and she was beginning to wonder if he had forgotten her. She laid it next to her plate and reached for the bacon.

"Aren't you going to open it?" Lexi asked with one eyebrow raised.

"Later."

"I hope he's doing well out there."

"Mike does everything well. No doubt he'll be the leading rider at that track by the end of the meet."

Lexi shook her head. "I miss him around here. He sure loved my pancakes."

"Who's Mike?" Sylvia asked.

"Mike is one of the best jockeys I've ever known," Lexi said. "He can make a horse do things in races that even their trainers don't understand."

"The irony is that he hated every minute of it," Tonya added. "What he really wants is to be a veterinarian. But he had to keep riding races to support his family in Mexico. Do you know what he did once? He saved Henry's life."

Sylvia looked down at Henry sitting by her chair. "This Henry?"

"Yep. That Jeffers guy we told you about? He tried to kill Henry with a wire around his neck. Mike did CPR on Henry and brought him back to life. He has a real gift for vet work. Now here he is, back riding again. He must be miserable."

"Well, that's a shame," Sylvia remarked. "But he's to be commended for taking care of his family. Do you think he'll ever come back?"

"We hope so," said Lexi.

Tonya swallowed the last of her coffee and excused herself from the table. She took the letter upstairs to her room, closing the door after Clive and Henry had scooted in behind her. Sitting on her bed, she opened the envelope. Tonya was disappointed to see there was only one sheet of paper, but she knew how difficult it was for Mike to write in English, a language that always mystified him. A small smile spread across her face when she saw that he had crossed out "their" in one sentence and replaced it with "there." It brought back tender memories of their grammar lessons together and made her miss him more than ever.

The letter was mostly an update on his trip to San Francisco, a two-day bus ride that must have been agonizing for an active young man used to physical activity. He wrote that he had won a few races already and was attracting the attention of the top trainers at the track. He had found a place to live with several other jockeys and complained about the cost of living in the Bay Area. He asked about Royce and the horses and said he hoped Tonya wasn't working too hard.

He doesn't know Luis is here, she thought. *I'll have to write and let him know.*

The end of the letter, which Tonya hoped would include something more personal, said simply that he missed her and hoped to come back to ride at the local track in the summer. He ended by asking her to write back and signed it simply "Mike."

She leaned against the wall and let the letter drop to her lap. As she gazed out the window, memories of his eyes and their last embrace came flooding her mind. It made her ache to think it would be months before she would see him again, if then. If he was successful at a big track like Golden Gate Fields, why would he want to come back to the small track here?

Her cell phone buzzed and interrupted her thoughts. It was Adam.

"Hi," he said. "Are you busy?"

"No, what's up?"

"I've got some news for you. Leo Jenkins has been remarkably cooperative lately." He chuckled and added, "I think he's come to realize it's to his advantage."

"What did he say?"

"He let me look at his financial records. I didn't even have to get a court order. He admits paying Caine to keep him quiet about the illegals he was smuggling. That's where the money in the locker came from. That's also why Leo was struggling financially. He was paying Caine five hundred a month."

"Poor Leo. I feel sorry for him. He was just trying to help those people."

"Yeah. Anyway, what I found looking into his payroll records is that Alec, the clerk that works there? Her name isn't Alec. It's Emma Beiser. And she came here from—"

"Let me guess. Ohio."

"Right."

"And she moved here in November, like the other two. Right?"

"Wrong. She came in September. Leo hired her the same week he hired Caine."

"Did she and Caine know each other?"

"Leo says they didn't."

Tonya's mind was spinning as she tried to make sense of the information. "So the four of them all came from Ohio. Caine and Alec in September. Tissy and Meggie in November. And those two met in the grief support group." She sighed. "I don't know, Adam. What's the connection? Aside from three women who changed their names."

"Four women."

"Four?"

"Diana Wilkins changed her name to Lexi Parr."

Tonya was stunned. "You don't think—"

"I don't think anything. I'm just trying to sort out the facts."

"But you know why Lexi changed her name. To get away from Caine. The other three may have been following him, but they weren't trying to hide from him like Lexi was."

"All I know is that the four women came from Ohio, all changed their names, and all ended up in the same town with Caine, who is now dead."

Tonya struggled to control her temper. "You know Lexi was here at home the night Caine was killed. How can you suspect her?"

"A person can be involved with a killing without being at the scene of the crime."

Tonya bit her lip, trying not to explode. Her father was in jail for a murder he didn't commit. Now Lexi was suspected too? It didn't seem possible.

Could Adam believe that the two of them conspired to have Caine killed?

"Thank you for calling, Adam," she said stiffly, "and for the information." She was so angry at him that she decided not to tell him she suspected someone was watching the farm. He would probably come up with another lame idea, like blaming Luis or something equally ludicrous.

"You're welcome. I'll—"

She disconnected him in mid-sentence and threw her phone down on the bed with such force that it bounced onto the floor. The cats looked at her quizzically while hot tears of anger and fear welled up in her eyes.

∽∾∽

That evening, Sylvia and Jack had retired early, and Lexi and Tonya sat at the kitchen table drinking coffee. Tonya hadn't told Lexi that Adam had lumped her in with the list of suspects in Caine's murder, but Lexi sensed she was disturbed about something. "Anything wrong?"

"I just wish I could make sense out of all this," Tonya said after explaining about the Ohio connection to Caine's murder.

"I know," Lexi said. "Hey. Remember how you figured out that it was Jeffers who killed Alana and the other two? It was the entry forms with the three horses circled. Remember? The names of the horses. That's what tipped us off."

"Oh, yeah, but we don't have any entry forms this time."

"But we have the two notes that were sent to Adam." Getting up from the table, Lexi pulled a sheet of blank paper from the drawer and sat back down. "Remember how we made a list of the information from the entry forms and zeroed in on the names? Maybe we can do that with the notes."

Tonya was skeptical. "But those notes don't tell us much. Just that Dad is innocent, which we already know, and a warning not to get involved. What good is that?"

"Who knows? But it can't hurt to try. Now, can you remember what was in those notes? Word for word?" Lexi stared at her, her pen poised over the paper.

Tonya had gone over them in her mind often enough to recall everything in them. "Okay. I guess it can't hurt. The first one said that the police had the wrong man in custody. Dad didn't kill Caine. They did. And it was signed The Furious."

"Okay," Lexi said, making notes. "What about the second one?"

"It said Adam should tell his girlfriend to be careful. That's me, I guess. And that they killed once and could kill again. It was signed The Furious Three this time."

"Hmm. Not much to go on."

"Adam said it might not even be three people. That could just be a way to get the police looking in the wrong direction."

Lexi stared at the paper. "What's strange is the signature. Whether it's three people or not, the word 'furious' keeps coming up. What do you suppose that means?"

Tonya took out her phone and typed the word "furious" into her browser. She read from a website that gave word definitions and origins. "Furious is defined as extremely angry. From the late Middle English: from Old French *furieus*, from Latin *furiosus*, from *furia* 'fury.'"

Lexi rested her chin in her hand. "Doesn't tell us much, does it? What about 'fury'?"

Tonya typed again. Then she read, "Fury: a spirit of punishment, often represented as one of three goddesses called the Furies. In Greek and Roman mythology, the Furies were female spirits of justice and vengeance. They were also called the Erinyes—pronounced Erin-ees. Most tales mention three Furies: Allecto, Tisiphone, and Megaera, who executed the curses upon criminals. They carried torches, whips, and cups of poison with which to torment wrongdoers." She sat in stunned silence, staring at her phone. "Allecto, Tisiphone, and Megaera," she whispered. "Alec, Tissy and Meggie."

She looked up at Lexi, whose eyes expressed her shock. "Can it be? Read it again," Lexi said.

Tonya read the passage a second time.

Lexi gasped. "Torches, whips, and poison? Oh, my God. Caine was beaten with a whip. Beaten so hard the popper came off. He was poisoned with arsenic, and the room set on fire."

Tonya stared at her phone and read again, more slowly this time. "Female spirits of justice and vengeance." She looked up at Lexi, almost afraid to breathe. "They executed justice and vengeance on Caine for what he did to them. It must have been Caine who abused Tissy and gave her that scar. Meggie said her sister got involved with someone in racing, and she is now dead, and Alec's daughter was paralyzed in some kind of accident at the racetrack. But she said it had nothing to do with horses. What if the accident was something caused by Caine? What if all three of them were Caine's victims? What if he is the one who damaged all three of them with his abuse and violence?"

Lexi continued to stare at the sheet of paper.

Tonya's heart was pounding, her mind in turmoil as she tried to put it all together. Suddenly she shouted, "*The oath.* The one I heard them talking about in the bathroom. The one the woman was trying to get Tissy to recite. She mentioned the power of something that sounded like Pyrenees. It was 'Erinyes,' another name for the Furies. See here? It says it's pronounced Erin-ees. That woman threatening Tissy must have been Meggie. That's why Adam didn't see anyone but Tissy come out of the hallway to the bathroom. Meggie went back through the kitchen."

"Wait. Wait," said Lexi. "How——"

By now, Tonya was up and pacing back and forth. "They must have all met in Jack's support group. He said some of the members bonded. I'll bet they got together, shared their stories and realized it was Caine they all had in common. They made a pact and swore an oath to one another to become the Furious Three, and they dedicated their lives to finding and punishing Caine. They changed their names to resemble the names of the Furies. Maybe they thought that way, they could go back to Ohio after they killed him and probably wouldn't be traced."

Lexi grabbed Tonya's phone off the table and read about the Furies again. "Can this be true? Could they have planned this from the beginning?"

Tonya sat back down, her hands on either side of her head. "Think. Think," she commanded herself. "What else?"

"Lucas came here in September," Lexi said. "Isn't that what Adam told you?"

"And so did Alec. Probably because she was the only one Caine wouldn't have recognized. He knew Tissy by sight, but it was Alec's daughter he was involved with, so he must have never met her mother. So Alec followed him here and got a job at the same place he did. She watched him to see if he'd stay put, and then she sent for Tissy and Meggie."

"Then the three of them waited for the right time."

"Right. And they really took the Furies thing to heart. They were so determined to imitate the Furies that they changed their names to names similar to the three Furies. They even made up an oath about it. Then they plotted to kill Caine with whips, torches, and poison, just like Allecto, Tisiphone, and Megaera. Jenkins said some-one had stolen a whip and some arsenic from his store. That must have been Alec. Michelle said she was missing some alcohol from the salon. Adam said they found the empty alcohol container behind the motel. Tissy must have dumped it there after she set the fire. It all fits!"

"This is unbelievable!" Lexi said. "What about the poison? How did they do that? Oh, wait. Didn't the cook at Hank's say Caine looked sick the night he left for the motel? Maybe Meggie slipped the arsenic to him in his dinner."

Tonya could feel the blood drain from her face. "My God. She tried to poison me, too. That's why Tissy spilled my iced tea and said not to drink anything else. She was trying to warn me."

"So maybe Tissy was having second thoughts? About the murder?"

"She's different from the other two. She's the soft-hearted one. No killer instinct. She loves animals too much. And remember the day she was here? She left suddenly when I told her someone attacked me. Remember she asked me if I was sure it was a man? She must have realized it was Alec because she had told Alec about my solving the murders at the track last summer."

"I'll bet Tissy's the one who sent the notes," Lexi said. "She doesn't want to see Royce in jail when she knows he's innocent. And she's trying to protect you, to warn you."

"Tissy must be feeling guilty about what they did. It's the other two that have no consciences. They'd love to see Dad executed for Caine's murder. That's why Alec lied and told the police she saw Caine and Dad arguing. She was trying to implicate him to take the suspicion off herself."

They sat in silence for several minutes, hardly able to comprehend what they were thinking. Finally, Lexi said, "But how are we going to prove all this? All the evidence points to your father, not to the three women. I mean, I think you're right, but I'm afraid it's going to sound ridiculous to Adam."

"I think we have to start with the support group. Jack told us Meggie was in it. I knew from his reaction when I mentioned Tissy's scar that she was also one of the group. If we can just get him to admit Alec was there, too, we have motive and opportunity for all three of them. Adam will have to pay attention then. We have to work on Jack."

Lexi looked skeptical. "I don't know. He's got that whole professional ethics thing going."

"To hell with his ethics. This is Dad's life we're talking about."

CHAPTER 21

The next morning, Tonya and Luis were out in the pasture, carefully checking each one of the mares. She watched as Luis ran his expert hands over the dapple gray mare's side and leaned over to check her udder. He straightened up and said, "She is not far from foaling. See, her udder is beginning to swell."

Tonya shook her head. "Another premature one. She's not due for another three weeks." *Does this mean another visit from Doc Frey that we won't be able to pay for?*

"The little ones come when they are ready," Luis said, stroking the mare's neck. "It should be another few days, maybe a week."

They moved on to the other mares and Luis pronounced each one healthy. Maisie's colt was his usual curious self. He moved confidently through the herd, following Luis and Tonya. Several times Tonya had to keep him at arm's length when he started pushing her with his nose and chewing on her jacket. "You're a bossy little thing, aren't you?" she said, laughing at his playfulness.

"Is a very good sign," Luis affirmed. "This is why he survived his early birth. He is *machismo*."

"That aggression will make him a good racehorse. Competitive."

"*Si.*"

Tonya was reminded of the time she had called Mike a macho jerk, and almost as though Luis read her thoughts, he said, "You have heard from Miguel?"

"Yes. I got a letter."

"He is well in San Francisco?"

"He's seems to be," she said briefly, afraid the emptiness in her heart would become too painful if she said more.

But, of course, Luis read her thoughts almost before they formed in her mind. He touched her arm gently. "He will return to you, *mija.* This I know."

Luis never ceased to amaze her. He seemed to know how much she cared for Mike without being told. "I hope so. Are you coming up to the house for breakfast?"

He started to decline, but she pressed him. "Please come, Luis. Maybe you can help me with something."

"Oh? You want Luis to make his *huevos rancheros*?" he said with a grin. "Very famous. *Muy caliente.*"

Tonya laughed. "I'll bet they are hot. No. Lexi is in charge of the food. I would like you to meet Lexi's uncle. You know how you can tell things about people, things others can't see. This man is keeping a secret, one that might be able to clear my father and get him out of jail."

Luis gazed at her kindly. "Some secrets are better kept secret, *mija.* But Luis will come and meet this man if it pleases you."

"It pleases me very much."

They left the pasture together and walked toward the house. Luis carefully cleaned his boots on the scraper attached to the porch floor, smoothed his hair, and followed Tonya into the house. Sylvia and Jack were seated at the dining room table while Lexi puttered in the kitchen. Tonya introduced Luis to the two, and he bowed slightly to Sylvia and shook Jack's extended hand.

"Come into the kitchen, Luis, and we can wash our hands."

"Welcome, Luis." Lexi's delight at seeing Luis glowed in her eyes. She nodded to Tonya. "Finally got him to come for breakfast. Good for you," she whispered to her while Luis was at the sink.

Once they were all seated at the table, Lexi passed around the plates of French toast, bacon, and scrambled eggs, and they helped themselves. As they began to dig in, Tonya noticed Luis quietly bow his head for a moment and then cross himself. *I didn't know he was religious,* she thought. *Something else to add to the list of things I don't know about him.*

Everyone seemed to be in a happy mood this morning, and they talked about the food, the weather, and the trip home they would soon be taking. Tonya said, "I guess you're eager to get back to your patients, Jack?"

Jack sat back. "To tell the truth, I've been glad to get away for a while. I mean, I love helping people, but sometimes their problems can be overwhelming. It can be hard to divorce myself from them."

Tonya decided to jump in and see how much she could get out of him before he shut down. She looked directly into his eyes. "This group we were talking about, was there a woman named Emma Beiser in it?" She watched him carefully, hoping his reaction would tell her what she wanted to know, as it had when she mentioned Tissy's scar. But Jack's gaze was stony behind his thick glasses.

"I know you don't like to talk about your patients," Tonya continued.

He set down his coffee cup and gazed kindly at her.

"It's not a matter of what I like or don't like. I am prevented by law. I've probably said too much already. You realize I could lose my license if I'm not careful."

Tonya spoke as sympathetically as she could. "I understand. But we think three women are responsible for Lucas Caine's death, and two of them were in that group. Meggie and Tissy, who you know as Erin and Celeste, followed Caine here from Ohio. We believe Emma Beiser was the third one. She goes by the name Alec here, and she works at the same place Caine worked. All I need to know from you is whether she was in the grief support group with the other two. That one piece of information could free my father—" She touched Lexi's arm. "—and Lexi's husband, from jail."

Jack looked down at his plate. It was obvious that he was conflicted and struggling.

Lexi's eyes pleaded with her uncle. "You said that under certain circumstances, like to save a life, you could reveal information about your patients that could save that life. Please. It's Royce's life we're trying to save."

Jack sighed and looked kindly at his niece. "Yes. Emma Beiser was in the group with Erin and Celeste. They became very close, and I always thought there was something that drew them to one another, something I wasn't aware of. Now I know what it was. Lucas Caine."

Tonya leaned toward him. "From what you know of those women, do you believe they are capable of murder?"

Jack thought a moment. "I don't like to believe any of my patients could do such a thing—"

Tonya held her breath.

"—but yes," he admitted. "Maybe not Celeste, but definitely the other two. If you only knew what they suffered. Things that could warp anyone's mind."

Tonya sat back in her chair and looked gratefully at

Jack. Lexi patted his arm and said, "Thanks, Uncle Jack."

When they finally left the table, Tonya walked Luis to the door and out onto the porch. He thanked her for breakfast and started down the steps, but he stopped halfway and turned back to her. "You didn't need Luis's help to get that secret, but some secrets, once they are told, can cause great harm. Be careful, *mija.*" His eyes were full of concern.

"Always," she assured him.

Tonya returned to the house and ran up to her room to change, taking the stairs two at a time.

"Where are you going?" Lexi called from the dining room.

"Into town. I won't be long." *Just long enough*, she thought, *to look into the eyes of a murderer.*

℮↶℮↷

Tonya drove toward town, well above the speed limit, pushing the old pickup until the motor whined in protest. The white three-railed pasture fences along the road were a blur, mirroring her thoughts as they raced through her mind. Now she knew that the three women, the Furious Three, had plotted to follow Lucas Caine to Centerville, drawn together by their mutual hatred of the man they believed had ruined their lives. They took him to his motel room, already under the influence of the arsenic Meggie had put in his food or drink at the diner. They gave him coffee with more arsenic in it, then, once he was incapacitated with the pain, they beat him with a whip and set him on fire. And now her father, the kindest man she had ever known, sat in a jail cell for the crime the three women had committed. *Well, not for much longer. Not if I can help it.*

She forced herself to slow down as she turned down the main street of town. The first shop she came to was Michelle's beauty salon, and Tonya decided to confront Tissy. She parked in front of the salon and saw there were ten minutes left on the meter. That would be plenty of time.

Tonya was surprised to see Michelle sitting alone behind the counter with the cash register on it. She looked up from the beauty magazine she was reading.

"Hello, Tonya," she said with just a little less perkiness than usual. "Can I help you?"

Tonya looked around the empty salon. "Is Tissy here?"

"She doesn't work here anymore."

"Really? Since when?"

"Since a few days ago."

Tonya wondered if Tissy had left for Ohio and if so, did that mean the other two would be going as well? "Is she leaving town or something? Or did she get another job?"

"Not that I know of. The truth is I fired her."

"Oh. That's too bad. Can I ask why?"

"Lately, she was coming in here looking like she hadn't slept or was hung over or something. Her hair was dirty, she stopped wearing makeup. Not the kind of impression I want to give to my customers, ya know?"

"I see. Maybe she needed help or something."

Michelle squirmed in her chair. "To be honest," she said, licking her lips, "she was starting to scare me."

"Oh?"

"Not only did she look awful, but she would talk crazy. Sometimes she just mumbled to herself, like she was arguing with someone. Other times she had this wild look in her eyes, and she would look right through me when I talked to her. Like I said, she was starting to scare me."

"That's too bad."

Michelle shrugged her shoulders and turned a page of the magazine. "I'm just glad she's gone."

"Any idea where she went?"

"No. I haven't seen her since she left here that day."

Tonya thanked Michelle and left the salon. She stood on the sidewalk, gazing down the street and thinking about that poor, damaged girl whose life had been shattered by violence. Anger welled up in her as she thought about the lives Lucas Caine had destroyed. Even from the grave, his evil was still wreaking havoc on people. Could there be forgiveness and redemption for such people? She would have to remember to ask Luis what he thought about that.

Tonya backed the pickup out of the parking space and turned toward Leo Jenkins's feed store. She didn't even know what she hoped to accomplish by confronting Alec, and she was sure Adam would be angry at her, but she didn't care. The more evidence she could gather about the Furious Three, the sooner Dad would be home again.

Entering the front door, she noticed that the parrot sat quietly in his cage, eyeballing her suspiciously. She almost missed his familiar greeting.

As she approached the counter, she felt an oppressive, dark atmosphere that seemed to have settled over the store. There were no more illegal aliens in the cellar, but Leo still had criminal charges hanging over him for his part in the smuggling. Then there was Alec's presence in the store. Surely that was part of the oppressiveness she was sensing.

The store was empty. She cleared her throat and said, "Leo? Anyone here?"

Alec stepped out from behind the curtain that separated the back room from the rest of the store. "What can I do for you?"

"Hello, Alec," Tonya said. She zeroed in on the woman's beady eyes. "Or should I call you Emma? Or maybe you'd prefer Allecto?"

Tonya watched Alec's black eyes glitter with smoldering hatred. Alec took a deep breath that seemed to enlarge her brawny frame even more, and she exuded a malevolent power. *She's the one who attacked me that night*, Tonya thought. *I'm sure of it now*.

"Excuse me?" Alec said with feigned innocence.

"You heard me. I know who you are, and I know what you did. You and the other two."

"I don't know what you're talking about," Alec said quietly. She looked around the store and started to come out from behind the counter.

Tonya suddenly realized she was in a precarious position. She was alone here and no match for this powerful woman who might have any number of weapons behind that counter. But she had what she came for. Alec's reaction had told her all she needed to know. Now it was up to the police.

"You'll be getting a visit from the cops soon, Alec. And it won't have anything to do with smuggling illegals." She backed toward the door, keeping her eyes on Alec, and nearly knocked over the parrot's cage in her haste.

The parrot squawked, and Tonya righted the cage. Then she retreated out the door hastily, looking back one last time at Alec's face, which was twisted in rage.

She got into the cab of the truck and gunned the engine, the tires squealing as she raced toward the police station, her heart pounding.

❧❧❧

"You did what?" Adam asked, glaring across his desk at Tonya. "After I told you to leave the police work to me?" He leaned toward her. "After I warned you to stay out of it? But your stubborn Irish pride just wouldn't let you, would it? You were going to take care of this all by yourself, is that it? You're letting that incident last summer go to your head. The truth is if it wasn't for Lexi coming into the locker room at just the right time, you'd be dead now. And yet you persist in playing detective."

Tonya's anger matched his own. "I found out who killed Caine. I just told you their story, about the support group where they met, about the oath they took. What have you been doing? What have you found out?"

Adam was clearly trying to control himself. "I've been trying to gather evidence. Evidence," he nearly shouted at her. "Ever hear of it?"

Tonya narrowed his eyes at him. She had never known him to be this sarcastic. "How much do you need? After what I just told you."

"Well, let's see what we've got," he said, no less sarcastically than before. "Fingerprints or DNA at the crime scene? No. Eyewitnesses that put any of the three at the motel that night? No. Confessions? No. All you have is a supposition based on the fact that all three were in the same support group and all moved here from Ohio. Is that about it? And we couldn't even prove that in court because your uncle wouldn't testify. He'd claim doctor/client privilege, wouldn't he?"

Tonya was silently fuming.

Adam bored in on her. "Is there any proof that Alec is the one who stole the whip and the rat poison?"

Tonya shook her head.

"No. But we do have proof your father bought rat poison and that there are whips in your barn. Correct?"

Tonya just glared at him.

"Is there any proof that Meggie poisoned Caine? That she was in the motel that night? Or that she put something in your iced tea?" He answered his own question. "No, there isn't. But we do have proof your father was in that room, don't we? His fingerprints."

Tonya could feel her face flaming. She didn't know whether to throw something at him or burst into tears.

"Let's talk about motive. You've heard of motive? Is there any proof that these women even knew Lucas Caine before they moved here? No? I didn't think so. But we do have proof that your father knew Caine and knew what he did to Lexi. He also knew that Caine said he wasn't leaving town without her. Correct?"

Tonya sat with her arms crossed in front of her, scowling at this man she had once been so attracted to.

He sat back and ran his hands through his hair. "I'm sorry to have to be so blunt, Tonya," he said, his manner softening, "I know this is painful. After what you've told me, I have no doubt the three women followed Caine here intending to kill him. In fact, they probably did kill him. But without some kind of proof, my hands are tied. If I go to the captain with this story, he might find it interesting, but he won't release your father." He sighed, and his shoulders sagged. "Go home, Tonya. Stay away from those women. Stay away from the feed store. Let me do my job. If they are guilty, we'll prove it eventually."

Tonya felt foolish and like a child who had been reprimanded by the teacher. But she wasn't about to let Adam see the effect he had on her. She stood up and squared her shoulders. "I'd like to see my father now, if you don't mind."

"Of course. Sergeant," he called toward the outer room. The chubby-faced, young uniformed officer appeared at the door. "Take Miss Callahan to the interview room and bring the prisoner to her."

Tonya cringed inwardly. *The prisoner. What an awful way to describe my father.*

Without another word, she left the office and followed the cop down the hallway, fighting back tears of anger and frustration. As she sat at the table in the dreary little room, she took deep breaths, determined not to let her father sense how upset she was.

Royce came in and sat at the opposite end of the table. "You know, Dad," she said brightly. "Orange is really your color. You look great in it."

"Thanks," he said with a smirk. "Maybe we should change our stable colors. We can call it jailhouse gold."

Tonya relaxed to see him in good spirits. She related all she had learned about the Furious Three and their relations with Caine, but she purposely left out the warning to her in the second note. He listened intently and asked a few questions. Then they talked about Lexi and the farm and the horses. Tonya assured him things were going well, especially now that Luis was there to help.

Their time was over all too soon, but Tonya assured her father that things were coming to a head and that he would be coming home soon. If only they could all hold on a while longer.

As she left the station, she glanced down the street toward the feed store, wondering what her next step should be. She considered going to see Meggie at the diner and confronting the waitress with what she knew, but the memory of Adam's angry eyes—the same eyes that had always looked at her with such affection— stopped her. She got into the pickup and started toward home, thinking that something precious may have been lost today.

CHAPTER 22

Tonya pulled into the driveway and slowed down as she passed the pastures where the yearlings and the mares were relaxing in the late afternoon sunshine. Jake and Gus were in their paddocks, and she noticed the calico cat standing on top of one of the fence posts. Gus stood close to her, occasionally rubbing his muzzle along the cat's back, while the calico arched her back against Gus's massaging movements.

She parked the truck in front of the barn and went to get Gus's halter. He hadn't had any exercise for days, and Tonya felt guilty at having neglected him. Gus wasn't the only one who needed exercise. Tonya's neck and shoulders were aching from tension and the lack of physical activity over the past few days.

She opened the gate and led Gus from his paddock, while the cat trotted along the fence beside them. Then she jumped down and followed them along the path to the training track, which was starting to harden due to the lack of recent rain. They passed the huge hay barn behind the main barn, a building that had once held hundreds of bales of hay, along with various farm implements, tractors, and equipment. Since the Warrens had left and sold all the equipment, the barn's only inhabitants now were the rats that had escaped Royce's efforts to eradicate them before he was arrested. The calico cat turned off the path and slipped into the hay barn through a slit in the door.

Tonya led Gus past the two foaling sheds next to the hay barn then out onto the track where she and Mike had been dragged along by Gus that day weeks ago. She smiled to herself at the memory. She led Gus into the three-stall starting gate that sat empty at the head of the chute on the backstretch. All the gate doors were open, and Gus walked calmly through from back to front. Tonya remembered his last race and how he had stumbled out of the gate, nearly unseating her. But they had overcome the bad start to win the Futurity by a nose. She wondered if there would be more racing in Gus's future. It all depended on how he recovered from his tendon injury.

They walked together down the track's long backstretch and around the turn. They passed the place where Tonya had felt someone watching her days before, but everything seemed peaceful and secure. As they rounded the turn, she chirped to Gus and pulled on the lead rope. He broke into a slow trot, and they jogged together down the length of the track toward the barn.

After one more lap around the oval, Tonya pulled him up and back to a walk. They returned to the barn, and she put him back in his stall to wait for his dinner then went out and brought Jake in, too. She had planned to ride him, but suddenly she felt very tired and decided to go inside for a quick nap before the afternoon feeding.

As she closed Jake's door, he looked down at her with his usual imperious gaze. "Yeah, yeah, you're the king around here," she told him. "We won't forget it, your highness." His tongue protruded from the corner of this mouth as though he was making a statement, and she couldn't help laughing at him. This was a horse with a personality.

She was trudging up the porch steps just as the front door opened.

"Hi," Lexi said. "Do you have any plans for the rest of the day?"

"Nothing much." She decided not to tell Lexi all about her visit to town until later.

"I'd like to take Mom and Uncle Jack to dinner and a movie. They're going home tomorrow. Come with us?"

"Thanks, but I don't think so. I'm really tired, so I think I'll take a nap until it's time to help Luis with the feeding."

"Okay, if you're sure. There's plenty of leftovers in the fridge, so help yourself. We should be home by eleven."

After the three of them left, Tonya climbed the steps wearily. She found the cats curled up on her bed, and they moved over as she lay down and pulled the blanket over her. All three of them were asleep in minutes.

ೆೊ೧ೊ೧

Tonya woke to the sound of Henry scratching on her bedroom door. It was pitch black, and she was disoriented for a moment. *What day is this?* Then she remembered and rolled over to look at the clock. The red digital readout told her it was eight o'clock in the evening. She sat up and looked out the window. The barn and Luis's trailer were dark, the pale moonlight just able to show the outline of the mares in their pasture. Luis must have fed the horses and retired early.

Clive and Henry were pacing by the door, and Tonya

realized they hadn't had their dinner. Her growling stomach reminded her that she hadn't eaten since breakfast.
She swung her legs over the side of the bed and sat holding her head in her hands, feeling groggy. Could she really have been asleep for four hours?

The house felt chilly, so she pulled on a sweatshirt
and opened the door for the cats. They scampered down
the stairs and into the kitchen. When Tonya got there,
they were pacing next to their bowls and meowing. She
poured dry cat food into their bowls and opened the refrigerator. The last of Lexi's chili sat in a small bowl on
the shelf. She put the bowl in the microwave and stood
watching the cats as it warmed up. She shook her head,
trying to clear the cobwebs. Never had she slept so long
in the afternoon.

The cats padded after her as she settled on the couch
with her bowl of chili. Clive took up his usual position on
the back of the couch, while Henry sat by her side and
busied himself by grooming his face and ears with his
paw. As she stared out the window eating, the events of
the day came back to her in a rush. Alec's malevolent
eyes and Adam's sarcastic mocking were equally odious
in her mind, and she couldn't decide which was more
painful to her.

After nearly a half hour, Clive suddenly pulled himself into a crouch and looked intently out the window toward the barns. He froze in position, only his whiskers
quivering and the very tip of his tail twitching. Tonya followed his gaze, wondering if Luis was making a final
check of the horses, but his trailer was still dark, and
there was no movement anywhere around the buildings.
She wondered if the calico cat had ventured too close to
the house, arousing Clive's territorial instincts, but she
didn't see the cat anywhere.

She finished the chili and decided to take a quick trip to the barn to check on the horses. Two successful race-horses, one a stallion just beginning his breeding career, were too valuable to take any chances. Going into the kitchen, she rooted in a drawer until she found a flash-light. Then she left the house and walked across the drive, pointing the light into the grass and hoping to see the cal-ico's yellow eyes staring at her. But the cat was nowhere around.

She flipped on the barn lights and walked down the shed row aisle, stopping first at Gus's stall. He blinked at the sudden light and gazed questioningly at her. She stroked his nose and then moved on to Jake's stall. Be-fore she even got to his door, she heard him snoring. She tiptoed to the door of his stall, and just as she expected, the big brown horse was stretched out on his side, his eyes tightly closed, and his sides rising and falling. She moved quietly away from his stall.

As she turned off the lights and left the barn, she heard a sort of screeching noise coming from the hay barn next door. She shined the light on the building's windows but could see nothing. She stopped and listened and heard it again, this time a little louder. *Maybe that barn cat has caught herself a mouse or one of those rats*, she thought. *Well, good for her.* But was that really the sound she heard?

She knew she should go back to the house or perhaps wake Luis before investigating, but her curiosity got the better of her. Or maybe it was that pride that Adam warned her about. Feeling just a little irritated with Ad-am, she slid open the hay barn's big door. She played the flashlight's beam around, and the first thing she saw was the calico cat peering down at her from the rafters. Unless she had dragged a mouse or rat up there, the cat wasn't responsible for the sound she had heard. Tonya moved farther into the barn, her boots crunching on the dry hay and straw scattered over the floor.

Suddenly there was a rustling sound behind her. Before she could turn around, she felt something like a cord wrap around her neck, pulling her backward. Then she was grabbed from behind, and the memory of the attack in the parking lot caused her stomach to lurch and terror to flood her mind. The pressure on her windpipe was causing her to struggle to breathe. She tried to pull the cord away from her throat, at the same time kicking out wildly. Then her flailing legs were grabbed by someone else who forced her feet together and wrapped something around her ankles. She was pushed to the ground, still struggling violently. Then she saw the face of the one tying her legs. It was Meggie. Looking up and backward as she was lowered to the ground, Tonya could see Alec's stringy black hair and pockmarked face.

"Tie her hands. Hurry up!" Alec snarled at Meggie.

Meggie complied, wrapping baling twine around Tonya's wrists. Then the two women sat her up and leaned her against a post. Her hands and feet were tightly tied, immobilizing her.

"Should we gag her?" Meggie asked.

Alec, clearly taking the role of leader, sneered at Tonya. "No. Let her yell all she wants. There's no one to hear her."

Tonya struggled against the restraints as her mind raced through a number of possible outcomes to this evening, none of them good. Luis was sound asleep in his trailer, Lexi and her mother and uncle were at the movies, and their nearest neighbor was over a mile away. Alec was right. There was no one to hear her. She cursed herself for not bothering to learn to handle Royce's rifle, standing unloaded in his closet. If she had learned how to use it and brought with her when she came out to investigate, she wouldn't be in this position. She continued struggling against the ropes.

Then a strange sound caused her to stop scuffling. It was that same screechy sound she had heard before. It was like a weird, ethereal song, tuneless and inane. Tissy moved slowly out of the shadows, humming to herself and staring into space. She ambled closer to Tonya but seemed not to see her, focusing on some unseen phantom born of her own twisted imagination.

Tonya's breath caught in her throat as she saw that Tissy was carrying a can of gasoline. Images of Tissy's face at the fire in town mingled in Tonya's mind with Jack's words about pyromaniacs who set fires as a way to relieve unbearable tension and emotional stress. Poor insane, warped Tissy, damaged beyond repair by a man who gave her the brutal abuse she somehow believed she deserved. Now here she was carrying the means to relieve her stress, at the same time destroying this dry, old wooden building and Tonya with it.

"Come on, stupid," Alec sneered at Tissy. "We don't have all night."

Tonya knew she was doomed unless she could break through to one of these women. She also knew Alec was unreachable in her rage and Tissy equally so, lost in her own mind. Tonya appealed to Meggie. "Erin, please," she said desperately, hoping the use of her real name would get through to her. "You don't want to do this. I know you don't. This won't bring your sister back."

Meggie continued to stand at Tonya's feet, looking down at her with a blank expression, saying nothing. She glanced up at Alec, awaiting her orders.

"Celeste," Tonya nearly shouted at Tissy. "Look at me. Do you know where you are? You're here at the farm. Where the horses are. Remember the little colt?

He's outside with his mother. If you burn down this barn, you could kill him. And all the rest of the horses. Don't do this. You don't want to hurt the animals. I know you don't."

Tissy seemed to be trying to focus on the voice, but couldn't quite manage it. Tonya tried again. "Look up, Celeste. See that cat up there? What will happen to her if you set fire to this barn? You don't want to hurt her, do you?" She saw Tissy's eyes flicker for a moment then gaze unsteadily up at the calico cat who was staring wide-eyed at the scene below.

"Put the gas can down, Celeste," Tonya coaxed. "Please. You don't want to hurt anyone."

"Shut up," Alec snarled, giving Tonya a savage kick in the side. Tonya groaned and gasped, her breath taken away. "And you," she barked at Tissy, "don't just stand there. Spread that gas around. Or do I have to do it for you?"

Tissy seemed immobilized, her gaze ping-ponging between Alec and Tonya as though she was watching a tennis match.

"I'll do it," Meggie said, grabbing the can out of Tissy's hands. Tissy sat down on the floor, her head in her hands, rocking back and forth in her traumatized condition. Meggie started pouring the gasoline all over the hay-strewn floor, the acrid smell reeking throughout the building. As it wafted up, the calico darted across the rafters and out the opening used for loading hay bales into the hay loft. *At least she'll be safe*, Tonya thought, relieved that something good could come out of this nightmare.

Meggie tossed the empty can aside and said to Tissy, "Give me your lighter, Celeste."

Tissy continued to rock back and forth, now with her

legs drawn up and her arms wrapped around her knees. She started to wail that high-pitched, otherworldly song again.

Meggie rooted through Tissy's pockets and found the lighter, the same one Tonya remembered Tissy playing with at the coffee shop, probably the same one Tissy used to start those fires in town.

Tonya watched in horror as Meggie used her foot to scrape together a small pile of straw and bent down to light it.

As it smoldered and a small flame flickered, Alec stooped and leaned close to Tonya who turned her face away from the woman's reeking breath. "Aw, are you afraid, little girl?" she mocked with a voice full of venom. "What good will all your snooping do you now? Hmm? Well, we have to be going now. Bye, bye." She stood up and said, "Let's go."

Meggie grabbed Tissy by the arm and pulled her to her feet. The pile of straw was ablaze now and starting to spread slowly across the floor, the smoke rising toward the rafters. Tonya's heart was in her throat, and as she realized these might be the last moments of her life, her thoughts turned to her father and the sorrow he would have to endure. Her second thought was of Mike Torres, who would hear of her death from Luis or Lexi. What would his reaction be? She would never know. Tears came to her eyes, partly from the smoke and partly from the knowledge that she would never see either of them again, never know whether she and Mike might have a future together.

As the three women headed toward the door, it suddenly flew open, and Tonya heard Adam's voice shout, "Police. Put your hands up."

Tissy sank to the floor again, and Meggie stopped. Raising her hands above her head, Meggie screamed, "I don't care! Do what you want to me. We finished what we started. He's dead! *Dead.* He'll never do what he did to Jacque again." Her huge eyes were wild, the growing flames reflected in them as she shrieked at the policemen. "I killed him! I'd do it again."

At that moment, Tonya saw Alec back up, looking wildly around the barn. She spotted a stack of tools leaning against a post and lunged to grab a three-pronged pitchfork. Holding the fork in front of her like a soldier's bayonet, she ran straight at Adam with a blood-curdling howl that sounded like something from the pit of hell. A shot rang out, and Alec fell to the floor in mid-stride.

Adam and two other policemen rushed into the barn. The two uniformed officers handcuffed Meggie and Tissy, while Adam and Luis, who had come in behind the policemen, stomped on the spreading fire, both men using their jackets to beat out the flames. When the fire was out, Adam went to Alec and put his fingers to the side of her neck. He stood up and looked down at Alec with both sadness and relief on his face. Tonya wondered if he had ever killed anyone before.

Luis was suddenly at Tonya's side, untying her hands and feet. "You are not hurt, *mija*?"

"No," she said, burying her face in his shoulder. "I'm not hurt." He tenderly smoothed her hair back from her face, and Tonya wrapped her arms around his neck and burst into tears.

❦❦❦

Tonya sat at the back door of the ambulance, shivering in spite of the balmy night, a blanket wrapped around her shoulders. As the paramedics carried Alec's lifeless body on a stretcher to the ambulance, a plastic covering encasing her bulky frame, Tonya moved away. They slid the stretcher into the vehicle and closed the doors.

Meggie and Tissy were handcuffed in the back of Adam's cruiser, while one of the officers stood guard next to it. Meggie glared out the window, her eyes blazing and as defiant as ever. Sitting next to her, Tissy stared blankly at the seat in front of her in a catatonic stupor.

Adam was taking a statement from Luis, and Tonya walked toward them. "I shudder to think what would have happened, Mr. Mendes," Adam was saying, "if you hadn't called us." He glanced at the hay barn, wisps of smoke still wafting up through the upper windows. "We put the fire out before it could really get started, but the fire chief will probably have to come out tomorrow to check and make a report. In the meantime, it will help if no one goes in there."

"I will see to it," Luis said.

"And you will need to come to the station to make a complete statement. You, too, Tonya," he said as she stood mutely by. "But there's no hurry. When you're up to it."

Tonya nodded, hardly knowing how to process what had just happened. When she thought about the past two hours, the events seemed to replay in her mind in slow motion.

"Well, good night now," Adam said. His cruiser, the ambulance, and the other police car moved slowly up the driveway just as the pickup carrying Lexi and her family pulled in and parked near the hay barn. Lexi's wide eyes mirrored her fear and shock as she jumped from the cab and raced to Tonya and Luis.

There would be many questions and hours spent talking about tonight, but before Lexi had a chance to say anything, Tonya said, "Good news, Lex. Dad is coming home."

CHAPTER 23

The old porch swing creaked as Tonya sat rocking it gently back and forth. She had first noticed the swing the day she and Royce first came to the farm. She had been afraid the Warrens would take the swing with them when they moved out, and Tonya remembered her relief at seeing it still on the porch when they drove up on moving day last November. Lexi's joy at seeing her new home, the one she would share with her new husband, also came to her mind, along with the way Royce's eyes had danced with happiness. A new home, after years of living like nomads in that little trailer, and a pretty new wife.

The laughter coming from inside the house reminded Tonya that nothing, not even their first days on the farm, could compare to their present joy. The moment Royce got out of the police car several days ago and came toward the house is one she would never forget. The memory of the embrace she shared with him and Lexi, their little family back together again, at last, brought a lump to her throat.

Could it really be only a week since their world was nearly destroyed by three mad women bent on burning down the barn with Tonya in it? She shut her eyes, pushing away thoughts of that awful night, determined to enjoy this celebration.

The calico barn cat came strolling toward the house, her tail straight up. She trotted up the porch steps and stopped in front of Tonya. The cat's yellow eyes expertly surveyed the distance from the floor to the swing. Then timing her leap perfectly with the movement of the swing, she sprang effortlessly and landed gently in Tonya's lap. She purred loudly as Tonya stroked her silky fur.

Tonya wondered if perhaps she should go back inside to the party, but it was just too comfortable and peaceful out here. Besides, the cat had curled up in her lap, and Tonya didn't have the heart to move her. "I'll have to give you a name," she told the cat as she stroked her, "one of these days."

The sound of a car's tires on the gravel woke her out of her reverie, and she looked up to see Adam's police cruiser coming down the driveway. He pulled up in front of the house and got out of the car. Tonya gazed at him, admiring his tall, well-toned body. As usual, when she thought about Adam, the differences between him and Mike always came to mind. Mike had the classic jockey's build—small, compact, and wiry, while Adam had the good looks of an actor or a *GQ* model. Two men, each unique and so different from one another, yet each one so attractive to her.

"Hello, Lieutenant," she called to him. It was the name she always used when she wanted to tease him. "Come to join the party?"

Adam climbed the steps. "I wouldn't miss it."

She made no move to go back into the house, so he sat down beside her. The calico looked up at him, decided this large stranger was no threat, and closed her eyes again.

Adam gazed around at the scene. "Peaceful here, isn't it?"

"Yes," she sighed, watching the horses in their pastures. The mares and Maisie's colt relaxed under the tree, while the yearlings played and raced each other along their fence. Jake and Gus stood side-by-side on either side of their fence.

Tonya and Adam sat quietly together, listening to the birds calling to one another from the trees surrounding the old house and smelling the wood smoke that drifted up from the chimney. Royce loved to build fires in the big brick fireplace, even on fairly warm days like today.

"So," Adam said finally, "have you recovered? From that night, I mean?"

"Yes. I don't think about it much anymore. Just sometimes I wonder..."

"What? Anything I can help with?"

Tonya hesitated. "Oh, I don't know. So many things."

"For instance?"

"Like what will happen to Tissy? She won't go to jail, will she?"

"She'll get the help she needs. But it may take a long time. She had a lot of emotional issues before she even met Caine. So she has a lot of therapy ahead of her."

Tonya nodded. "I don't know if she even knew what she was doing that night. It's so sad. What about Meggie?"

"She'll have to stand trial for her part in the murder of Lucas Caine and the attempt on you. She made a full confession. She almost seemed proud of what they had done."

Adam's nearness, his gentle voice, and his basset-hound eyes helped to reassure Tonya that the world had righted itself at last.

"Anything else bothering you?"

She almost hesitated to bring it up, but it was the one thing she couldn't reconcile in her mind. "I understand why Alec went after Caine, but why me?" There. It was out in the open. Had Tonya done something to provoke her? Was she somehow at fault? She glanced up at Adam, and he seemed to see the fear in her eyes. He put his arm around her shoulders and pulled her close to him.

"You know that it was Alec's daughter that got mixed up with Caine?" Tonya nodded, and he continued. "Alec, or Emma, was the instigator of the revenge killing. I think her mind got warped watching her daughter suffer. She's the one who came up with the Furious Three idea. She convinced the other two that they needed to make a pact and take an oath of vengeance. The idea of the Furies who executed justice on criminals was appealing to all of them."

"It was Tissy and Meggie I heard in the bathroom at the diner talking about that oath."

"Right. They thought there was some kind of power in it. But once Caine was dead, Alec became more and more irrational. That's what Leo Jenkins told me. Maybe she thought emulating the Furies and taking vengeance on Caine would give her satisfaction, but vengeance never satisfies. Apparently, when the relief she thought she would feel didn't come, she looked for someone else to take out her anger on. She met you, and she might have seen in you what her daughter had hoped to become."

"What was that?"

"Maybe a jockey. Maybe just a girl with a happy life. Someone who was healthy. She compared you to her incapacitated daughter. Whatever it was, she certainly had you in her sights. Did you know her daughter died recently?"

"No," Tonya whispered.

"Yep. A couple of weeks ago. That may have pushed Alec over the edge. Then when you confronted her in the store that day and told her you knew all about the Furious Three, she realized it was over. We found packed suitcases in her room. She was going to hit the road as soon as she took care of you."

Tonya shuddered, thinking of how her life had nearly ended that night. "Adam, how did you know to come here that night?"

"Luis called me. He heard noises in the barn and went to investigate."

"Thank God he's a light sleeper."

"He saw you all through the window and gave me a blow-by-blow description of what was happening as I was on my way. I told him not to go in until I got there. I'm not sure he would have waited much longer."

Tonya smiled at the thought of Luis charging into the barn armed with nothing but his cell phone.

Another burst of laughter reminded Tonya that she was neglecting her guests. "Come in and say hello, Adam. We have champagne." Tonya lifted the cat and placed her on the swing. She held the door open for Adam, and he moved past her into the house.

The living room seemed unusually crowded. Doc Frey was there, chatting with Lexi's Uncle Jack and stroking Henry. Clive had taken up his usual position on the back of the couch. Sylvia bustled back and forth filling everyone's glasses and offering plates of hors d'oeuvres. Even Leo Jenkins was there, sitting on the couch beside Luis. "We have to do more for them," Tonya heard Leo say, and Luis nodded. If Leo was intent on helping people cross the border, legally this time, he couldn't find a better ally than Luis.

Royce was sitting beside the fire with Lexi perched on the arm of his favorite chair. "No champagne for you, little mother," he teased her. "Adam," he said, standing up as Adam and Tonya entered. "So glad you could join us."

Adam shook his hand. "No hard feelings?"

"Of course not. You were just doing your job. Have a glass of champagne. We're celebrating today. In fact, I want to propose a toast." He raised his glass, and everyone stood up. "To freedom. And to my family, present...and future." He winked at Lexi.

"To the family," everyone repeated.

"Future?" Adam whispered to Tonya.

"Lexi's pregnant."

Adam grinned. "Well, good for them. A man can't ask for more than a wife and children. Don't you think so?"

Tonya felt a bit uncomfortable, fearing what Adam might be hinting. She ignored the question. "Sit down, Adam. I'll get you something to eat." She left him hastily and started to fill a small plate from the table which sagged under the load of food.

Doc Frey walked up to the table and began sampling the sauces. "I'm so glad your father is home again," he said. "You must be relieved to be all together again. Just like old times."

"Not quite all," she said. There was that feeling in the pit of her stomach again. "Have you heard from Mike?" she asked nonchalantly.

"Yes. I wanted to be sure he was trying to keep up with his studying as much as he could. He said he reads his *Merck's Manual* every night."

"So he hasn't given up on vet school?"

"Not at all. He knows he has a long road ahead of him, but if anyone can do it, he can." He leaned down closer to her. "He asked about you."

Tonya brightened. "He did?"

"Of course. He wanted to know how you are, what you're doing, and if you are going back to the track this summer to ride. I said I didn't know for sure. Are you?"

"I haven't thought much about it. I think Mike's afraid of the competition," she said with a grin. She glanced around the room at the people she loved and knew something was missing. Or someone. "I'll give him a call later," she said, "and we can talk about it."

"Good idea. I know he'll be happy to hear from you. He has a bright future ahead of him. You both do."

Doc patted her shoulder and walked away. Tonya surveyed the room. Lexi was sitting on Royce's lap, the two of them completely engrossed in each other. Luis's eyes found hers, and they exchanged warm smiles. A feeling of joy and relief came over Tonya, and she felt sure that if the future was half as bright as the present seemed to be, she'd never ask for more.

About the Author

DM O'Byrne's first job was as a waitress. Now she's a writer of mystery novels. In between, jobs included English teacher, racehorse exerciser, jockey, accountant, golf resort assistant manager, writer, and editor. Her places of residence ranged from the Jersey shore to a lengthy sojourn in California and finally to the Colorado Rockies. Each profession, each location was rife with life lessons, fascinating characters, potential plot lines, and wide-ranging experiences. Sooner or later, they will all end up on the written page. O'Byrne is the author of *Dangerous Turf* and the sequel, *Three to One Odds*.

Printed in Great Britain
by Amazon